Christine

Once upon a time there was a little girl who wanted a nice office job. Personal assistant, maybe. I'd have been happy with a cubicle, but a small office would've been my dream. People would depend on me to answer the phone, and placate clients, and bring coffee.

Something boring like that.

And the man in my life would've been my boss. He'd wear a suit and a tie. He'd look at me like I was saving him when I made excuses for him on those days when he just wasn't feeling the job. He'd have flowers waiting on my desk for Personal Assistant Day, and take me to lunch somewhere I could never afford for my birthday, and have me buy gifts for his girlfriends because he was too busy.

We'd have been partners.

We would've trusted each other. Respected each other's talents. Known our places in this world.

And we'd have been happy with it.

I don't know if any of that is true, but I think it is.

Because no one would wish for the life I have now.

Not even me.

I woke up yesterday in a strange place. This tiny basement apartment, to be specific. There was blood on the pillow and a long stitched-up gash on the back of my head. My fingertips explored that gash. Counting. One. Two. Three… seventeen stitches. About four inches long. Blood clotted in my hair.

Someone had fixed me up. Obviously.

And they took care, I think. Not to shave too much hair. Because when I hold a small compact up as I look in the bathroom mirror, I can't see the gash through my thick, auburn mane.

Today I have a headache. A bad one, actually. But there are painkillers on the cheap coffee table in front of the couch. One of those orange pill bottles with the caps that are impossible to remove and a white label that says CHRISTINE KEENE on it in someone's sloppy handwriting.

So I take those and feel dizzy, and stop wondering what's happening and just… float.

I think I'm Christine but I'm not really sure.

It feels like it's my name so I'm gonna go with it.

I don't really have an alternative option because I don't remember anything.

I don't know who I am, how I got here, or why I stay.

I don't know why there's a shotgun in the closet, a sniper rifle under the floorboards, or a pistol under the bloodstained pillow.

When my fingers explore the scar under my chin and I wince at the pain in my shoulder every time I try to reach higher than my chest, I know I'm not that boring office girl. I am the opposite of boring.

The Triangle

SHAPE OF LOVE

HA HUSS

J McCLAIN

Copyright © 2018 by JA Huss & J McClain
ISBN: 978-1-944475-60-4

Edited by RJ Locksley
Cover Design by JA Huss

description

Alec. Christine. Danny.
This is how you say our names.
There is no her without him.
No me without them.
No we without us.
We are Alec, Christine, and Danny.
And this is the shape of our love.

I don't even know how I knew about the sniper rifle. I was staring down at my dirty bare feet and just *knew*. There's a rifle under the floor.

But I think I'm intuitive. Because there's this *thing* inside me saying...

There is no cubicle, or flowers, or desk to put them on.

There is no boss.

There is only me and these weapons.

That same thing inside me says, *Be still, Keene. Lie low. Say nothing. Call no one. Just disappear.*

And it's not even that hard to listen because I don't have a single contact in my phone. If that's my phone. The only thing on that phone is a text from a virtual currency site telling me a two-million-credit transfer was completed two days ago.

Even if I did have a contact I don't have anything to say. No questions to ask. And there's food in the fridge and painkillers on the coffee table.

So it's easy.

There's no panic inside me.

I give that little thing in my head total control.

Until that knock on the door.

CHAPTER ONE

Christine

I stare at the door as my heart thumps inside my chest.

"Keene," a man growls on the other side of the door. "Open the fuck up."

I get up, the floorboard hiding the sniper rifle creaking under the weight of my dirty feet, and straighten the long t-shirt I woke up wearing yesterday.

"I'm gonna count to three, Keene. And if this door doesn't open—"

I pull the door open. Stare at the surprised face of a man on the other side.

He's no office boss, that's for sure. Tall, broad frame hiding underneath a heavy leather biker jacket. Piercing blue eyes shooting anger as they find mine. They dart back and forth, scanning me. Searching for answers, or intentions, or... something.

And then he sighs, pulls me into his chest, and wraps his arms tightly around my body.

It's such a nice hug. So comforting. And it makes that thing inside me go silent long enough for me to close my eyes and kinda enjoy it for a few seconds.

But just as quickly as he took me in, he pushes me away. "Fuck you," he says, forcing his way into my apartment, grabbing my hand to take me with him as his foot kicks out and closes the door behind us. "Just fuck you! What the fuck, Christine? What the fuck?"

He pulls on my hand, yanking my shoulder. Not hard, but it's fucked up and I squeak out a cry of pain.

"Shit," he says. "Shit. I'm sorry." And then he's hugging me again. "I thought you were fucking dead when he called. I thought that was it, man. I thought we were fucking done."

He pushes me away and I get the feeling this is how it is between us. One moment we're together, the next we're apart.

I get the feeling I should get used to that.

"What happened?" he asks, holding me at arm's length. "What the fuck happened? What did you do?" His eyes are doing that scanning thing again. Searching for answers inside mine. "What the fuck did you do?"

If I thought I had answers I'd say something. If I had context I'd lie. If I had any idea at all I'd just go with it. Because I think that's who I am. I think that's what I do.

But I'm empty. Even that thing inside me is gone. I have absolutely nothing inside me. So that's exactly what I say.

I just stare at him.

"Jesus. You look…" he starts, then stops. Runs his fingers through his hair again. "Someone betrayed you," he says. I screw up my face as I stare at him. Mostly because betrayal… I hadn't thought of that. "It wasn't me. I'd never fucking betray you."

"Do I know that?" I ask, finding my voice surprisingly low and throaty. Not what I thought it would sound like.

"Christine," he says. "Don't fucking do this. Not now. I need you."

10

I get the feeling lots of people tell me that and none of them really mean it.

"Tell me what happened, OK? Just start from the beginning and tell me everything. I can fix this. You know I'll fix this, right?"

He's holding me at arm's length again. Still scanning me for answers.

But there's something else in his eyes now. Something soft when normally there's nothing there but hate and anger. I know this even though I can't possibly know this since I don't even know if I really am this Christine girl.

I just know.

"Why are you looking at me like that?" he asks. "It wasn't me. It wasn't fucking *me*, OK?"

"Then who was it?" The question comes out like an instinct. Like it's something Christine would ask the day after waking up from a night gone wrong. "Him?" I ask. Even though I don't know who 'him' is. Just another instinct.

This one chews the inside of his lip as he shakes his head. "No. I mean…" He sighs. Loud. Heavy. Runs the fingers of both hands through his thick, blond hair, pushing it away from his face. "Usually I'd blame him first but *he* called *me*, Christine. Told me you were here. And just what the fuck, man? Why the fuck didn't you call me?"

It's unfortunate. This moment. Because decisions have to be made. And that little thing inside me—the one that probably saved my ass when… whatever went down and I got this gash on the back of my head—it's telling me to shut up. Get rid of him. Then pack up my painkillers, ditch the guns, and disa-fucking-ppear.

But that voice doesn't seem to have the full story. There's no indication that it understands I don't know who the fuck I am. What I did. Or where to go.

So a decision has to be made.

Trust this guy or kill him.

Option two should worry me. At the very least should give me pause.

But it doesn't.

Because this is my reality whether I remember it or not.

"Christine," he whispers. And now all ten fingers are threading through my hair. They pull away—I'm getting used to that—when they find the blood-crusted gash on the back of my skull, and then, just as quick, he's turned me around, bent me over, and gently—so gently—pushed the hair aside so he can see what's there.

"Jesus fucking Christ." He stands me up. Roughly, but I like it rough—don't know why that thought popped into my head—and takes me by the shoulders again. "What. The fuck. Happened?"

So we're back to that moment of decision.

"I don't know," I say, choosing a path forward. "I don't remember anything."

"What do you mean you don't remember?"

My arms move instinctively. Up, open, and break the hold he has on my shoulders like I'm a pro at that. He doesn't startle but he does lean back. Uncertain.

"I mean," I say, looking down at my dirty feet, letting my hair fall in front of my eyes, "I don't remember." I tip my head back up, look at him through the hazy curtain of auburn mane, and say, "I don't know who I am. Or who you are. Or what I did. Or how I got here. Or—"

He just stares at me.

"Or if I should kill you now."

His mouth slackens a little, slightly open as he breathes in my confession. His blue eyes softer. His shoulders slightly slumped in… disappointment? Sadness? What? Why is he looking at me this way?

"What?" I say.

"You don't remember me?"

I shake my head.

"Do you remember *him*?"

I'm about to shake my head no to that too, but… "Alec," comes out instead. "He's… Alec."

CHAPTER TWO

TWO NIGHTS AGO

Ag, man. I hate being fokken shot at.

"Mr. van den Berg, sir! Get down!"

That's what the laaitie closest to me says before a bullet chases him back behind a fortunately-for-him bulletproof SUV. He can't be more than nineteen. Maybe twenty. He darted out from his hidey-hole to try to pull me back. And I appreciate that level of commitment and loyalty. I truly do. I'll have to remember to do something nice for him later. If he lives.

Hell, if I live.

"Sir! Get down!"

I don't.

And I know that gives the impression to everyone currently cocked up in this unnecessary gunfight that I'm tough or possibly crazy. Which is just fine by me, because it's to my great advantage in life to have people believing that I'm both tough and crazy. And I can be. But the actual reason I don't get down now is that we're in a dusty warehouse and this is the first time I've worn my new suit, and I'm not keen to get it all filthy just yet.

I figure it like this: If I die, it won't matter. But if I live, I'll have to keep wearing this suit for at least the next few hours and I don't want it to be all mucky. I need to maintain the respect of the people who work for me and seeing your boss in a mucky suit that got that way because he was cowering for his life don't seem like it's likely to garner a lot of admiration.

Also, it's a fokken lekker suit and the thought of ruining it over someone else's proper craziness makes me wince.

Shit.

This didn't have to happen this way. This should have been a simple exchange. We hand over diamonds to you, you hand over money to us, we all smile, laugh, pat each other on the backs, and head off on our merry ways.

But Americans. Eish, Americans love to shoot their fokken guns, man.

Right now, I'm depending very much on something my father once told me: If, in the face of mortal danger, you look like you're not frightened, it will cause the other oke to take up that fear in compensation. And then you will hold the advantage and he will be made weak and vulnerable.

It does occur to me, however, that it may have just been another in the long litany of bullshit things my dad said to me over the years that appeared useful at the time but turned out to just be poor parenting.

I reckon I'll be finding out shortly.

Oof, the bullet that just winged by me was a mite too close. Perhaps I should reconsider how much I like this suit.

But I don't have to, because as if on command, a deus ex machina of sorts arrives in the form of my ringing mobile. I'm able to glance at the screen and see that it's Lars ringing. Deus ex Lars. My concern, however, is that Lars usually only ever rings when something's gone wrong. If everything's fine, I'll just receive a text saying so. And the fact that he's my point person on the thing with Christine makes this particular perturbation feel even more amplified than it otherwise would in my current state.

"Yeah?" I answer as I spin behind a column of metal boxes which may or may not contain explosives, and which, in turn, may or may not have just served to make my life worse. I wink at the laaitie who was worried for my safety. I don't really consider the action, I just do it. It seems to give him courage or embolden him or something because he pops his head up and caps off two of the guys shooting at us. Good for him. I like this lad.

"Howzit, bru?" replies Lars. "Can you talk?"

"Yeah, bru, not too busy. What izit?" The sound of metal hitting metal ricochets off the boxes guarding me. Not explosives, I suppose. Good times.

"Problem."

"I guessed. What happened?"

Just then someone starts up with a goddamn machine gun. One of the Americans.

"Fok is that, bru?" asks Lars.

"Hold on," I say. And when the blast of machine-gun fire dies down long enough for someone to replace a clip, I seize the opportunity to shout, "Fok is your problem, man? How the fok did this get so cocked up?"

My American counterpart, Wallace, shouts back at me in his thick American accent, "Fuck you, you cracker-ass motherfucker! Racist piece a' shit! Trying to cheat me out of my ice, cocksucker? Who the fuck you think you dealing with? Dirty-ass blood-diamond-dealing son of a bitch!"

Does Wallace not see the irony in impugning my integrity for selling this particular type of diamond when he is, in fact, the one *buying* this particular type of diamond? Apparently not. "Racist? Bru, I'm coloured!"

"Colored? That's some racist shit right there, motherfucker!"

"No! That's what I am! There's white, Zulu, Swazi, coloured... The list goes on, boet! My great-grandad was a Zulu oke! Technically, I'm mixed-race, bru! Coloured!" This is an odd time to be offering someone a lesson in South African ethnology, but...

"I ain't give a fuck what you call it! You look white to me, motherfucker! And you still a racist, cheating, blood-diamond-dealing motherfucker! Motherfucker!"

I can't help but ruminate, *Bru, you knew the diamonds had conflict when you agreed to buy them. That's why you wanted them. Quality, purity, and at a portion of the cost of lesser diamonds mined more... legitimately.*

But, I suppose, the racist accusation isn't completely without some rationale. Illogical though it may be. Wallace heard one of my guys call him a *kaffir* last month when we were all in New York putting this deal together on paper. Which is not OK. And I get why he might still be upset. I mean, I beat the living fokken daylights out of a schoolmate once when he used that word in reference to me when he found out I had mixed blood.

But, I mean, fok, man... That particular employee of mine who said it is now dead. Quite dead. I'm certain. I killed him myself. And I did that as a show of good faith *and* as an apology for his unconscionable behavior.

Jesus, Wallace.

Some people harbor their negative feelings far too close to their hearts. And that is simply terrible business.

"Wallace, my china, you didn't come to Cape Town for this! You came for product! Let's—"

"Product you're fuckin' light on!"

"Hey! I'm a lot of things but I'm not a cheat, man! Maybe it's just your scale! Do you have it set to ounces and not grams, by chance?"

"Suck my dick!"

"C'mon, bru! Honestly! Let's just lay down guns and talk for a tick!"

"Fuck you, bitch!" And the machine gun commences again.

Yes. Fuck me, indeed.

"Lars? You'll have to yell! What happened?"

"Christine took a tumble," is what I hear in reply.

And then I hear nothing else. Not the sound of Lars on the phone. Not the machine-gun fire. Not the screaming and yelling. Nothing.

I've known people to describe a sensation like getting cold chills up and down their spines when they are confronted with situations or information that might give them worry. I don't. Get cold chills, I mean.

No, when confronted with information that taxes my nervous system, I get something akin to a throbbing headache but that pulses in my limbs instead. It feels like my body is swelling to twice its normal size. I imagine it's what that oke Bruce Banner feels like when he turns into that Hulk fucker.

"Fok do you mean, 'she took a tumble,' bru?"

"Details still coming in. Seems she wasn't exactly where she was supposed to be."

"What do you mean? Where the fok was she?"

19

"She took care of the thing she was supposed to but then she told Reggie and Lex there was something else she had to handle."

I can't process everything he's saying to me. Because it's confusing. And because of the fire fight. And because Hulk is taking over. I cut to the chase.

"Is Christine all right, man?"

"Yes and no."

"Fok does *that* mean?"

I don't like losing control in front of anyone. But right now, with the chaos swirling all around, I don't think anyone will notice.

"It means that... we're not totally sure! Somebody..."

"Somebody what, bru?"

The laaitie has his head poked from round the SUV. There's a red dot in the center of his forehead. In an act of impulse, I spin round from my metal barrier and immediately spy the oke holding the pistol with the laser sight attached. I have no laser sight attached to my pistol. Because it's foolish and serves largely to just give away your position. Also, it has always suggested to me that it signals that you don't know how to aim terribly well.

I do know how to aim terribly well.

I pop a single shot into the head of the oke who don't know how to shoot, look at the laaitie again to make sure he's still there, see that he is and is looking mightily and rightly grateful, and I duck back behind my improvised safety wall.

"Somebody fokken WHAT?" I ask again.

"It seems like somebody might have thrown her off a roof."

If I really was that Hulk fucker, this would be the point where the buttons would begin popping off my shirt and the seams of my lekker suit jacket would start to rip.

"Fokken say that again." I realize that my voice may be too quiet for Lars to hear over the noise in the warehouse, but I can't seem to make my vocal cords vibrate above a whisper.

"Reggie and Lex was out front of this other building, keeping watch while she was handling whatever she was handling, and they heard something up above, like a gun going off—"

"Her?"

"Not her. Someone else. Like from a pistol, they said. And they looked up and saw what they say looked like a struggle. Reggie says he was about to run up and see what the fok, but then suddenly a body came spilling over the side."

This is where my feet would be swelling and smashing through my shoes, and my pants splitting down the sides. It feels like that's what's happening anyway.

Lars goes on, "Lex says he could tell it was Christine right away, so he stepped to try to catch her. Figured she was only four stories up, maybe he could break her fall."

"And?" I shout with what I hope sounds like impatience rather than fear. Which is actually what it is.

"He mostly did. Broke his arm in the process."

"No offense to Lex, but I don't give a fok. What happened to Christine?"

"She hit her head. Hard."

I close my eyes and take two breaths. Suddenly what I'm going to have to do in a matter of moments is becoming very clear. And I need to focus.

"Is she alive?" I ask.

21

"She is," he says.

Thank Christ.

"Where is she now?"

"Reggie and Lex took her to doctor."

"One of ours?"

"Of course."

I breathe in again through my nose and say, "Aces."

"And I have her in apartment thirty-six."

"What? Why?"

"Because she'll be safe there."

"Fok, man! I can think of twenty places she'd be safer and I'm not in a position to be problem-solving right now!" A bullet wings past. "Are you with her?" I ask.

"Not at the moment."

"Fokken hell, Lars!"

"I can go back."

"No! No! God damn it, no."

"Well then, who do you want me to have stay with her?"

"No one."

"No one? What—"

"Fokken no one, bru! She has weapons?"

"Yeah. Course."

"Fine. I'll have someone check in on her straight away."

"Who?"

I press 'end' on the call and slip my mobile back into my lekker suit pocket. Then I give Wallace and his men the only chance they're going to get.

"Wallace!" I shout. And maybe the Hulk has crept his way into my throat, because suddenly everything stops. It's almost like I'm imagining it. "Wallace, I'm fokken sorry that that pielkop who worked for me insulted you and I'm sorry that you think we're trying to fokken cheat you, man. But he's proper dead and we are not cheating you. If there's a mix-up, I promise you, bru, on my mother's soul, that we will make it right. But I'm gatvol with this shit. Something's come up and I have to go. So, unless you and everyone standing within twenty feet of you want to die in the next ten seconds, I recommend you put your fokken guns down and let's sort this later."

There's a beat wherein it sounds like Wallace is maybe mulling it over. My men, including the laaitie whose name I need to learn, are all staring at me like I've gone round the bend. Then, after about eight or so seconds, Wallace shouts, "Fuck you *and* your mama, motherfucker!"

I close my eyes, take one last breath, and think, *Don't you die on me, Christine. I'll be there as soon as I can. In the meantime, I'll be sending the only person I know I can trust, one hundred percent, to watch over you. Maybe it's an insane idea, but simply, I love you more than I hate him.*

And I don't know if my father's advice was actually right or if it's just that when the Hulk shows up, everything changes. But the absence of fear I feel as I march toward Wallace and his men, their bullets whizzing by me, is authentic.

And the fear in their eyes as I place a single bullet into every. One. Of. Their. Brains. Is very, *very* real indeed.

CHAPTER THREE

Danny

"Sure," I say. "Sure. Alec. Right." And all that comes out low. It comes out angry. It comes out dangerous. I breathe through the next few moments, my eyes on hers, doing my best to keep it all under control.

She's staring at me with those wide hazel eyes of hers. Looking at me like I've got something she needs. Looking at me like I've got answers.

I've waited a long time for that look. Long time. Three years? Four, maybe?

And now here it is.

Fake.

She doesn't even know who I am.

She closes her eyes, my intense glare becoming too much for her, and then her hand drifts up. Her fingertips absently swipe at the soft fluttering of hair just behind her ear. She turns her head, sighs like... I dunno. Like she's sad, maybe. That's probably just me projecting. And then I see the moment when her fingers find the gash on the back of her head.

Because she winces. Even with her eyes closed.

"Are you OK?" I ask, the old me back.

"I don't know."

"Come on. Get your shit. We're outta here."

25

"But. But something happened…"

I hear what she doesn't say. Those ellipses at the end of her sentence tell me more than I want to know right now.

"Danny," I say, filling in her blanks. "I'm Danny. And yeah, something happened. You've got Alec to thank for that. Now get your shit and let's go."

Fucking asshole Alec. Who the fuck does he think he is walking back into our lives after all these years? After all that bullshit. I'm gonna make him pay for this. For all of it. Every fucking thing he ever did is coming due for that motherfucker.

"No," she says, stepping backwards. "I'm not going anywhere with you. I don't even know you."

"I know you," I say, poking my finger into her chest. She hates that. But instead of slapping me in the face or punching me in the gut, she just says…

"Not good enough."

"What he said, Christine, whatever he promised you— it's a lie. That's all that motherfucker does. Don't let the dreamy accent fool you. He's one hundred percent evil. And the whole reason you're here in this shit hole is because he asked you for a favor and you said yes. I told you a long time ago. That motherfucker ever comes asking, your answer is always no. But do you ever listen?"

"What favor?"

"What do ya fuckin' think, Christine? What do ya fuckin' do?"

Her eyes dart three places in quick succession.

A blood-stained pillow on the couch.

The floorboards in front of the couch.

The closet.

So she's got three guns in here. Probably the ones she used for that job. Which means we've gotta get rid of them. And that pisses me off. "We'll ditch the guns along the way."

"No," she says. "I'm not leaving here. Not with you."

"You don't have a choice. I'm not askin' you. I'm taking you."

"You can try to take me." It comes out like old Christine. Little sixteen-year-old badass Christine.

And goddammit, that hurts. Fuckin' hurts every time I get those little glimpses of how things used to be.

"Look," I growl. "I don't have time for this shit. I just spent the last two hours thinking you were dead. That your fucking luck finally ran out. That your skills just aren't what they used to be. That your past came back, or some enemy got you for some long-ago hit that you forgot all about but he still remembers like it was goddamned yesterday. And," I say, putting my hands up on either side of my head, fingers outstretched like I want to grab her neck and strangle the stupid out of her, "and that you left me. For him. That the two of you have been on some fucking yacht off the coast of the Cook Islands counting your goddamned diamonds, yucking it up on how you pulled one over on that dumbass Danny."

I stare at her. I'm breathing hard. Like a fucking bull staring down a matador. Ready to charge.

"Or," I say, barely a whisper now, "that he had you. Because you fell for his shit again. His lies. And he got you into something new. Something bad. Something worse than all the other motherfucking somethings he's already gotten you into."

I stop. Swallow.

She just stares back at me.

27

"You being dead would, of course, be the worst-case scenario. But that last one was a very close second. Because Christine, if he's gotten you tangled up in his web of lies again you might as well be dead. It's only a matter of time before that payment comes due. And I know you don't fear death. You've said it so many times I can hear you screaming it at me now, even in your silence. But this won't be death. You have no idea what kind of shit he's gotten himself into these days. They won't kill you, Christine. They'll rape you first. Torture you until you're begging for death. So save your I'm-all-good bullshit for someone who doesn't know better. You're not all good. You don't even know who you are. Or what you did to earn this day. And you're not staying here. So get your fucking shit together and let's fucking *go*."

She turns her head. It's almost a no. Almost.

But then she bites her lip and exhales.

There's a vulnerability in her expression that's not usually there. And last week if she'd given me that expression I'd have fucking melted like a piece of chocolate in the glove box on a hot summer day. My heart would've exploded with satisfaction.

But today it scares me.

Something happened to her.

Something bad.

But what else is new?

Bad things happened to all of us.

LONG TIME AGO

"Just do it," Alec is telling Christine. "He's drunk. He won't even see you."

"What the fuck do you mean, he's drunk? You said he wasn't gonna be there."

"Relax, bru," Alec says. "He partied hard last night, it couldn't be helped. Only way to get the information, yeah? So just go in there, do it the way I showed you, and all is good. Life is good."

Christine's hazel eyes find mine. She's not asking me to save her. God fucking forbid she asks someone to save her. She's asking for backup.

My grin back says everything she needs to know. *I'll be there for you,* that grin says. *I got you.*

I love her. It's dumb because she's almost like my little sister. I've been taking care of her since she was ten years old. The minute I turned eighteen I busted her out of that last foster home and she never looked back once.

Almost like my little sister. But almost doesn't count in biology.

Right now she's my number-one partner in crime. She's the main reason I get up in the mornings. Maybe the only reason.

We live together now. With Alec. It's actually one of his dad's places, but that guy is never here. Always flying somewhere. I swear to God, Alec talks about taking planes the way most people talk about taking buses.

But there's a price to pay if we want to stay with Alec. And that's why we're standing here in this alley looking over at the house across Race Street.

"You're sure about the safe?" she asks him.

"I'm sure," Alec says, petting her hair like she's his favorite pet. It makes me angry when he does that. Like he's got a claim on her. Like she's his when she's mine. "And don't worry. I'll distract him."

29

His South African accent is thick. His t's come out like a machine gun. His skin is still tanned from the rays of some faraway sun. Everything about him is exotic compared to the cold, gray day in this upper-class city neighborhood.

"Just get the diamond," he says. And then he does something that will change her life forever. It might be the most formative moment she's had in all fourteen years of formative moments.

He lifts up her dirty t-shirt and tucks a pistol into the waist of her pants.

TODAY

"There," I say, pointing to the floorboards. "Get the sniper rifle. I'll get the shotgun in the closet, and you stuff that pistol under the pillow into your pants like old times, and let's get the fuck out of here."

I pull my jacket aside so she can see I'm carrying too. Her eyes don't move, but she sees it. I'm sure of that.

"Christine," I say. "You need to trust me. Don't keep making the same mistake over and over again. You just know his name right now, but pretty soon all the other things you know about him will come crashing back. And then you're gonna thank me."

CHAPTER FOUR

Christine

We don't go to my place. If I actually have a place I don't know where it is and even though Danny asks me over and over again to try to remember, there's nothing there. It's just dark. Just black and empty.

But I feel like my name is Christine. The pill bottle in my hoodie pocket says so. And Danny says so. And even though I don't know who Danny is, I feel him to be Danny just as much as I feel me to be Christine.

He's driving an old Willy's wagon that's outfitted like a tank. Four-inch lift kit, thirty-five-inch tires, and glass thick enough in the windows that surround me to be bullet-resistant.

We end up across town in some dumpy garage filled with custom motorcycles. The sign on battered metal door says Fortnight's with a picture of a skeleton riding a chopper through flames underneath the name. Mad toothy grin on his skull face like he's about to challenge Satan for control of Hell.

It's cold inside. Empty too, except for the bikes. There are seven workstations but today must be Sunday because it all looks very much put away.

He closes the door behind us, locks it, then arms an alarm system that looks way too state-of-the-art for this

31

dump. Then he leads me across the large space to a beat-up old metal staircase and we go up to a door, deal with another alarm system, and enter what must be his apartment.

We didn't ditch the guns. Turns out the sniper rifle was all packed up in a convenient carrying case, the shotgun was sawed off, and the pistol was a suppressor-ready CZ in urban gray that just looked pretty. We placed them on the cheap coffee table and looked them over with the same expression.

Nice.

That's what our silent voices said in our heads.

Too nice to ditch and too difficult to replace.

So I took the rifle and pistol, he stuck the sawed-off into his leather jacket, and that was the end of it. Old habits dying and all that shit, right? It's hard to let go of a nice piece of equipment, even if it could be your downfall.

His apartment is warm.

That's the first thing I notice. It's fuckin' freezing outside and I'm only wearing a dark gray hoodie over the threadbare t-shirt I woke up in.

So I breathe in the heat as he tucks the shotgun away in the coat closet—I think that's where all shotguns live—and then takes the sniper rifle from me and goes in the bedroom to put it somewhere safe.

I keep the pistol and it jabs me in the back when I sink down into the soft couch cushions, aware that my body is bruised and achy and the gun isn't helping matters, but the pressure of a gun against my lower back is something that makes me feel better. So I don't care.

He comes out of the bedroom sans rifle, taking his heavy leather jacket off as he crosses the room, my eyes tracking him the whole way. It jingles from all the zippers and that's all I concentrate on until he hangs it over the back of a chair at the small table next to the kitchenette and things go silent.

I look at him.

He's nice to look at.

Dark blond hair, blue eyes, thick, muscular body, and a square jaw with at least a week's worth of golden stubble on it. His arms are bare now but full-sleeved with tattoos. Skulls and skeletons, mostly. Which makes me think of the logo on the garage door.

"Danny Fortnight," I say, putting two and two together.

He smiles, which almost changes him into a different person. "Christine Keene."

"So now what?"

He sighs, shrugs, then walks over to the couch and sinks down into the cushion next to mine.

There is some deep desire hiding inside me. Something that makes me want to sink into him. Rest my head on his shoulder, wrap my hands around his upper arm, and just... forget about everything else but us.

But I don't do that. I want to, but I don't.

"I'd make small talk," he says. "Ask you what you've been up to these past few years, but I'm gonna assume you don't know. So..."

He lets the word dangle there. Waiting for me to pick it up.

"So..." I say, thinking. Thinking about what's missing between us. Because clearly there's a lot.

"So I got this place," he says, saving me from myself. "It's going pretty good."

"You make bikes?" I say, staring straight ahead. Because something tells me if I look at him I'll do

33

something stupid. Like hug him. Or kiss him. Or something worse. Or better, depending on how you see things.

"I make bikes." He sighs. And then he sorta chuckles. Which—I'm so fucking weak—makes me turn my head involuntarily so I can see him. "I sold one last week for a hundred and fifteen grand so I got money."

That last part reverberates in my head for a few seconds. It implies whatever history we have between us didn't involve a lot of money. "I don't need money." It's true too. According to the text on the phone I'm rich in virtual currency. And the thing inside me says if I think hard enough about that little fact, I'll know how to liquidate it into something real pretty quick.

"Maybe not," he says. "But I got some."

"Now what?"

"We wait, I guess."

"For?"

He huffs out something that isn't quite a laugh. "For fuckin' Alec to call. Just like old times, right?"

"Is it?" I ask, still looking at him.

"Look," he says, reaching for my hand. He folds his fingers over mine and squeezes. "Whatever it is he's got you into, I'll get you out. OK?" His blue eyes do that searching thing again. They scan me like a laser that knows how to read my barcode. "Don't worry about what happens next. I got you."

I want to pull away and make him squeeze me tighter at the same time. Both urges running deep. Both desires simultaneously confusing and comforting. His hand is so warm, his whole body radiating heat that calls my name.

He lets go of my hand and puts his arm around me and pulls me close.

34

I sink.

Absolutely sink into him.

And we just sit there in silence. For long, drawn-out moments. For eternity.

"I'm glad you're back," he finally says. "I don't care what you did or how you got here, I'm just glad you're back."

"Me too," I say. And I mean it. I don't know who I really am. I don't know who Alec is. I don't know why I love this man holding me right now.

I just know I do.

CHAPTER FIVE

Danny

We almost did it once. Almost stepped over that imaginary line and changed our relationship from friends to lovers. But I stopped it.

Her fingers were already dealing with the button on my jeans. Our mouths heading in the direction of a desperate kiss. My hands wanted to touch her everywhere all at once. It felt so inevitable in that moment and then like a dumbass I let myself imagine what things would be like tomorrow. Not *tomorrow* tomorrow. It might take weeks or months. Hell, years. People go years blinded by that one mistake they made, refusing to see it for what it was.

But even though I want one—desperately—there's no way Christine and I could have a relationship. Not after all we've done together. Not after all we've been through. There's too much sadness there. So much anger. And blame.

Blame for all the things that went wrong. For all the reasons why we're here right now. Dealing with whatever the fuck she's into. Sitting in this stupid one-bedroom apartment above a dingy garage that has become my whole life.

She got down on her knees and I don't know why, but that scared me. And then her fingertips were about to wrap around my cock and pull it out. Her lips puckered up against my swollen head were just moments away.

But I got a glimpse of the future and it was not pretty.

She wasn't even eighteen. After all that time together, after all those jobs, after all that killing… she wasn't even old enough to vote yet.

She would've blamed me when it all went to shit. And then I'd have lost her. For good.

She blamed me anyway. She left me anyway. And I lost her anyway.

What was my point again?

"You have a nice security system."

"What?" I turn my head slowly to look at her. God. I shouldn't even fucking look at her because those hazy green-brown eyes are staring back at me. I could get lost in them. So easily.

"I mean," she stammers. "You seem to take your security seriously. Two alarms. And it's a good company. I don't know how I know that, but… forget it."

I let out a breath and a smile comes with it. "You know how you know that?"

"How?" she asks, leaning into me a little.

"Because that's the only company we never got past."

She squints those beautiful eyes. Searching for the memories, maybe.

"That's why I use them. They're the best and we never got past them."

"Oh," she whispers. "I only meant… I just meant I feel kinda… safe with you. That's all."

And that sets off a cyclone of what-ifs and coulda-shoulda-wouldas in my head. How I could've done things different. How I should've been there for her, even after she walked away. How I would've been so much better off if she was in my life these past few years.

But that's the thing, right? What's good for me was never good for her.

"I used you," I say. "For a very long time. And one day you just said, 'Fuck you, Fortnight.' And we were done."

She takes a deep breath and holds it. I count to five in my head and she lets it out.

I know her so well. Even when she has no idea who she is or why she does things. I know her.

"Maybe," she says, turning her back to me. Turning her body. Stretching out on the couch. Reaching for a pillow and laying her head on it as she tucks her hands underneath. Her legs find their comfort zone across the top of my lap.

Like old times.

"Now what?" she says.

I shrug. "We wait for Alec, I guess."

"Why?"

"Because... I guess... he's the one who knows things."

"Should we care what he knows?"

I press my lips together and reluctantly nod my head. "We should."

There's ten minutes of silence after that. I feel very exposed for some reason. And I don't know why. Is it because she's back and she brought him with her? Is it because I still want her and can't have her? Is it because there's an opportunity here? One that ends the way I always thought it would?

I think back on the day I first met her. We were in a foster home. She'd been there a while, but it was my first day. I'd gotten busted for stealing food from a local grocery store and just finished a few months of juvie time. Most kids like me have no hope of getting placed with a family, but it was my lucky day. The family had a baby on the way and needed some quick cash. So they took as many kids as the system would let them and packed us all into this big, old house down on Second.

Christine was ten years old. I was fourteen and those four years seemed like an eternity between us. She was sitting on the grass in the ratty backyard poking a beetle with a stick. I remember this because the beetle was blue, and it shouldn't have been.

"It's a mutant," she said, still poking at it. "That's why it's blue."

I remember thinking she was a mind reader when she said that.

But she turned those hazy green eyes up at me and said, "Do you ever feel like crushing pretty things?"

And it stopped my heart, I swear to God.

I said, "No," because I thought she was pretty and if I told the truth and said yes, then that would mean I'd want to crush *her*.

"I do," she said. She poked the bug again. Not hard or anything. And it scrambled up a tall, weedy stalk of grass to get away. "But only because I want to see what's inside. I need to know what makes it so pretty."

I remember thinking, *Damn, this little girl is fucked up.*

But I didn't say that. I just took that stick and tossed it over a fence. Then I reached for her hand, pulled her to her feet, and said, "I got a couple bucks. Wanna blow this place and get some ice cream?"

Because it wasn't fair. She wasn't a kid anymore. She was old and someone did that to her. Someone stole her childhood. Maybe she'd never been a kid and it just wasn't fair.

"Do you have a bathtub?" Christine says in the here and now.

We were a team after that.

I look at her without turning my head. "Yeah."

"Can I take a bath? I'm so fucking sore. I just want to soak."

I swallow down the opportunity. Tell myself I don't want to kiss her right now. Tell myself I don't love her that way. Tell myself—

"Please?"

"Sure," I say. And then I push her legs off my lap, stand up, walk over to the little dining table, put on my leather jacket, and say, "I'll be back in a couple hours. There are towels in the hall closet."

Brasil is my Alec these days. He's a tall guy with reddish hair and beard—both going gray at vastly different rates—who lives on the west side of the city near the waterfront on the top floor of one of those newly renovated old buildings that spent its youth as a rubber factory or some shit.

He's only like twelve years older than me but the guy has been around the fuckin' block and he's got the scars and lines to prove it.

We chop cars.

High-end motherfuckin' cars.

41

We don't do it here. This city is way too industrial for the legitimate über-rich. Not enough sun, not enough sand, not enough glam.

We got an operation out west. About thirty-five up-and-comers do the dirty, put them on a train, ship them to another city down south, and then we have 'em picked up and spread out to about two dozen different shops to be chopped. We sell that shit online through a website hosted in Mexico.

Like me he learned to keep his distance from the product the hard way. Like me he's got a business and like mine, it's not a front. I make custom bikes because I love the work, and he breeds and sells racehorses because he likes the smell of premium alfalfa hay and the sound of that bugle on race day.

He told me that. I'm not just talking out my ass.

But it feels like we're at the tail-end of closing up shop. Ready to retire. At least I am. I've got money socked away in various offshore accounts. When I told Christine I got money I wasn't lying. When I said I sold a bike, I did, and that's how I got it. I don't touch the dirty money. Not one fuckin' cent. Everything I spend comes from bikes. All that other green is locked up tight in faraway banks.

But if she needed piles of money I'd get it for her. If she wanted it, I'd hand it all over.

I owe her.

Brasil has even more security than I do. He's one paranoid motherfucker. But we're partners so I got a special biometrically-coded app to open his garage door, which lets me pull the Jeep right onto a lift that will take me up to his personal parking spaces. When I get up there I ease the Jeep out, take a reserved spot next to his Escalade, and make my way to the door where his security pats me down (no one gets past this door without a pat-down), finds my gun, takes the magazine out, empties the chamber, and then hands it back with nothing more than a nod.

No one gets past this door locked and loaded either.

"Be careful," the door-thug warns me.

"Why?"

"He's pissed off today."

"Noted."

Brasil isn't one of those Zen guys. He throws a fit about pretty much everything. But the second I open the solid-steel door I can hear him yelling. It's his I'm-about-to-off-one-of-you-stupid-motherfuckers yell.

When I walk the hallway leading into the vast, open loft space I see a line of men—tough men—standing up against the wall like they're about to get hit by a firing squad. My age. Hard men. Experienced men. You get the point. They're not fresh-faced babies.

And Brasil is pacing in front of them, screaming, his face red with anger, his yelling so loud it makes my throat hurt. I can practically see the vein throbbing in the side of his neck as he points to the guy with the gun.

It really might be a firing squad.

"What the fuck?" I ask.

Brasil stops mid-stride to stare at me. It takes a lot of self-control and a few seconds to halt the threats he was about to hurl at me, but he does it.

"We have a fucking problem."

"OK," I breathe out.

"Get the fuck out of here. And you do not come back until you know who the fuck is responsible for this."

The line of men scatters instantly. They don't look back. They don't make faces or throw each other sidelong glances as if to say, *What the fuck is up his ass?*

They just leave.

Brasil pours himself a whiskey, downs it in one gulp, and then slams the glass down on the concrete kitchen counter so hard it shatters.

"I... am going to assume something went horribly wrong with that last order."

"You assume correctly." He's calm now. Like that whiskey was the golden ticket to peace. And he walks over to the office section of the loft, takes a seat in the absurdly large leather chair, and leans back with a creak. "Our last shipment is gone."

"Gone? Like never got here? Or someone got to the freight cars before our guys did?"

"What's the difference?"

I shrug. "Well, if it never arrived then you don't need to yell at our men. It's not their fault. But if they fucked up and let it get away, then yeah, we got a problem because that means we got a rat."

"We got a rat," he says, his Irish accent thick. He was born in the U.S., but he's spent a lot of time in Ireland over the course of his lifetime. Just got back a week ago and the accent is always thicker when he comes home than it was when he left. "And we've got competition."

"Who?" I ask.

"If I knew that do you think I'd waste my time yelling at those dumb fucks?"

I shrug and take a seat in another smaller leather chair in front of his desk, just kinda waiting for him to get over his anger. I'm not afraid of Brasil, but I give him his space and he gives me mine. It works well for us.

"I heard rumors while I was gone."

I pause to think about that for a second, but it doesn't make much sense. "Rumors? In Ireland? About us?"

"We have a problem. And David is dead."

"Shit," I say, raking my fingers though my hair. "What the fuck? When?"

"Two nights ago. Some girl got him and—"

I stop listening at the word 'girl.' I picture Christine instead.

"And she was a professional."

"How do you know?"

"What did I just say? He took a bullet to the head and my guys say it came from the top of a building almost a mile away. A sniper."

David is not a partner. Not like me. But he's pretty high up in our little organization. He runs all the out-of-towners. Keeps the trains on track, so to speak.

"A very talented fucking sniper."

"How do you know it was a girl?"

"We got footage of her."

Fuck.

"From a gas station CCTV across the street from where she did the hit." He turns in his chair, swings his laptop around so I can see the screen, and yup. Her face is blurry but sure as fuckin' shit, that's Christine. I see her so clear, this grainy image might as well be HD.

The video cuts out and Brasil asks, "Who is she?"

"How the fuck would I know?"

He stares at me. Long and hard. It's kind of a challenge. A dare to keep this lie going. But I'm an excellent liar and I don't care how many cars we've chopped together, if it comes down to Christine or Brasil,

I choose Christine. "Why the fuck are you looking at me that way?" I growl the words out.

"Because you had a girl once, right? That girl you used to talk about long time ago."

"She's gone. Been gone since before we got into business, Brasil. You know that already."

"I hear she's back."

"I think you've heard wrong."

"Why's that?"

"Because I'd know."

"Maybe you're not as important as you think?"

"Maybe you'd better shut the fuck up before you say something I don't let you take back?"

"Are you threatening me, Danny?"

"Depends," I say. "Are you accusing me?"

We stare each other down for the better part of ten seconds. Then he opens his desk drawer, takes out a pack of smokes, lights one up, and blows out the hit with the words, "We have a problem."

I lean back into the chair, prop a leg on my knee, and shove my hands into the deep pockets of my leather jacket to let him know I've got all day.

"Someone used our cars to smuggle diamonds."

And there it is.

The who, the what, the when, the why, the where.

Alec is back. And this time he brought Christine with him.

But I rally. I don't even miss a beat. "That's dumb. No one needs to smuggle diamonds these days. No one gives a fuck about where diamonds come from anymore."

"Not true," he says. "There was a UN resolution last month about it. Cracking down pretty hard from what I hear."

"And you know this how?" I ask, but I don't need to. And he doesn't answer. Because he saw this coming. Maybe not the fucking hit on David or the actual car robbery, but he knew something was up and he never told me.

I point my finger at him. "Do not fuck with me, Brasil. I might not be the muscle I used to be, but I've got a contingency plan for every possible scenario."

"You better," he says. "Because we lost something else in that shipment. Something we didn't own and something we now have to pay back."

"What the fuck are you talking about?"

"Women," he says.

"What?"

"Russian women. Asian women. All kinds of women."

"What?"

"We've been trafficking people for over two years, Danny. And the fact that this got past you really disturbs me."

CHAPTER SIX

Christine

There's this leftover breeze in the air after Danny leaves. Like the cold rushed in when he opened the door and it decided to stick around afterward.

I sit on the couch for a few minutes trying to wrap my head around things. There's this hazy fog in there. Like memories trying their best to come back. My hand involuntarily goes to the stitched-up wound and I absently count the stitches again.

One. Two. Three. Four... still seventeen of them.

I know what I do. Which means I kinda know what I did to deserve this. I know my name. I know Danny is Danny and some guy named Alec sits between us. I know I should take this opportunity to leave, but I also know I'm not gonna.

I get up, find the hall closet, grab two towels, and cautiously enter the bedroom because there's no bathroom out here so that's where it must be.

The bed is messy. Sheets strewn about like a good night's sleep is some elusive pot of gold at the end of a rainbow. There are clothes on the floor, T-shirts and jeans all stained with the blood of bikes, and the smell of transmission fluid and brake dust in the air.

I breathe it in, liking it for some reason.

I have an urge to snoop but the urge to wash the days-old blood off me overrides it, so I give in to that and make my way to the bathroom.

It's surprisingly modern. Like he put a lot of thought into it. Marble floors and tile. Large soaker tub and a separate standing shower.

For a second I debate taking a shower instead. There are four shower heads pointing down at the drain from different locations and a control panel on the outside that looks like it might have magical powers a tub can't conjure up.

But I really do want to soak. Just slide down under hot water and listen to the hard thrum of power pouring out of the faucet while I think.

I take off my clothes, start the water, and get in before it fills. I like the feeling of buoyancy a tub offers. I like feeling heavy like stone and then, as the water level rises, the feeling of weightlessness. So I lie there, my body pressing down on the cold porcelain, close my eyes, and wait for it.

Gunshots make me sit up, water splashing around my body and spilling over the side of the deep tub.

Shit. I think I fell asleep.

Were those gunshots real? Or was I dreaming?

I grip the side of the tub—forcing myself not to move—and listen.

There's nothing. But the feeling... that feeling that I'm in danger... it doesn't quite fade with the realization that I'm alone, I was dreaming, and no one is shooting.

I reach over and turn the water off, then sink back down into the liquid heat.

Alec.

Christine.

Danny.

This is how you say our names. In this order. We are Alec, and Christine, and Danny. I don't know why that matters, I just know that's how it's done.

I'm in the middle. They surround me.

I know this. I feel this. But I have no memory of it.

There's a bar of white soap waiting for my fingertips when I reach over to the marble tile insert on the wall. There's a black bottle of shampoo too. I wash, breathing in the thick steam, and then reluctantly pull the plug and get out before the buoyancy feeling fades and the weight of the world comes back.

The towels are scratchy and for some reason that makes me smile. Is it a memory? Are cheap towels some little quirk of his that feels like home? Some kind of rebellious stand he took once, long ago?

Shit. What the fuck is wrong with me? I don't know much about who I am, but I have a pretty strong feeling that a towel's softness factor isn't something I give two shits about.

I wrap the second towel around my head, swipe my hand across the fogged-up mirror, and stare into unfamiliar eyes.

What happened to you?

There's this moment when I feel something floating up to the surface the way my body floated up in the tub with the rising water—the soft *thoomp* of the bullet leaving the suppressed barrel of the rifle. The recoil of a powerful weapon pulsing through my body. The kill shot exploding his head—what was his name?

It's on the tip of my tongue when it disappears.

Shit.

I throw the bathroom door open, slamming it against the wall so hard, a picture tilts on the wall revealing a…

Holy fuck. What is that?

I walk over to it, take it off the wall and smile.

A safe.

Not just any safe. A Starling HC900. A 1999 model that everyone said was uncrackable back in the day. It's still a good safe today. Not like the digital ones lazy people keep. An old steel dial with barely visible black-inked numbers carved into the metal stares back at me as all this comes back.

This safe…

LONG TIME AGO

He sticks a gun into the waistband of my jeans, the cold metal pressing against my lower back. "What's that for?" I ask, looking up into his bright eyes. They're the eyes of a privileged boy who has everything and doesn't even know it. A boy with a family, and a home, and a history that doesn't involve pretend relationships you gather up and discard every time opportunity knocks and then, sure as shit, slams the door in your face.

He has blood ties and I am jealous of that.

And he's pretty. Like that blue beetle. And I have an urge to poke him until all the pretty spills out.

But I look at Danny instead. Danny isn't pretty. He's strong. And rough. Like a wall. And he's got the same things inside him that I do. And he won't let me poke the beetle or this golden boy either. He takes my mind off the ugly inside with just one look.

"Just in case, nunu." Alec winks at me and some of the sickness inside me dissipates into the air like a misty day at the end of summer.

"OK," I say, even though the gun is uncomfortable. "But should I use it?"

"If you have to," he says.

"No," Danny says at the same time. And then he turns to Alec. "You said this was a done deal. No one was inside. Why the fuck—"

"Just in case, bru. Precautionary tale and all, yeah?"

I like the way he talks. I like the way words come out of his mouth like poetry. Doesn't even matter what he's saying, I just get lost in it. I like the pretty inside him. And he's got enough to share with me. With us. So I don't care if I have to use the gun to bring him back what he's sending me inside for.

"Now, you go in there," Alec continues, "And do it just it just the way I showed you, K?" He places his hand on my cheek and it's surprisingly warm. "Four turns to the left. Stop on the first number. Then three turns for the second number and—"

"I know," I huff, irritated. "You told me all that a million times last night."

"Good," he says, petting my hair. "Then go. We'll meet you in the alley with the bikes."

"Be careful," Danny says, reaching for my arm.

"Shit," I say, shrugging him off. "Don't start, Danny." I hate it when he treats me like his little sister. We're not family. Not real family. I'm his best friend, not his stupid sister.

TODAY

The memory comes rushing back like a slap in the face. Makes me recoil and want to fall into it completely at the same time. And it occurs to me—I have these opposing feelings a lot. Even in my unreliable memories.

This safe in his bathroom wall is the same model as the first one I cracked lifetimes ago. Not that I had to crack it that day. I had the combination, I remember that much. It was an inside job. Some friend of the family—I roll my eyes, can't help it. Some family. Some friend, for that matter.

You don't steal a seven-carat diamond from your friends and family.

Unless your name is Alec van den Berg.

How did he get that combination? I try to dive back in the flashback. Look for that answer. But it's not there. It's all gone.

I tug my towel up, straighten it out and tuck the edge in to keep it tight as I look at the safe.

Could I open this? I didn't crack that safe that day, but I have a feeling cracking safes is something I do well. Maybe as well as I shoot people.

Funny, haha, Christine, that thing inside me says. *You shoot people so well you wake up in strange apartments with a gash on your head you don't recall getting.*

Fuck off, thing. Alec and Danny put the pretty inside me and I don't need you anymore.

I press my ear to the side of the safe and start turning the dial. If I had the right equipment I'd know what to do, that's a fact.

But my fingers already know what to do…. four turns to the left, each time briefly stopping on the faintly visible tick mark for the number thirty-three. The dial is already rotating to the right, briefly stopping on the second tick mark. At the end of the last two rotations to the left I smile.

I rotate the lever and the safe silently opens when I pull.

Still got it, Christine.

And dumbass Danny is still using our combination.

None of this is normal. Most friends don't share combinations. You give them the spare key to your apartment in case you ever get locked out. Or your spare car key in case you go to jail and need someone to pick your car up from the bar for you.

But not us.

I want to think about that for a long time. Get lost in it. But the little stainless-steel box inside the safe steals all the thoughts in my head.

The brushed-metal box with a triangle etched on the top. The brushed-metal box that, when opened, reveals one seven-carat loose diamond sitting on a plush cushion of black velvet.

"Holy shit, he still has it." I don't know how, or why, I breathe out those words because the memory of what happened that night I took the gun inside that house has no ending.

But they come out anyway.

And a moment later it all comes back.

This diamond is the very first one I ever paid for in blood.

CHAPTER SEVEN

The fight isn't pretty. It's not some good-natured rumble between friends or a small hitch in a plan between partners. I have Brasil pinned up against the wall behind his desk, gun pressed into his throat so hard, he's gasping for breath.

His gun, not mine. Took it right out of the fucking holster he wears under his arm.

Jack, his top security man, has another gun pressed against the back of my head, but I'm growling as I stare into Brasil's bloodshot eyes, "Underestimate me, Brasil. Do it."

"Back off," Brasil chokes out to Jack. "Back. The fuck. Off."

Jack pulls his gun away and I feel the space he creates between us as he does as he's told.

I don't take my eyes off my partner. "What the fuck did you do?"

"Your turn to back off," Brasil gasps. "Now, Danny. You won't get out of here if you don't."

Yesterday I wouldn't really care if I walked away from this. Finding out your business partner of almost five years has been trafficking humans behind your back and now you're responsible for a debt you never signed on the dotted line for is enough to make a guy snap.

And, oh, man, do I ever feel like snapping right now.

But Christine, that little voice in my head says. *Christine is back. She's taking a bath in your apartment right now. If you die here she'll die there. Sure as fucking shit. They'll go there, find her, and then all those things I said would happen to her will happen. Torture, rape, death…*

Only I'll be the one responsible, not Alec.

And that kind of weight isn't something I can die with. I won't take that burden down to hell with me.

So I grit my teeth, tilt my head, and say, "You know what I find really disturbing, Brasil? The fact that my business partner has not only been lying to me, but doing it with such conviction I didn't even suspect him capable of such betrayal."

And then I spit in his face.

He blinks, but that's it. Just takes it. And Brasil Lynch might be a lot of things, but he's not a man who cowers from a well-deserved insult.

I press the gun into his throat even harder, but only so I can grab a moment to look over my shoulder at Jack. I'm still his target, but he's good at his job and has followed orders. So I back off, step away, Brasil's own gun still pointed at his face, and say, "I'm out. Whatever the fuck you've gotten us into, you're gonna remove me from it and I'm gonna walk away now."

Brasil laughs, a good-natured chuckle that even comes with a smile. "Brother—"

I pull the trigger. The bullet smashes through the wall of his apartment, mere inches to the left of his skull, and shards of concrete go flying.

"Do not," I say, feeling the temperature in the room rise up to boiling, "call me your brother."

Brasil brings his hands up to chest level, palms out. A small calm-down-dude-it's-all-good-here gesture meant for both me and Jack, because Brasil's looking at his muscle when he does it, not me.

"We are not brothers, got it? We're over. I never signed up for this bullshit."

"May be the case," Brasil says. "But you're in it anyway. What? You think I can just call up the Russians and say, 'Little problem. We lost your people in the last shipment and oh, by the way, my business partner is out so let me take all the responsibility for this?' Do you really think they give a shit which one of us costs them money?" He laughs. "You are out." He's not laughing now. "Fuck you, Fortnight. No one ever gets to pull a gun on me in my own fucking place. Least of all you, motherfucker. We're done here. But you will help me find out who did this. And you will take them down. Maybe get that girl to help you, huh? We know she's alive. We know you probably have her. So now who's the liar? Now who's the cheat? Now who's—"

"Still you, Brasil. I have no idea what you're going on about, but my girl is gone and has been for a very long time."

"Nice try." He chuckles, pulling his shirt down as he grabs his stupid king-sized office throne, spins it around, and takes a seat. "She killed David. I was gonna tell you about the women this week. Give you a nice, clean escape route. Let you walk away rich, fat, and happy and let David take your place. But guess what?" He shrugs, palms up, like this is an actual question.

59

"David's dead," I finish for him. "Boo fucking hoo. Got what he deserved. And you're gonna get yours too."

"Do you really think you're in a position to threaten me?" He's got this maniacal, amused look on his face. Like this is all good fun.

"Yeah," I say. "I do. Because I know who stole your shit. *Your shit*," I say again, just to be clear. "Not mine. And if you want out of this fucked-up mess you find yourself in, and don't want to end up with your brains splatted all over the wall of this loft, then you're gonna shut the fuck up and let me handle this."

"Who?" Jack asks. He's standing right next to me now, gun at his side instead of pointing at my face. *Nice, Jack. Good to know you're not really gonna shoot me after all these years.*

I think.

"Alec van den Berg."

"Who?" both these assholes say at the same time.

"South African diamond smuggler. Old acquaintance of mine. And I know where he is."

Which is a lie. I have no clue. But I know where he'll be.

Here. Very soon. Because Christine is back with me and there's no way in hell he's not gonna show up to try to steal her back.

CHAPTER EIGHT

YESTERDAY

Somewhere over the Atlantic, I remember that I have yet to ask the laaitie his name.

"Ou! Laaitie!"

Everyone turns to look. The laaitie's head snaps up. He happens to be sitting up front in a seat with its back to the cockpit, facing the rear of the plane, so we make eye contact through an open doorway straight away. I crook my index finger to summon him over.

His eyes dart around to the other okes on the Bombardier Global 8000 for just a moment, as if to question if anyone has an idea of what being called up to speak with the boss might mean for him.

"Not just now, man. Now now," I tell him as gently as I can, so as not to give him the idea that he's in any kind of trouble. It doesn't seem to convince him, but I try. Finally, he pushes himself up out of his recliner and makes his way back to where I'm trying to look like I'm lounging casually on the sofa, even though I don't feel terribly casual or much like being in repose. But appearances are, as ever, important.

He's a good-looking kid. High cheekbones and dark skin. He's tall, and even though he's still got the gangly limbs of youth about him, he carries himself with the sure-footed gait of a much older man.

I let him stand in front of me, waiting, as I lift a tumbler of Van Ryn's to my lips. I take a moment to consider the golden-brown liquid inside, then close my eyes, take a sip, and allow the spill of brandy to caress my tongue and wash its warmth along my throat, causing me to forget for a moment that I'm still hours from being able to see Christine with my own eyes. From being able to make sure for certain that she's all right.

It took ten fokken calls to get Danny to answer the goddamn phone. Everybody on the plane has a secure line and a restricted number. It's no surprise that he would never pick up a call from a blocked line. Finally, after witnessing my growing aggravation, someone exclaimed, "I think Gerry has an unsecured mobile."

Poor Gerry looked as if he'd been betrayed and then stared up at me with a lowered head as would the cliché puppy who just had a wee on the carpet. He shook his chin back and forth tightly once or twice until it became clear to him that in this rare instance it was an asset, rather than a liability, that he has an open line to the great big world outside.

I can't blame him for initially resisting. Normally he would be right to panic a bit. Under usual circumstances, having such a thing would be grounds for immediate termination and dismissal. And at ten thousand meters, being dismissed from the organization would probably smart a mite upon hitting the ground. But fortunately for Gerry, I was so distracted at the time that I didn't even bother to question what the fok he's doing with a phone he bought at Cellucity or wherever, just grabbed it and started dialing Fortnight's number. I assume that nine separate rings from an unknown caller, seeing the number twenty-seven country code appear on his screen, gave him a fair indication that his attention was needed urgently.

What the fuck are you doing calling me?

Until I heard his voice, I didn't realize how long it had been since we'd spoken. He sounded different. The same. But different.

Christine, I said.

Historically, I'd be pithy or smug or insufferably charming with him, as is my custom, but I couldn't risk the possibility that he'd hang up straight off. Or that he might, in any way, misinterpret the call as anything other than what it was: the best possible option I had to ensure that the only thing on the planet more important to me than diamonds was safe.

Christine what? he asked, the anxiety in the asking both appropriate and shared.

The rest of the call goes like this:

There's been an accident.

A great deal more silence than I might have expected lingers on the line. I certainly expected some, but it goes on for a length of time that seems almost designed to encourage me to speak again first.

I don't.

Finally, he says, *Say more.*

I don't have a great deal more. Christine and I were engaged in an affair—I don't choose those words by accident—*and something appears to have gone awry*—

Fuck have you done?

And right now, my china, I don't know who I can fokken trust. Except you.

I'm not your fuckin' china. And what the hell makes you think for a second that I'll do anything for you?

Not a thing in the world, bru. But I do expect you'll do what's right for Christine.

Again, silence.

I continue, *Or—*

What happened?

I'm not precise on that. I'm not there—

Where are you?

—but from what I can glean, she took a bit of a knock on the head that required some attention.

Fuck does that mean?

Honestly, it's probably the most straightforward thing I've ever said, bru. It means what it means.

I used to know precisely how to get Danny to do things. I knew his triggers. What would work, what wouldn't, how to best manipulate him into giving what I needed.

The man on the other side of this call is not the Danny I used to know.

I'm not entirely sure how to proceed, and I don't have the luxury of figuring it out, so I opt for something resembling the truth. I proceed to fill him in on all the information that Lars provided me.

Then, *Are you in town?* I ask.

Yeah. I'm in town.

I need you to go to her and make sure everything's hundreds.

Again, another lengthy silence.

Eventually, *How the fuck am I supposed to trust anything you're saying?*

No clue, boet. I wouldn't trust me. But, simply, either I've turnt up, after all this time, to telephone you with an elaborate plot designed to somehow cock you up—which, if we stop to consider it, is the stupidest fokken thing I ever heard—or else I'm telling the truth and really, really *have no better option.*

I don't get short of breath very often. Usually the opposite. Like the Hulk thing. I breathe deeply into myself and then myself grows and expands and becomes bigger than life. I never even practiced that or had to learn it. I think I inherited it.

But waiting for Danny to say, *Where is she?* I find myself not breathing at all.

Where is she? he finally, finally asks.

I close my eyes and breathe again, giving him all of the particulars on where she should be. 'Should,' because even though Lars is Lars and even though Lex and Reggie weren't chosen to watch out for her because they won a contest—it's because they've proved themselves loyal—somebody threw Christine off the roof of a fokken building. And that means that someone is either trying to kill her, trying to weaken me, or both.

And in any of those scenarios, I need someone with her who would be willing to lay down their life for her without pause. And there are only two people in the world whose CVs suggest that to be true. One of them is on the phone with me right now. The other, I'd like to believe, is me.

But, in all truth... If asked to pick a sure bet between us, I'm not certain I wouldn't still go with Danny. That's a hard thing to admit. So I don't dwell on it for very long.

Are you coming here? Danny asks.

Don't know, man. I guess that might depend on what you find when you arrive .

Of course I'm fokken coming there. I'm halfway there right now. But I decide that Danny doesn't need to know everything. I mean, I already know he doesn't know *everything*. Because if he did, we wouldn't be in this situation. But irrespective of anything else, he doesn't need to know that I'm on my way, because my old bru, Danny Fortnight, has never been the kind of oke who's big on 'reunions' or 'nostalgia.' Not too keen on 'surprises' either, but some things can't be helped.

Ring me back on this line when you've seen what's what, yeah? I say.

Go fuck yourself.

And then he hung up.

"Mr. van den Berg?"

The voice of the laaitie stirs me out of my brief stupor. I assume it was brief. I don't know how long I had my eyes closed. I think I might be quite a bit more knackered than I realized. The last several hours have been taxing.

Looking at him standing there, he appears nervous but eager. I continue to like him.

"Uphuma kuphi?" I say.

"Sir?"

"Where are you from?" I repeat, slowly.

"Oh, yes, sir. Sorry. I just... You speak Zulu?"

I nod slowly and take another sip from my tumbler. "Why does that surprise you?"

"I don't—I heard what you said to them at the warehouse. To the Americans."

"I would imagine. I was yelling."

He looks at me for a moment, confused, then I finally smile. Which gives him permission to smile. He shifts his feet. Makes a small face. I smile again.

"What's your name?"

"Solomon, sir."

"Solomon what?"

"Bophela, sir."

I nod. "How long have you been with me?" I ask.

"Um, about three weeks, sir."

"Yeah? How is it? As a job?"

"It's very, very good, sir."

"Izit?" I regard him for a long moment. "What were you doing before?"

"Not… not much, sir. Just trying to… you know." He looks away.

The feel of the tumbler in my hand is comforting for some reason. I'm not sure why.

"Do you have a family?"

His eyes dart back to mine. He lowers his head, gives a tiny shake, and although I could well have predicted his response, a wave of emotion that I wasn't expecting pours through me. I down the remainder of my brandy in one gulp, stand, and say…

"Well, you do now, bru." I clap him on the shoulder. "Like how you handled yourself out there today. Good man."

"Thank you, sir. You too, sir." He cringes, worrying he's been insulting, I reckon. It's clear that he wants to feel proud but is still unsure if that's OK. Yet another thing I like about the lad. Then he says, "Is there anything I can do for you, sir? Anything I can get you?"

"No, bru. I'm all right." I begin to head toward the back when his voice stops me.

"Oh… Mr. van den Berg?" I turn. "May I ask where we are going, sir?"

I laugh inwardly, then catch a tiny grin and nod at him.

"Get some rest, man," I say as I again make my way toward my bedroom.

Just as I'm about to close the door and see if I can try to sleep at all, which I most assuredly won't, I turn back to him one last time. "Solomon Bophela..."

He hasn't moved. He faces me.

"Ninety-five years ago, my black great-grandfather married my white great-grandmother in a secret ceremony on the outskirts of Jo'burg. They had my grandmother, she married an Afrikaner called van den Berg, they had my father, my father amassed a fortune, met my mother, had me, I have continued my father's business, and as of the last time I checked, I was—off the public record—the forty-fourth wealthiest person on the earth."

He looks at me, waiting for more.

After a second, I nod and say, "I wouldn't be here today if, ninety-five years ago, that Zulu oke and that yarpie woman hadn't come together. And the fokken courage it took for my great-grandparents to do what they did, especially then, is beyond reason, my boet. I mean, can you even *imagine* how much they had to love each other to take that kind of risk?"

His face remains blank.

I sniff in a tiny laugh and say...

"I hope someday you can."

And then I close the door to my suite so that I can lie on my bed and stare at the ceiling for another eight hours.

CHAPTER NINE

The year after Christine left me was weird. It was just fuckin' weird. We'd been partners for so long I didn't know what do with myself after she walked out. I kept waiting for her in not so logical ways.

Like… I remember wanting to go out to dinner. Not fast food. I'm not talking about the drive-through. I'm talking about sitting in a restaurant and eating something nice. A steak with a fat, baked potato. Candles on the table. Hell, a tablecloth too. And good craft beer. I wanted it so bad, but for weeks, in my head, I kept thinking… *When Christine comes back. Then I can go out to eat.* Because eating out was something we always did together. It felt impossible to eat out if she wasn't there.

And then one day… I dunno. Maybe six months later. I was driving by Caseon's Steakhouse and I just stopped. Went inside. And ate. By myself. Just like that.

And just like that I was someone else.

Someone who didn't have a girl named Christine by his side.

For the first time in as long as I could remember, I was just Danny.

I had a little bit of money that day. Ran into an acquaintance who owed me about ten grand for a job I did, but never got paid for because the dude went to jail. It's funny how money is so relative. When you're fat with cash you don't think about it but when you have none, that's *all* you think about.

And the day before that I had none. Like, I was fuckin' broke. I didn't even have an apartment. I was crashing at Brasil's warehouse. I did a few jobs for him back when we first met. Stole a few cars. So he was letting me sleep in a back room. And when I was driving home from dinner I saw this bike in a driveway with a for sale sign on it. I pulled in, talked to the guy who owned it, handed that guy almost all my cash, and then called up Brasil's towing company and took it home to the warehouse.

There were tools there and cars were already something I knew a lot about. Plus, I'd done two semesters in a body shop at a vo-tech school back when I was still in the foster system, so I knew a little bit about how to fix a fucked-up fender. And Brasil had a guy who could do a nice paint job.

I sold that bike for double the money three weeks later and bought myself two more. Fixed those up, made an even slicker profit, and one year after Christine left I was this guy.

Fortnight's Custom Choppers.

Whenever Alec disappeared I didn't have this existential crisis. I *never* thought about that motherfucker when we weren't together. Barely remembered he was part of the team.

But Christine was there to keep me in check. Christine filled up all the empty spaces Alec left behind and yeah, even back then I knew a day of reckoning would come eventually, but I was busy. When he was gone, I was glad he was gone.

But the way shit ended... that still sits bad with me.

The feelings I have for him now are nothing at all like the forgettable bad taste he left behind when the whole operation fell apart.

The feelings I have for him now are real.

Men are just like that, I guess. When we're ragey teenagers all pumped up with new testosterone our anger is tempered by ignorance. Twenty-eight is different. At twenty-eight those hormones have pretty much evened out, the body has filled itself in, you know who you are, what you're capable of, and that anger is dangerous.

What I feel for Alec right now isn't some desire for revenge. It's not even jealousy that he had Christine for God knows how long and I never knew about it.

It's rage. It's hate. It's that gut-wrenching feeling of betrayal that makes you sick because you didn't even know you were betrayed until the whole shit-show was over.

He's got all the money. But that's not why I hate him. I've got all the money now too.

He's got the looks, and the suits, and the fuckin' houses and the cars. But that's not why I hate him either. If I wanted suits and summer houses, I could make it rain.

He's got Christine. Not physically, of course. But he's weaseled his way back into her life. She did this job for him. She got hurt because of him. She has some misplaced sense of loyalty, or nostalgia, or whatever.

He got a hold of a stick and poked her until all the pretty spilled out. He only ever wanted to ruin her. Turn her into what he thought she *should* be.

And that's not something I'll ever let him do again. Never again.

So do I feel guilty for setting the asshole up and handing him over to Brasil so Christine and I can skip town and start a new life? The life we were *meant* to have?

Fuck. No.

There's a moment when I'm climbing the stairs up to my apartment in the garage when I feel like I made a mistake. That leaving Christine alone was a mistake. That when I pull open the door and step inside she's gonna be gone. No trace left behind just like last time.

But she's there. Sitting on my couch, wearing my t-shirt, dark hair still damp, legs all tucked up underneath her the way she always liked to sit because her small body doesn't quite fit on the furniture the way a large man's does.

And she's holding the box with the triangle etched on the top.

I can't see it, but I know what she's looking at.

Her eyes meet mine as I kick the door closed and toss my keys on the little dining table. "You didn't sell it?" she asks.

I take off my jacket, hang it on the back of a chair, and say, "Not mine to sell. And uh… how do you know what it is if you can't remember anything?"

She turns the box around so I can see the diamond. Holds it up like an offering. "I remember this. I remember this day."

I suck in a breath of air and nod. "Remember anything else?"

She shakes her head. "No. Not really."

I grunt. "Well, that sucks. And it figures."

"Why does it figure?"

"Because, Christine. You and I have been partners since you were ten years old. Like fourteen fuckin' years. And the only thing you can remember is the day we let fuckin' Alec in?"

"In what?"

I grunt and shrug again. Louder. More deliberate this time. "Into *us*."

She just stares at me.

"Us," I repeat. "Me and you were a team. A damn fuckin' good one too. And then his rich, punk-boy ass comes along. And he charms us both. And he's got everything we want but don't have. And we just let him…" *Poke the pretty right out of us*, I don't say. "In," I finish.

She shrugs now too, unable to give as many shits as me, I suppose. "We must've let him in for a reason."

"Yeah, because that's what he does. That's who he is. He's a dirty fuckin' con man and you really don't want to know the story I just got from my partner about what he did now." I run my fingers through my hair. "You really don't."

"I killed someone."

"Yeah." I kinda laugh. "Thanks for that. I guess I owe you."

"What?"

"Turns out that asshole you killed was probably gonna kill me."

"What do you mean?"

"I mean shit is going down, Christine. Shit is going down and I'm in the middle of it. I think my partner was trying to get rid of me."

"Get rid of you how?"

73

"Doesn't really matter," I say. "The only thing that matters is David, that guy you offed? He was gonna take my place." I walk over to the fridge, take out a beer, pop the top, and gulp. When I come up for air I'm staring at her. "And you took that off the table. So uh, yeah. Thanks."

She stares back at me.

I get a weird feeling. Like... shit, I dunno. Her intense gaze just kinda affects me that way. I lean my hip against the kitchenette counter, unsure what to say next.

"I think it's really good to see you," she says.

Which makes me smile. "Good to see you too, Mean Keene."

She giggles. "No."

"Oh, yeah," I say, unable to stop the grin as I nod my head. "That's your name. And you know what's worse?"

"What?"

"You picked it out."

She almost snorts. "I did not. That's stupid."

"Hey." I shrug. "You were ten. Lesson number one in the Book of Thugs. Wait until you're old enough to wear a training bra before you choose your gangsta name."

She stands up, snaps the metal box closed, tosses it on the couch, and walks towards me.

I think... I think my heart is beating too fast. I lock eyes with her as she slowly walks across the small living room. My t-shirt is too big on her, so it ends high-thigh. Her bare legs capture my attention and I have a second to wonder if she's wearing anything underneath it.

She stops in front of me, one hand reaching for my beer, setting it on the counter, the other on my waist, sliding around to press against the hard muscles of my back. "What are you doing?" I breathe.

"I want to touch you for some reason." She moves forward. Her breasts against my chest. Her head finding a home against my shoulder. She's looking up at me with… with… I dunno. I don't know what that is, but she's got her arms wrapped around my middle now and it makes me want to…

"Christine," I say, reaching around to grab her wrists and pull her off me.

"What?"

"Don't."

"Why?"

"Because"—I sigh—"that's not what we are."

"You're lying."

"No," I say, so frustrated. "No, I'm not. We're just friends."

She pulls away a little so she can see my face. "Friends? Do friends come back to kill enemies for you?"

"Partners," I say.

She smiles a little. Just the corners of her mouth lift up, which makes me look at her lips as she talks. "I don't remember everything but I know… I know this is right. I have wanted to touch you since you first rescued me from that tin-foil apartment."

I don't know what to do.

I want to kiss her so bad right now. Not the kiss of a friend, either. Or a partner. I want to kiss her whole mouth like we're lovers.

But I'm afraid. I could ruin everything if I kiss her. I could ruin us, and this, and everything I ever hoped for since she left. I want her to stick around. I don't want to disappoint her again. I don't want to fuck things up. I don't think I could live through another breakup.

75

But I can't tell her any of that, either. Because I know what she'll do. She'll lean up on her tiptoes, place her hands on my cheeks, and kiss my mouth like we're something we're not.

And I'll forget that's not what we are, and I'll let her, and kiss her back, and then tomorrow—

"Christine," I practically beg.

But she's not listening. Her hands are pressed against my cheeks. Her eyes are only looking at mine. And then she does it.

She kisses me.

And I know. This is the moment that defines who we are. It's the beginning of something we can't have. And everything that comes after is just an ending.

CHAPTER TEN

Christine

He grips my wrists, still in the act of trying to remove himself from my embrace. But he loses the battle almost instantly. The moment our lips touch we close our eyes and sink into each other.

It's everything I imagined. A sense of complete peace. The longing fades and satisfaction takes its place. My fingertips slip under his shirt and the heat of his body increases both my desire and the feeling that this is how things were meant to be.

It's not an urgent kiss though. Not some prelude to us ripping each other's clothes off. It's just... nice.

And I might not remember everything that makes up Christine Keene, but I do know one thing: Nice isn't something I've gotten a lot of in my short life. So I take it. I sigh into our kiss, my hands pressing against the hard muscles of his waist as I invite him in.

"Christine," he says, pulling back in the very moment I'm opening up.

"What?" I ask, irritated that he's still putting up this stupid pretense.

"We can't—"

"We can do whatever the fuck we want."

His grip on my wrists is real now. And a second later my hands are no longer touching his body.

"What?" I ask, pleading with him as I gaze into his blue eyes. "What?"

"This isn't what we are. It's gonna ruin everything if we..."

But he can't even say it. "If we what? If we fuck? Jesus. I might not remember everything, but I seriously doubt you've never thought about this. You want to fuck me. I can tell."

"Stop being so goddamned vulgar."

I push him away, angry at... I don't know. The rejection. The fact that this feels like who we are and he's telling me it's not. Which means my instincts are off. And that kinda scares me. And—

"Look," he says. I glance up at him through my hanging hair and he stops. Sighs. "I'd be lying if I said I didn't love you like that. I do. But we're in a world of shit right now, Christine. And it's not the time to start a brand new chapter in our lives. We gotta finish what we started and then maybe..."

But he never ends the thought. Just shakes his head, pushes me so I have to take a step back, and extricates himself from the situation.

"Maybe what?" My words come out hard. Accusatory, maybe.

He turns to face me once he's in the middle of the small living room. "I'm glad you're here. No," he says, shaking his head. "Glad isn't even close to what I feel about you being here. Fuckin'... fuckin'..." He holds his hands up, palms towards each other, like he wants to choke me. Because he feels something for me and he doesn't even have a word for it. "I can't lose you again. I

78

can't, Christine. I'll fuckin' die this time. I'm not gonna lose you again."

"I'm offering myself to you," I say, taking a few steps towards him. "All you gotta do is accept me."

"Jesus," he says, fingertips threading into his hair like his frustration has reached a new level. "Can we just take it slow?"

I smile at him. Not because I'm happy or anything. I am a little happy though. Because this all feels good. It feels right. I should be scared right now. And if I was alone and not with Danny, I would be scared. But I'm not alone. I am with him.

He smiles back at me. "I missed you," he says. "So much."

I nod, walking towards him. Trying to erase the space between us. Get back to where to where we need to be. Where we should be. But I go slow this time. Like he's prey that might get away.

God, that's a disturbing analogy.

"I want you, Christine. The way you want me. But I don't want to give up what I just got back, do you understand that at all?"

I nod. Because I do.

"And hey, if when all this blows over you're still interested, if when we get somewhere safe you still want this—"

"I will," I say, feeling very sure of myself.

"—then we'll… give it a try, OK? But business comes first."

That stops me. "What?"

"We gotta take care of this situation. You have no idea how much shit we're in. Both of us. And fuckin' Alec is gonna get here soon and—"

"Alec is coming?"

He winces at my question. Because there's excitement in it. And then the wince goes hard. "Yeah, he's coming. But it's not gonna play out like some family fuckin' reunion. You're never gonna see him again."

"Why?"

"Because Alec van den Berg is the lying, cheating motherfucker who got you involved in all this, that's why. He's on his way to get what's coming to him. And from this moment on, you're out of this goddamned deal."

"Wait," I say, feeling a little irritated. Because he's treating me like I'm a child. "I thought I was some kind of assassin."

"You are, but—"

"And my right hand is actually a sniper rifle hidden somewhere in your bedroom."

"Christine—"

"And I'm not ten years old anymore so—"

"Will you just fucking hear me out for once?"

"—if I want to get involved, I will."

We stare at each other.

"I will," I repeat.

He shrugs. "What can I say? The answer is no."

"Who the fuck are you?"

He steps forward and pokes me in the chest. Hard. I swipe his hand away. But he grabs both my wrists and holds them. Tight. "I'm the only guy you can trust. And the fact that I refuse to take advantage of you tonight should be all the proof you need. Because believe me, if you were with Alec right now, sure as fuckin' shit he wouldn't give you that same respect."

"I'm not asking you for respect, Fortnight. All I wanted was a goddamned kiss. All I wanted was a fuckin' hug, OK? So you can shove your respect up your ass because all you gave me was rejection."

He lets out a long breath of frustration.

"And I think..." I say. "I think that's typical of you."

He lets go of my wrists and pushes me backwards at the same time. "That's because you don't remember anything."

"So when that memory comes back I'm gonna feel different, Danny? I'm gonna realize that you weren't the one responsible for the long gap of time we've been separated?"

"I wasn't."

"I don't believe you. In fact," I say, lowering my voice, "I'm gonna go out on a limb here and say... I bet when Alec does get here he's gonna have another perspective on that whole situation."

"Yeah, and it's all gonna be lies." He practically growls the words at me. "I've been telling you that for almost ten years, Christine. He's a con man. I get that your memory is in the shitter right now, but surely that brain of yours understands what a con man is."

"Don't talk down to me," I snap. "I'm not a fuckin' child."

"Then for fuck's sake, act like a goddamned adult and hear the words coming out of my mouth."

"Why are you being such a dick? My fuckin' head hurts, my brain feels like it's got holes in it, and pretty much every muscle in my body feels like it's on the other side of a really serious goddamned fight. I mean, Jesus Christ. All I wanted was a little comfort."

He threads his fingers through his hair as he sighs, frustrated with me. But I don't care. I'm frustrated with him too. "Look," he says. "Can we just... go to bed or something? Sleep this day off and talk this through tomorrow?"

I look around his small apartment, then glance down the hallway at the single bedroom.

"I'll take the couch," he says.

Which is not what I was looking for. In fact, the thought of him and me sleeping in separate rooms tonight, so close, but still so far apart, just... I dunno. It's just the last straw.

I turn away, hot tears burning in my eyes. I don't want him to see me cry. Something inside me says I don't cry. Not even in front of Danny Fortnight.

But I can't help it. The tears run down my cheeks before I'm even done processing that part of my missing self. "You know what?" I say.

"What?"

"I missed you."

He huffs out some air. "I missed you too, Christine. More than you can ever imagine."

"And I don't remember everything between then and now. But I know I love you. I know I'm happy to be here with you. And I know I'm not gonna make the same mistake I did when we fell apart." I turn to face him and the moment he realizes I'm crying everything about him changes. His hard body, his severe stare, his tough exterior—all of it softens. "And I don't want to sleep alone. I just... want you to hold me, OK? To be... whatever it is you are to me. Because right now, I need that. That's all I'm asking for. So if you refuse to give in on that one request, I swear to God, Danny, I will never fuckin' forgive you. I will—"

"Fine," he says. "No problem." He covers the space between us in three long strides and then his arms are around me. Holding me tight. "I surrender, OK? I give in. We can share the bed. I'm here for you. You have to know that."

He lifts a stray strand of hair away from my eyes and tucks it behind my ear. So I'm forced to look at him, except it's not forced at all. I can't take my eyes off him. I never want to take my eyes off him.

"Hey," he says.

"What?" I say, sniffling as I wipe the tears away.

"I'm just trying to protect us, that's all."

"Us," I say.

"Us," he says. "Me and you. Just because I'm not giving in to what you want tonight doesn't mean I don't want to. Doesn't mean I never will."

"When will you?" I ask. "When Alec comes and tries to steal me away?"

His eyes dart back and forth, scanning me again. "Why would he send me to get you, Christine?"

"What do you mean?"

"I mean, he called me. He told me where you were. He told me to go get you. Why? Why would he do that?"

"To keep me safe?"

"Or maybe... it was to get us both together in the same place again."

"To what end?" I ask. "To hurt us?"

"That's what he does best."

I can't anymore. I just can't deal. My shoulders slump and I bow my head and stare down at my bare feet. "Why does he have to be here for you to admit you love me?"

"I don't need him to admit that. I love you."

"Then why—"

"Because the timing is wrong, OK? Just... just heal a little. Let your memory come back. Let me figure out

83

what's going on. Put together an escape plan. We've got all the time now."

"That's such a fuckin' lie. There's people after me. You too. I don't know how you control yourself. How can you not want to take everything you can as quick as possible before the fucking timer runs out? We could be dead tomorrow—"

"We won't be," he says, brushing the back of his fingers against my cheek. "We're a team, Keene. The best team there is. We've passed all the tests. We've crossed all the finish lines. This is just a victory lap as far as I'm concerned. One last task before we take the trophy and go the fuck home."

I draw in a deep breath, hold it for five seconds, and then let it out. "Yeah," I say. "Let's just go to bed and kick this world's ass tomorrow."

He leads me down the hallway to the bedroom. Points to the bed and takes off his shirt.

Jesus.

My eyes start at his shoulders and follow every curve—every hill and valley of muscle—as they travel down his body. Linger on the tattoos that run the length of his arms. Pause to watch him unbuckle his belt, unbutton his pants, and drag the zipper down as he kicks off his boots and steps out of his jeans. He stands there for a few seconds trying not to grin as I study the way his boxer briefs hug the corded muscles of his thighs.

"Now get in and scoot over. I'm gonna hold you all fuckin' night, OK? Never let go once."

I sigh, then do as I'm told.

Because the moment the comforter flops over us and his arms gather me up, everything is right in my world.

Everything.

CHAPTER ELEVEN

I met Alec at a boxing gym that ran an after-school program for hood kids like me. I had Christine in school by then. I took care of a little problem the liquor store owner down on Seventh had with thieving kids and instead of paying me in money I got him to take Christine over to the junior high school and register her as an incoming homeschool kid.

You wouldn't think something like that would work but then again, if you've been in the system as long as I have, you would. And it did.

We were living in a pay-by-the-week motel down on Juniper Avenue and by this time it was starting to feel like home. Which sucked and felt pretty good all at once. At least it was ours. We had heat, hot water, TV with a few cable channels, and free wi-fi that mostly worked.

I managed to graduate a semester early the previous December. That was the deal I made with Christine. Or, rather, the deal she made with me. She'd go back to school if I finished.

So fuck it. I signed up for one of those remedial night schools for asshole thugs, did the work in between jobs, and there you go. My part of the deal was done. I'm sure she came up with that idea because she thought I'd never do it, but she was wrong. And even though I had to drag her out of bed every goddamned morning and threaten her with anything from slave labor to jumping on a bus heading down south to live on the beach and leaving her behind, she did get up every day and go.

So that's where she was when I wandered into the boxing gym that fall morning.

I was a sort of regular. I knew pretty much everyone, so the guy in the ring trading jabs with a big guy called Curtis caught my eye immediately.

Even then—all sweaty, eye swelling shut from the blows he took from Curtis' meaty fists, breathing hard like he was about to collapse—I knew he didn't belong here.

He was wearing blue slacks for one thing. Shirtless though.

I knew he and I were about the same age but his body, like mine, had filled out early. He wasn't thick the way Curtis was. Or the way I was. He was lean, but the muscles were there. He was cut like a goddamned sculpture. And his skin was golden. Like he grew up on a beach and even though he and I were in the same drab, gray city now, that wasn't where he belonged.

I guess the word to describe him was exotic. At least that's the one that ran through my head at the time. And pretty. Not like a girl, either. There's nothing feminine about Alec. He was pretty like Christine's blue beetle. The beautiful hard exterior was just the beginning of what makes up Alec van den Berg. And the minute that thought popped into my head I knew she'd want to poke him. See what's so special inside him that he gets to be blue.

I wanted to know too.

I wandered over to the ring to get a better view of the fight and spied a pile of clothes on the ground next to a pair of expensive leather shoes. There was a white dress shirt, a tartan maroon tie, and a blue jacket. Not a hoodie like I was wearing, but a real fucking jacket. The kind that goes with a suit. Which explained the blue slacks.

The clothes were on the floor like they were worthless, but the emblem on the pocket of the blazer said St. Francis of Assisi Upper School on it.

What the fuck was this kid doing in our gym?

That's the next thing that went through my head.

But just as quick, I forgot about it. Because there was this loud, sickening crack and I thought, *Well, that's the end of this dumbass.*

But when I looked up to see what I missed, it was Curtis on the floor of the ring. Blood pouring out of his mouth, broken tooth stuck to his lip.

I squinted my eyes and looked at this new kid again.

He's blue on the inside too, that's what I thought next.

He was jumping then. Kinda circling Curtis, yelling at him to get the fuck up and finish what he started. His knuckles weren't even taped, so they were tore up from the blows he'd delivered. Bloody and sick, missing bits of skin.

Bare-knuckle boxing was forbidden in the gym. The rules on the sign hanging on the wall even said so. But that never stopped us.

Seconds later there were like a dozen people in the ring. Some kneeling on the ground trying to rouse Curtis, some blocking the new kid from approaching, two firmly gripping his shoulders, holding him back.

That's when I looked into his eyes and made a decision.

87

I liked this asshole. Because those eyes weren't the eyes of a kid who went to St. Francis of Assisi Upper School.

They were my eyes. They were blue, even if they weren't.

He was pretty and I wanted him.

Fast forward a couple of years and my life had taken a turn. Because that was the night we were in the fuckin' alley waiting on Christine to come out with the diamond and heard the gunshot inside the house.

That was the first time she ever killed anyone.

But it wasn't the last.

Over the next few years we did dozens of heists. All over the fuckin' world. Private planes became familiar modes of transportation. We ate caviar on crackers that taste like air, drank bottles of champagne that cost more than six months' worth of weekly motel rent, wore bespoke clothes, and shot more guns in more countries than we ever knew existed.

All in the name of money.

Ah, but that's not exactly true. Yeah, the money was the end game. But the excitement, the adventure, the fuckin' adrenaline. The feeling we'd get afterward. The way we'd laugh, all scrunched up together on some luxurious couch. The want we felt for each other. The knowing that this was the true meaning of pretty.

That's why we did it.

And even though the three of us spent years living the dream, the way it ended... well, that was the shit nightmares were made of.

CHAPTER TWELVE

BEFORE

Prague's cold, damp, winter air is filling my lungs as I run, and I'm drinking it in. I have Christine by the hand, pulling her along, glancing to the side to make sure she's keeping up. She is. She's the only one I've met in my life who can.

Danny's almost a full block behind. It's not that he's not fast. He most assuredly is. He's a strong runner, in fact. He moves quickly and efficiently. But Danny's built more for distance than speed.

Christine and I go fast and hard. Danny moves slower. But I suppose what that will ultimately mean is that he'll still be running and moving forward long after I've broken the barriers of sound and light and burst into flame.

It's no one's fault, I reckon. People just are the way they are. Constructed to serve whatever purpose it is they were put here to serve.

I'm beginning to realize that Danny's purpose is to be our conscience. The thing that keeps our merry band from spinning off the edge of the planet and out into space where all of us would be lost. Adrift in the soundless black of the cosmos. Where no one would ever hear us, and we couldn't find our ways home.

Conversely, my purpose is to keep driving. Faster. More desperate. Keep soldiering forward ever further in pursuit of what's mine.

Which is, as I once was told, everything.

When I was very, very young, I fell from a tree I was climbing on our property in—I actually don't remember which property it was. It may have been in the States? Or we might have been back home? I don't recall that detail anymore. All I recollect is that I scraped my knees and elbows and hands. Started crying. Because, as noted, I was very, very young. And I ran inside to see if I could find one of the house staff to patch me up.

But instead of finding house staff, I found my dad. He had just walked in the front door, so when I burst in, he turned and saw me. I was quite shaken, I remember. Not only did it hurt, but the wind had gotten knocked out of me.

Dad saw me sobbing, trying to get out the words of what had happened, and he rushed over and knelt beside me. He wiped the tears from my eyes and shushed me until I calmed.

I don't know where Mom was.

After I quieted, I remember vividly him saying, "Listen, hey, shhhh, listen to me, man. There's nothing to cry about. Yeah? Nothing ever to cry about." Then he gestured wide with his hands and said, "Nothing at all. Look... this world. The world we live in? It's yours."

I imagine the expression on my face was quite confused, because then he furrowed his brow, brought his eyes close to mine, and said it again, "Hear what I'm telling you, man. The world. All of it. Is yours. K? It belongs to you. There's nothing to cry about. Ever. There's no harm that can come to you. Nothing that can ever happen to you that you can't handle. Nothing that you can't control. OK? Nothing. You hear?"

My crying finally slowed to a stop and I looked up at him and nodded my tiny head.

"Do you believe me?" he asked.

I sniffed a bit, stilling myself and holding my small chin high, squaring myself off like the brave little man I was, and nodded again. I think I smiled at him a bit. I know he smiled at me. I remember that more clearly than just about any memory I've ever had.

And then he slapped me as hard as he could across the face.

And when my eyes got big and my breath caught in my throat, he slapped me again.

And then he stared at me. Daring me to let the tears start falling once more.

When they didn't—when I fought back the shock and the pain and stuffed it down—his smile widened, he said, "Good man," and then disappeared off into the recesses of whichever house it was.

The memory lands on me quite by accident just before we fling open the door of the flat we've been renting for this particular escapade, and Christine and I tumble inside. We're not high, but it very much feels like we are. The rush of adrenaline coursing through both of us amplifies the need we already feel.

In the less than handful of years since I met the two of them and we started adventuring together, I've watched Christine grow from an irrepressibly spirited and spunky girl into an impossibly sexy and capable woman. And since

I first began tasting her, I've needed to have her as often as possible. And so I have.

Because the world is mine.

Because she is mine.

I have her body suit ripped open and her back against the wall by the time Danny comes huffing through the door.

"What the fuck?" he gasps out.

Christine and I ignore him as we continue pawing at each other savagely.

He comes up behind me and puts his hand on my shoulder.

I don't think he does it to be aggressive as much as to draw focus. So, while not his intention, it is his mistake.

My fist, someone else's blood already drying on my knuckles, is made wet anew with the spray of blood from Danny's nose as it makes contact.

I don't know the last time I felt regret.

I don't know if I ever have before.

Kak.

As he stumbles away shouting, "Fuck! What the fuck is happening?" I go over to him, my hands up.

"Fok, bru! Are you all right?"

When I reach him and kneel down to see how badly I bliksemed him, the memory of my dad kneeling down to me is once again called into my mind. But Danny, of course, is not crying. Unlike me, I don't think Daniel Ryan Fortnight has ever cried once in his life.

No. He is definitely not prone to tears. But he is prone to vengeance. He rears back and slams his forearm between my legs and right into my ballas.

The searing, burning, vomit-inducing pain I feel right up into my stomach drives me into a rage and a clear, white heat takes me over as I grab him by the hair and slam his already broken face into the wood-planked floor.

Somewhere, a long, long way off, I hear the sound of Christine screaming. Not in fear. Never in fear. But in anger. I think I feel her on my back, but it's all quite muddy. I do know that Danny has now grabbed my wrist and twisted it backward in a manner that my wrist is not intended to be bent.

The three of us are now tangled together at odd and violent angles. Struggling and pulling and pushing. Arms and legs entwined, slick blood and—even though it's winter out—wet, sticky sweat making us slide off one another as we collide, and grunt, and fight, and strain.

And I'm sure that it means there's probably something about me that's not quite right—even more so than I'm already aware of—but my already hardened cock gets even harder.

But I know I will find no release tonight.

Because tonight will not end in reconciliation and understanding.

Just like the urgent need that had been building between me and Christine for years, this fracturing apart of all three of us was building right alongside it. Cloaked in the shadows, but no less needy and emergent.

Once this battle is over, tonight will be the last night all three of us are together.

How long that separation will last is hard to predict at present.

But somewhere inside I want to believe that it won't be forever.

JA HUSS & J McCLAIN

NOW

The recollection of the event plays in my mind over and over again.

Being obsessive is something I'm dead proud of about myself. It keeps me sharp, it keeps me focused, and it ensures that I don't miss anything. Which, given the danger of both my responsibilities and my hobbies, is most valuable.

I'm replaying the memory for the fiftieth time when a sound causes me to shake my head a tiny bit and bring myself back to the present.

It's the sound of Danny moaning as he stirs in bed, rolling his arm away from Christine and propping himself to a sit. His eyes flutter open and then he blinks to try to— I assume—understand what it is he sees.

Which is me, sitting in the chair across the room, watching them sleep.

"Morning, bru. Good to see you, man."

CHAPTER THIRTEEN

He's the same and altogether different. Still golden. Still arrogant. Still somewhere he's not supposed to be. Which, in this case, is my fuckin' bedroom.

I know what he expects of me.

Danny is all temper.

Danny is all muscle.

Danny is the one who hits first and thinks later.

But he doesn't know me anymore. He never knew me.

The half a second it takes for these words to form in my head as some cloudy moment of self-realization brings instant clarity. An idea of how to handle him has me raising a single finger to my lips.

"Shhhhh," I hiss.

He tilts his head, confused. Not the reaction he was expecting.

Christine is still sleeping. Her familiar light snore feels like home to me. My eyes dart to her, then back at Alec. He raises his chin, a sort of half nod of understanding, and stands up.

When I don't move he shrugs with his hands. *What the fuck, bru?* that's what he's asking me.

I give him the same half nod back and he understands.

The shorthand gestures we developed while we were global diamond thieves comes rushing back. And even though I'm using it to get him the fuck out of this bedroom—get him the fuck away from Christine—I think we both have the same nostalgic feeling coursing in our hot blood for days gone by. Jobs that were done and done well. A whole other life than the ones we're living separately now.

He leaves the bedroom without comment and I'm left here, in bed with the only girl I ever wanted to be in bed with.

We could be us, back then, in this moment.

In the Cristal Suite at the Le Place d'Armes Hotel in Luxembourg City. Still drunk on adrenaline from yesterday's job well done. Breakfast would be waiting in the dining room. A full spread of eggs, and bacon, and pastries laid out on the table. And carafes of bad European coffee.

I smile, thinking about the coffee. I was always complaining about the coffee. No matter where we were, no matter what everyone told me about the fuckin' beans, or the machine that made it, or the barista who mixed everything together... American coffee was the one thing I always missed. And you could tell them you wanted an American coffee, but it never mattered. It was always just the same dark, bitter European shit with fat-free milk mixed in.

Fucking Europe.

I kinda miss the bad coffee.

No, that's not it.

I kinda miss... us.

Get your shit together, Fortnight. You've got Brasil waiting on a delivery.

That's enough to get me moving. I slowly, gently, lift myself out of the bed Christine and I are sharing. I don't want her to see him. Ever, if I can help it. I want this conversation with Alec to happen downstairs in the garage. I want it to be over with before she wakes up. Before she realizes we're back together again.

I don't want the word *us*, as it pertains to our long-ago triangle, to ever enter her mind.

I grab yesterday's jeans off the floor and step out of the bedroom, closing the door behind me.

Alec's eyes are wandering over the contents of my apartment—perhaps wondering there's anything of value to steal from me—realizing there isn't.

But then they land on the silver box and as I step into my jeans and pull them on, I feel him hold his breath as he takes a few steps over to the couch and picks it up. Turning it around in his hand. Single fingertip tracing the etched triangle on the top. His sidelong glare over his shoulder says more than words ever could.

What the fuck are you doing with this?

I point to the door, head that direction—grabbing my leather off the back of the chair as I pass—and open it. It's my turn to glare at him over my shoulder. He's still holding the box. Still standing in the same spot.

But our silent conversation holds. And he turns, walks over to me—past me—through the door, and I follow him out as I shoulder into my jacket, zippers jingling in the silent, gray, pre-dawn morning.

His expensive shoes tap on the metal stairs, my bare feet silent and cold as I follow him down to the floor of the garage.

"OK," he says, turning to face me. "Explain."

97

He's holding up the silver box. Whatever's happening with Christine is not what he's referring to. Everything in the present gets sidelined to all the shit from the past. Because I am not supposed to have this diamond.

"I don't owe you an explanation."

"I think you do, bru. Because this was…" He doesn't finish.

I smile. "Fuckin' sucks, doesn't it? Realizing you were betrayed and you didn't even know it. That the betrayal happened behind your back. Kind of a gut-clenching wake up call, right, bru?" I mimic his stupid accent. Badly. Never could get those vowels to sound authentic.

He stares at me. He looks good, I guess. Still lean. Same golden skin. Same piercing amber eyes. Still wearing those nice suits. Still… *him*.

If he came from South Africa I'm impressed. Jet lag always had me looking like shit when I landed in a new time zone.

"Enough," he says. "How?"

He's still referring to the diamond. I shrug. And smile. Because it's hard to con a con man. And we did it.

"We stole it back," I say. Evenly. No emotion. No touch of pride in my words, even though I feel it.

"When?"

I laugh. "You never noticed? Not like you to overlook something like a missing fucking diamond."

"How?" It comes out genuinely perplexed. "How did you—?"

"Never mind the diamond. What the fuck did you do to Christine?"

"Me?" It's his turn to laugh. "Bru, I was in a fokken firefight when I got news of Christine's tumble. Almost ten thousand miles away. It wasn't me."

98

"Bullshit," I sneer. "You had her on a job, didn't you? You told her to kill David. You've been using her."

"Using her?" He laughs. "And who the fok is David?"

I nod. Back to the silent language. That nod says, *OK. That's how you're gonna play this? Fine.*

"You know what? I don't even wanna know what you're up to. Not even a little bit. All I care about is Christine."

"That makes two of us, man."

I lose a little bit of my calm exterior. Point my finger at his face. "You never cared about her. All you ever cared about was what she'd do for you. You dragged us in, used us up, and then you—"

He slaps my finger away and points back. "You're the one who walked out."

"You were fucking her," I snarl.

"She was fucking me!"

I don't picture how it ended. Never. I always go back to the day it started. To the gym. His bloody knuckles. To the night outside in the alley. To the gunshot. To the moment when I fucked everything up by letting this asshole in.

"But," he says, some of the excitement in his voice dissipated, "to be fair, she wanted to fuck us both. And you were never good at sharing." His eyes wander to my bare chest. They linger there too long. "It's not too late, ya know."

"Fuck you."

"I wish you would. Just fokken get over it, Danny. Accept that this is our future. And you can run—hell, you did run—but looks like we're right back where we left off if you ask me."

99

"I'm not asking you. I'm not here to ask you anything. I'm here to tell you something. Give you one last shot to move along and never look back." It feels generous. Because I already told Brasil I'd deliver Alec to him. I already made a deal to sell him out. And I should just shut up, let that shit play through.

But whatever. The warning is already out.

"You expect me to leave?" Alec says. "Now? When we're in the middle of all this shit?" He pans his arms wide, like it's us against the world.

That's how he did it back then too. Us against the world.

It's something Christine and I had together. We were us against the world. And then Alec shouldered his way into our lives and joined our team without even asking. Disrupted all the plans we had. Ruined all the futures we imagined.

She wouldn't be killing people for money if this asshole hadn't given her that gun that night in the alley.

But, that annoying, truth-telling, reality-checking voice in my head says. *But you'd still be this Danny, Danny. You'd still be working for Brasil. You'd still be right where you are now. Alec never poked the pretty out of you. You were never special to begin with.*

Fair enough.

But not the point.

"We don't need your help."

"I disagree," he says. It comes out solemn. A little bit sad, maybe.

"What the fuck is happening?"

Alec and I both turn our heads to look up to the top of the stairs. Christine is standing there wearing only a too-

100

large t-shirt. She steps lightly down the metal stairs just the way I did, trembling in the frigid air.

How long was she standing up there? What did she hear?

She trains her eyes on me. Then Alec. Then back to me.

I worry about her cold, bare feet. I worry about her shivering in the frigid morning air. I want her back upstairs. I want her back in bed. I want her anywhere but here with us.

Because I can deny it all I want. Won't make it true.

There is an us.

There has been since that morning I met Alec at the gym. Since that same night when I introduced him to Christine.

You can't undo the past.

We are the triangle etched on the top of that metal box.

There will always be an us.

CHAPTER FOURTEEN

Christine

"Morning, bru. Good to see you, man."

I hear him speak. Even lost in the depths of dreams there's no way I can't. His voice is like music I've been programmed to respond to. A code that unlocks something deep and dark. A fix for that part of me that is irrevocably broken.

"Shhhhhh…"

But the arms that held me all night don't belong to him. They belong to Danny. And Danny evokes all the same emotions, only on the gut level as well as the heart.

There's some kind of string that connects us. Some bond that attracts us.

But the voice. Alec's voice. Just a few simple words— they're enough to rouse me out of the fantasy life I'm living in my dreams. A life of parties, and planes, and money.

A life I was too young to really appreciate.

Or make the most of, if I'm being honest.

The bed moves, things get lighter.

I don't want the dream to end.

It's only then that I realize it's not a dream. It's my reality. And there are good parts, sure. But there's a lot more wrong with the life I've tried to forget than there is right.

That's a choice though.

I can see things one way or another.

I can choose. I can remember the good, or the bad, or both. And seriously. Who in their right mind chooses bad over good? Or both, for that matter.

There's a heavy click of a door closing from the other room and a wave of panic swells in my chest.

They're gonna leave me here. They're gonna walk out of my life in the same moment I realize they walked back in.

And that. Cannot. Happen.

I force my eyes open, swing my legs out of the bed, and wave aside the rush of cold air that chills my entire body. Out in the living room I try not to panic, even though I'm well on my way. My heart is fluttering wildly, my breath coming in short gasps.

But just before I pull the front door open... I hear them. I hear them talking down in the garage.

I glance over my shoulder at the couch. The silver box with the triangle on top is gone. One of these two men has it. Probably Alec since he wasn't in on that little heist.

I lean my head against the cold, gray metal of the door and smile. That night we stole the seven-carat diamond back from where Alec had stashed it... that was how it began for me.

I loved Danny for years before that job, but after that job I was *in love* with him. Because after that night I knew. He'd do anything for me. Anything.

And I don't care that I was only a kid. I don't care that he was more like a big brother to me than a guy. I don't care if it's weird, or sick, or whatever.

THE TRIANGLE

The only thing I care about are the feelings.

How he made me feel. How he took care of me. How he busted me out of the foster system like a superhero saving the day.

When we stole that diamond back that was it for us.

Me and him. Just the two of us. That's it. There was no Alec yet. He was there but he didn't matter. It would take months, maybe even years, for Alec to really be part of us.

But once he was... God, was he ever.

I sigh into the cold metal door, only half listening to the argument going on down the stairs. Only half listening to the one going on inside my head, too.

They're not arguing about the diamond anymore. No one gives a shit about that diamond. We can't sell it. Not easily. It's got a serial number. And it's heavy. And...

And there are people who would notice this seven-carat diamond.

But we didn't know that when we stole it back. We didn't care, either. We had no idea that the opportunity to steal diamonds that *could* be sold would present itself over, and over, and over again.

We thought, *This is it.* Our chance to change our lives. A little guarantee that we'd never go hungry again. We'd never be homeless again. And we took it.

Not because we're thieves, just because we could. And who wouldn't? If they were in our shoes? Who wouldn't seize the day and turn their shitty lives into the stuff of dreams?

I turn the handle on the door. Slowly ease it open a crack.

"You were fucking her," Danny snarls.

105

"She was fucking me!" Alec almost snorts. "But to be fair, she wanted to fuck us both. And you were never good at sharing." A pause. "It's not too late, ya know."

No, it's not. That's why I'm here.

I need them. Both of them. These past few years without Danny and Alec together have been a whole other level of hell. So much worse than the years that came before Danny anointed himself my knight.

But the situation is precarious. It's teetering on the edge. We are on the verge of losing everything. All of it.

No. That's not how this is gonna go down.

"What the fuck is happening?" I ask, stepping through the door and out onto the landing. The soles of my feet are tingling from the cold and my body is starting to tremble. But the frigid air inside the garage makes me shake like a kid trying to crack a safe with a gun to her head.

That happened, I realize. And in the same moment I also realize I remember.

I remember everything.

I remember the bond between us like it's still there.

And it is. We just need to find it again.

"Go back inside, Christine. I'll be up in a second."

I stare at Danny as the moments tick off, then slowly shake my head.

"Christine," he barks. "Do what I say."

"She doesn't take orders, bru. Not from you or anyone else."

"Shut the fuck up," Danny growls. "She's in this situation because of you."

"I'm in this situation," I say, forcing my voice to be loud and strong even though I feel so very soft and weak right now, "because of you, Danny Fortnight."

106

Alec huffs out a laugh. "See? She knows. So why don't you just calm down, shut your fokken mouth for once, and listen to what I'm trying to say."

Danny's glare is filled with rage.

But he doesn't scare me. The world is filled with unintended consequences. So many ways for things to go wrong. And I may not be sure of many things, but even in this leftover state of amnesia-induced denial I know one thing for certain.

He would never hurt me.

"I'll go inside," I say, meeting Danny's ragey stare, "if the two of you come inside with me."

"No, he was just leaving."

"Not so much, bru." And just like that, Alec is climbing the stairs. Coming toward me with outstretched arms. "Are you all right?" he asks, folding me into his embrace. "You gave me quite a scare, my luv."

I sigh, let myself accept the heat he's wrapping around me, and stare at Danny. "I will be. Now that I'm back here with you two."

Danny folds his arms across his chest. Defiant.

But Alec is already pushing me through the open apartment door. "Don't worry. He'll follow. It's his fokken apartment, isn't it?"

My eyes are still locked with Danny's when I disappear inside.

Alec kicks the door closed, pushes me up against the wall, places both hands on my cheeks, and kisses me on the mouth.

Fuck.

I sink into him.

Absolutely sink.

107

The door slams open, hitting the wall so hard I know there's a hole in the sheetrock. "Get your fuckin' hands off her," Danny says, pulling me away.

I spin into him. Bounce against the hard muscles of his chest. And an instant later his arms are wrapped around me, replacing the heat of Alec with the heat of him.

Sinking is something I could get used to. Because I do it again.

"Now you're getting the idea," Alec says.

"Oh, I've got ideas," Danny says. "I've lots of ideas. And all of them involve me cracking that pretty face of yours into pieces."

"Promises," Alec huffs, taking a step forward.

"Back the fuck up, van den Berg. Now."

"Sorry, bru. But she doesn't belong to you." He pauses, his eyes focused on Danny. And without dropping that challenging stare he says, "Tell him, Christine. Tell him why we're here."

Shit. Why are we here? Did I miss something? Are there still gaps in my memory?

"She's here because you're selfish," Danny answers for me. "She's here because once again, you got her wrapped up in some illegal bullshit."

"Why don't you ask her what she wants for once? Eh? I mean, I get it." He takes another step closer. I'm in the middle now. Alec in front and Danny behind me. I can feel the heat of both men and they are on fire. "You had her first. Your claim is older. But you let her get away, Danny. You let her walk out and face the cold, hard world alone. And I never did. That should count for something." He places his hand back on my cheek. Lets his gaze fall to me—"Right, luv?"—then rise back up to Danny.

Danny holds me tighter, the zippers of his leather jacket cold and biting against my back where my t-shirt has ridden up. God. Yes. "It counts," I say, betraying Danny in the same moment I pledge allegiance to Alec.

And then I turn to face Danny.

He wants to be angry. He wants to glare at Alec. Probably kick his ass. But that turn changes everything. Because he forgets about Alec and only sees me.

I slowly rise up on my tiptoes. My hands slip underneath his jacket and slide along the cut muscles of his waist. He closes his eyes for half a moment, sighing inside as we fall into each other. My lips gently caressing as my tongue probes against his hard mouth.

He gives in.

Maybe it's because he has to choose. This is a defining moment and he's up against a hard decision. That might be why he kisses me back. That might be why his fingers thread into my hair. That might be why he presses his hips against mine. Why he lets himself get hard.

But I don't think so. And I don't care, either.

His surrender is the only thing that matters.

Alec must feel the same way. And he's never one to miss an opportunity to get what he wants, I suddenly remember with stark clarity. His hips press against my back, pinning me between them. His hand brushes my hair aside, his mouth tenderly kissing my neck. Chills run up my spine and shoot out of my mouth and into Danny's.

Danny kisses me harder. His hands gripping my hair tight. Our open mouths and twisting tongues the only thing that matters.

Until... until Alec's hands slip inside my too-big t-shirt, slide up to find my breasts, and squeeze.

And this. This is all I've ever wanted from them.

109

To be their middle.

CHAPTER FIFTEEN

What am I doing?

I want to push them both away—especially Alec. But her kiss. It's our first *real* kiss. The first one I give in to. The first one where I know I won't back away. There's just no way I can stop myself.

I've always wanted her. She has always thought my rejection was personal. That I didn't want her like this. That I didn't dream of taking her whole body.

But I did. Not when she was a kid. Not then. But as she got older, as our relationship with Alec matured into a well-organized trio of pirates, we became more than just friends, but something less than lovers.

That's why it fell apart. Lovers was always the next step. Or betrayal.

Those were the only options left.

And as much as I hate to admit it—Alec was right.

She has always wanted both of us.

It was me who forced the second option when the whole thing fell apart.

I thought I could stop the inevitable by pushing her away. Keeping it professional. Keeping my distance.

But it was never enough. Her level of determination to get what she wants has always been a lesson in fortitude.

She was a master at remaking her shitty reality and turning it into something new. Something pretty. Something... *blue*.

The headstrong ten-year-old became the daring teenager, became what she is today.

A top-tier sneak assassin, safe-cracking, diamond thief.

Telling Christine, "No," is the same thing as telling her, "Yes, but not yet."

She was always going to win. And if she had to walk away and give me space to reconsider what we are to each other, she'd do it.

And it wouldn't surprise me at all right now if she looked me dead in the eye and said, "I fucked everything up on purpose. To get us all back together again. To make you choose one final time. Us. Or nothing."

She's just that determined.

And she's patient too. So patient. It was the very first thing I noticed about her when we started working as a team before Alec showed up. She could wait. She could always see the long game. I never had to explain it to her.

It was the first thing I loved about her. That she could wait for the prize and put up with the agony of denial if it meant she won in the end.

Is this that end? Is this the last chance I'm ever going to get?

So I guess I have to ask myself an honest question.

Do I want to fight her? Lose her? Mourn the loss of her for lifetimes to come just because—as Alec put it—I was never good at sharing?

Is it even a concession at this point? I mean, as much as I tell myself I hate him—hate what he did to us, hate what he turned us into—do I? Do I really hate who I am?

Because that's some bullshit, right there.

I don't hate myself.

I don't regret what we did. I don't think back and say, *I'd do all different.*

And I don't hate him either. I just hate the way he forced my hand. Because he was always ready for the next step. He was pushing it right along with her. It was always me drawing that imaginary line. It was always me who wanted stagnation.

But I can't see the logic anymore.

She's not a kid. I'm not a kid. And she doesn't need me the way she did back then. I'm not her only choice. She's got plenty of options. And one of those is Alec minus Danny.

And that… that I *cannot* stand.

I kiss her harder. My fingers—already threaded into her hair—tug. She hisses out a breath of pain and I remember her stitches. I loosen my hold but still force her closer, which isn't even possible. Her breasts are already crushed up to my chest. Alec, doing his part on that end. Because he's got her pinned to me. Both of his hands caressing her full breasts. His hips grinding against her ass as he nips her neck.

I am as aware of him as I am of her.

One day, I think absently as our tongues twist together, our mouths pliant against one another. One day I will look back on this moment and know—this is when it truly began.

Not back in that gym. Not back in the alley.

Here. This morning in my apartment. The cold seeping in from outside like a creeping arm of death and destruction.

And when that day comes—when the shit is probably falling apart all around us—I will finally take responsibility.

Because it's me.

I'm the reason for everything that happens that day in the future. I'm the reason the world ends.

Because I'm weak with love for this girl. And if that means Alec gets to come along for the ride…

Fuck it. I don't care.

I let go of her hair with one hand and find her hand inside my jacket. It's warm now. Our body heat mixing together. Our blood heating up with the moment, or the reunion, or the potential danger hanging like a dreary gray cloud all around us. Who the fuck knows why we're running hot right now. It's just not cold, that's all I know.

I drag it down and across my lower abs. Slip it inside my pants. Her fingers find my cock, instinctively wrapping around it.

I stop kissing her and close my eyes. Drop my head a little and let myself enjoy it.

Alec's mouth takes my place on hers. He smells like… Alec. Which makes me smile. He smells like money. He smells like the past, and danger, and something exotically erotic.

Her other hand comes up and rests on mine, which is still tangled up in her thick mane of auburn hair. She slowly pries it away, the kiss she's sharing with Alec more urgent, and she drags my hand down her body. For a brief moment it brushes against Alec's hand, still gripping her tit with insistent need, and then she moves on. Down to her hips, to her thigh, and then she grips my hand and my cock with the same squeezing pressure and blows my mind.

But she's not done. Because she moves on once again. Placing my palm against Alec's hip. His thigh. Then his thick, hard cock pressing up against his stupid dress slacks.

I don't know why I think about his clothes in this moment. I should be backing up. I should be shaking my head no. I should be coming up with all sorts of reasons why this won't happen.

But I think about his clothes instead. How his broad shoulders fill in his button-down shirts. How he always looks so put together. How every time we have a problem he's got the answer. Confidence. I think that's what seeps out of Alec. The con man confidence.

She lets go of my hand and forces me to focus.

In? Or out?

Make a decision and commit.

So I do.

I don't pull away. I lean in to them. Hating myself for letting them win, but loving the agony of defeat. And hating myself for that too.

Because I have already committed to Brasil. Because I chose a side too early. Because—it's true. I *will* be the reason the world ends.

I will blow these two people apart like a goddamned bomb.

And I do it anyway.

I lean into their kiss and join in.

And even though I thought that first kiss was the true first kiss, it wasn't.

This one is.

This is the moment it all begins.

CHAPTER SIXTEEN

People have called me complicated.

I'm not.

The motor that drives me to do the things I do in my life is fueled by a simple source: Power.

I'd love to pretend that it's more complex than that and that underneath it all I'm more sophisticated, but I ain't. I just like getting the things I want, and I like knowing I can. And I feel like what separates me from all the other okes out there who try, and fail, is that I'm honest about it.

With myself anyway.

I was already getting hard before Danny and Christine got swept up in the heat of the moment. I was hard as I sat, watching them sleep. I didn't know for certain that this would happen, but I had a fair suspicion. And the fact that I was right, and that it means that I'm responsible for making it so, fills me with as much energy as the heat of our bodies coming together.

I'm not the only one in this room who has wanted this for the last handful of years. I'm just the only one who's been willing to do what's necessary to make it happen.

My fingers twisting Christine's nipples cause her to bite hard on my lip. Her neck twists harder so she can

117

reach my mouth but not be pulled away from Danny. I gasp at the rush of pain and pleasure, a needy groan bounding out from deep in my lungs.

It's actually only been a few weeks since we've been together like this. Christine and I, that is. But it's been a lifetime since all three of us have been together. And never quite like *this*. Not for lack of desire, of course. The timing and the circumstance are not precisely how I foresaw this moment occurring, but that it is now is satisfactory enough for me.

I'm made even harder by feeling that I'm the one who orchestrated it. It's because I chose to call Danny and convinced him to do as I asked that this is happening. And there's nothing under the bright yellow sun that feels better than that. That knowledge that I win.

There is possibly only one thing that could soften the feeling of strength I have right here in the now of now. And unfortunately...

The bullets come pouring through the windows of Danny's apartment like a herd of stampeding rhino. Like a flash flood. No test shot. No delicate precision. Indiscriminate. An assault. Meant to shock and immobilize. It's not elegant or sophisticated. But it is effective.

The reflexive conditioning all three of us display is synchronized. It would be graceful if not for the fact that each of us tries, instinctively, to protect the other. Danny and I step to shield Christine. She tries powering past us to do the same. And the resulting action is an inept ballet, as the three of us inadvertently wrestle with each other to try to save the other two.

Much like the biblical account of Jacob wrestling the angel, it is a scene that in theory should be poetic and beautiful, but in practice is blunt and desperate.

It feels like we're the goddamn Keystone Kops.

"What the fuck?" Danny shouts as the three of us take refuge in the toilet. "What did you do?" he says, slamming the door and pushing me against the wall.

There's a moment where I almost yell back, but instead I take a breath, fill my body with air, and say, "I didn't do nothing, man. It ain't my house they're shooting at."

Danny starts to grab for my throat and I'm curious to know what he thinks he'll do, exactly, but Christine intervenes, stepping between us and saying, "Stop! You both have big dicks! How the fuck do we get out of here?"

I don't mean to smile, but I can't help myself. Both because she's right, we do, and also because I've missed this.

"Is there another way out?" Christine asks Danny.

"No. Just the stairs," he says.

"You don't have an escape route?" I ask him, somewhat surprised.

"Yeah. It's called the fuckin' stairs," he snaps.

"Shame," I say, drawing my pistol from inside my topcoat and reaching for the door handle.

"Wait!" Danny shouts. The sound of automatic weapons fire from the other room is like white noise in the background.

He pulls open the medicine chest, presses a release lever hidden inside, and the whole thing pops forward, revealing a small cache of firearms buried in the wall. I roll my eyes in spite of myself.

"Brilliant. And yet there's no escape route…"

119

He ignores me, grabbing two pistols for himself and handing a shotgun to Christine. He doesn't offer me any auxiliary form of protection. That's fine. I wasn't expecting it.

There is no further discussion. No conversation about improvised strategy or the best way to take flight. Like any act of muscle memory, the body knows how to react when conditions are familiar. And for the three of us, this something we've done a number of times before.

It's like going for a swim.

With sharks.

Or taking a bike tour.

Off the side of a mountain.

And just like those, what we're about to head into might be incredible and invigorating or it might very well kill us.

But of all the things we have in common, the most unifying is our shared lack of fear of death. We've never chatted about it aloud, but I know that our absence of dismay over dying is because the thing we share most—well above all else—is that we all came to accept, at a very early age, that death is an inevitability. A necessary payment for the privilege of living.

Eish, man, I don't think any of us expected to live past the age of eighteen. So every day since then has just been a bonus.

In any case, what takes the place of a colloquy on how we get out of this is a brief look between us. We make eye contact for just long enough to confirm that we're all still who we know each other to be, and once that's done, Danny grabs at the door, flings it open, and we get ready to fokken shoot our way out.

We sprint through the apartment, toward the lone front door which stands as a poor and shameful excuse for an escape route, taking our individual postures of choice to try to avoid being shot. Danny crouches and moves swiftly, Christine favors staying close to the wall, I face the windows, the direction from whence hot metal is raining sideways, and move laterally.

I don't so much try to avoid being shot as I dare the shots to hit me. I challenge them to try to take my life. Silently, I shout at them, *Fok julle naaiers!* The only thing that can kill Alec van den Berg is Alec van den Berg. I decided this long ago. And I'm not in the mood to die today.

When we arrive at the door and open it, it sets off the alarm. The wail of the siren is amplified by the wailing of another siren that also just went off. Not cops. Another alarm siren.

And as we step through the doorway, we discover, predictably, that a small platoon of large-ish okes is making its way up the stairs toward us.

They're not wearing body armor or anything, which seems ill advised, but they are all wearing masks that cover their faces. Nothing extraordinary, just ski masks. To me this suggests a hastily thrown together operation. No faceplates or tactical gear. Just big, lumbering okes, identities clumsily shrouded with hackneyed disguises, making their way oafishly up the stairs to confront our motley little band like they was in some second-rate gangster picture.

They fail to reach us where we stand, however. Christine's shotgun puts a rugby-ball-sized-hole in the chest of the daft fucker who presumed to be the tip of the spear. The blast echoes loudly off the metal steps.

Danny and I had squared off to face down the invading horde, but Christine pushed past us, edging us out of the way with the gun's barrel, and sent the first oke tumbling back down the stairs far quicker than he came up. She immediately racks another round into the chamber and blasts again. This time sending two more falling.

The shot must hit an artery on at least one of them, because arterial spray paints the stairwell wine red. And I suddenly realize that I'm going to have to accept... I'm simply not going to be able to escape without mucking up my lekker crocodile shoes. Shame.

The three remaining muscle are firing indiscriminately in our direction. One of the bullets catches the fabric of my topcoat, cutting through the lining and puncturing the cashmere shell. My mouth contorts on its own and I twist my neck sideways as I shove my own gun back inside my newly blemished finery and march in their direction.

"Alec!" shouts Christine. But it sounds a long way off because of the inharmonic duet being sung by the battling alarm systems, and because my limbs are now getting hot and growing in size. Inflating. Pulsing. The blood in my body pumping wildly but methodically, making me bigger than I am.

I don't know who these hol naaiers are, or who sent them, but I suspect they must be part of the same group who tried to harm Christine; who did, in fact, harm her, even if they failed to kill her, because my girl is hard to kill; who disrupted a beautiful moment that I was enjoying with her and Danny; who splashed blood everywhere, making my lekker shoes slick and wet with their cunting blood; and who have now ruined a perfectly beautiful topcoat.

And I'm gatvol with their fokken bullshit.

I wrench the handgun from the shaking grip of the masked naaier standing in front of me, shove it directly under his chin, and pull the trigger twice. A single pull of the trigger would have gotten the job done, but I'm frustrated right now.

It is, perhaps, the cloudiness that accompanies my frustration that disallows me awareness of the gun pointed at my temple. I'm so fixated on blowing this poepol's head off his shoulders that I neglect to see the barrel that's about to take mine own head from me.

But—in what I choose to think of as an act of love in spite of himself—Danny does see the pistol and comes flying down from one of the steps above me, tackling the would-be assassin to the ground. Why he didn't simply shoot him, I don't know.

Perhaps, like me, he's taking this all somewhat personally and wanted the feeling of taking a life from close range. There is something uniquely satisfying and intimate about it. I heard a rumor once that eating a bit of chocolate will rid one of blue balls. In the event that one experiences coitus interruptus, the legend goes that eating a bit of chocolate will trigger the same chemicals in the body and mitigate the throbbing ache in one's groin. Perhaps looking someone in the eye before you extinguish their candle triggers the same wave of chemicals.

Whether that is true or not, Danny is flooded with some type of energy from somewhere, because he lands on the oke with force, strips him of his gun, and begins whipping him with what can only be described as a sanguinary relentlessness.

It is beautiful to watch.

He pulverizes the poor bastard's face with the butt of his own bloomin' pistol until the ski mask he wears darkens further with blood. That's unfortunate. It must be embarrassing to be ferried to another dimension of consciousness by the ass end of your own weapon. Shame indeed.

The alarms continue to blare, mingled with the sound of continuing gunfire. I've been so distracted by watching Danny pistol-whip a person to death that I almost completely forget there's still another masked assailant inside our perimeter. It's not *his* gun that I hear now, however. It's the booming blast of Christine's shotgun once again, as she nearly removes the lower half of his legs just below the knees, and he sprawls onto the ground, pulling himself along the cold, concrete floor of Danny's garage.

Christine descends to stand beside me now, and we watch, for a brief moment, as Danny, almost mechanically at this point, continues thrashing the ever-softening brains of the oke on the ground beneath him. I suspect he feels us staring at him because he glances over his shoulder, sees us watching this grotesquerie unfold, and shouts, "What?"

At that, he stands, having dispatched the fellow to Hell or wherever he's gone, and the three of us walk in the direction of the near-half-legless fokker dragging himself along the floor of Fortnight's Custom Bike Shop.

Christine pokes him in the ass with the barrel of the shotgun and he stops struggling along. He rolls over to face us, pulling the ski-mask up above his eyes, I presume because it's likely now hard for him to breathe and also because at this point, honestly, who fokken gives a shit?

I don't recognize him. By the non-looks on their faces, neither do Danny nor Christine. Christine puts the barrel of the shotgun against his throat and over the still-blaring siren says, "Who are you?"

He strains to speak, but no words come out. Or if they do, they're impossible to hear over the wailing tocsin that blasts all about.

She follows up her own question with, "Who sent you? What's this about?"

I can't imagine that if he'll not answer a simple, "who are you?" that peppering him with more questions is likely to garner a different result, but to my surprise, he manages to sputter out, in a voice *just* loud enough for us to hear, "Fuck you, bitch."

American. Both in accent and in the almost cartoonish way he clings to his misogynistic machismo as he faces down his last moment. Eish, man. Have the decency to die with a little grace.

Christine pulls the trigger and relieves him of the burden of his brains.

We recognize, collectively, that there's no time to assess the situation further, although my eyes do pass over the carnage that surrounds us. It's really quite something. Even in our most daring and active moments in our shared past, we never left behind a scene like this. A wave of worry rumbles through me. A feeling that I do not care for and to which I am generally unaccustomed.

"Do you think there's any more?" Christine shouts.

Danny looks around. "Outside?" he yells.

She nods.

He shrugs.

His workshop-cum-apartment is in the middle of nowhere-industrial-no-place. You could park half an army on the street outside and virtually nobody would know or care.

I reckon we'll find out shortly who else is waiting for us.

"Do you have a car, man?" I holler to be heard.

Danny points at a poor-looking example of what was once likely a very handsome Jeep, now undermaintained and, to coin a phrase, beat to all fokken Christ. My gaze passes over several beautiful custom-built motorcycles, each one worth probably almost a hundred thousand U.S. dollars, and I shake my head ever so slightly at the irony. *Danny, Danny, Danny. You are the only one of you on the planet.*

I make my way to the car and through the window see the keys sitting on the driver's seat. I swing the door open, grab them, and hop inside. Danny comes flying to me, putting his hand on the door before I can pull it shut.

"Fuck do you think you're doing?" he shouts.

"I'm fokken out of here, man!"

"Get out of my fuckin' Jeep!"

"Fok jou, man! You think this is a fine place to stay at the moment?"

"Get out of my fuckin' Jeep!"

I hear him scream extra loud. Both because he screams extra loud, and because Christine, it seems, has managed to turn off the alarm. She marches over to where we are, comes around the side of the car, and hops into the passenger seat.

"What are *you* doing?" Danny asks.

"We can't stay here. Clearly."

"Where do you wanna go? What do you think we'll do?"

"I have a place, bru. Get in the car," I say.

"Fuck you."

I turn the key in the ignition and he levels one of the pistols he's still carrying at my head. I smile, turn to look at him, and say, "Fine. Kill me then."

There's a hint of a beat where I think he just might do it. But then, as quickly as the murder flashed into his eyes, it skitters away.

"Fuck!" he shouts. Then he moves around to the passenger side, pushes Christine over to sit between us, and slams the door.

I smile again. To myself. I don't dare let it alight on my lips, but inside, I'm beaming.

Danny says, "We don't know what the fuck is waiting for us out there."

I look over at him. He stares out the window ahead. Christine looks over at me and shivers, either because she's only wearing a t-shirt or because of something else. Regardless, the shiver goes direct to my heart and I reach up and stroke her cheek. The sound of Danny breathing heavily through his nose is the only noise now. It's strange how loud it seems, especially compared to the cacophony of before. But it does. It sounds like the loudest thing I've ever heard.

I stroke her cheek, listen to him breathe, watch the rising and falling of his bare chest under his leather jacket, and then put the car into drive and head out of the garage to discover what the fuck is, indeed, waiting for us out there.

CHAPTER SEVENTEEN

Christine

Streams of bullets are waiting for us. And I register that. I understand it. But my head is a swirling cloud of… something that is not fear. Because as the bullets cut across the windshield in an eerily straight-line about eye-level—*blat-blat-blat-blat-blat*—the shots don't blow our brains out. They're captured by some pretty kick-ass, military-grade bullet-resistant glass. Which of course immediately becomes a sheet of white as the rounds embed inside it.

So none of us die. We're not even injured. Maybe a cut or a scrape from some hot shrapnel, but that's it.

Alec's hand is between my legs, shifting into the next gear. We don't even stop. We don't even look back. Just take the corners of the maze-like alleyways inside the industrial complex and leave the whole mess behind us with three turns.

No one even tries to follow.

And a moment later, when the Jeep jerks our bodies so hard as Alec jumps a curb and gets us onto something that resembles a main road, jostling us together back and forth, I have to wonder with equal parts fascination and sickness why the only thing I really cared about in the five-second firefight was Alec's hand shifting gears between

129

my legs and Danny's hand on my thigh, trying to keep me from hitting my head on the roll bar directly above us.

Alec rolls down the window and leans his head out, no longer able to see through the windshield. Miraculously, the side windows never even got hit. They are clear as day. Well, with a blue-green tint that reminds me of shallow waters in the Mediterranean Sea near Greece.

"Fortnight," Alec yells, the adrenaline catching up with him. "I fokken love you right now, Fortnight."

"Me too," I breathe. Staring straight ahead. Unable to chance a look at these two men who fill me up like nothing else in the world ever could.

Exhilarating. All of it. Every fucking second. And I'm not talking about the firefight. Or the way we just slipped past like a trio of charmed gods. Or the fact that we're back doing what we do best. Shooting and being shot at.

I'm talking about the kissing, and the touching, and the fast-beating hearts of three people who fit together the way they're supposed to. I'm talking about the yearning, and the deprivation, and the energy it took to convince Danny that this is right. That love comes in many shapes and no one gets to define it for anyone else. That a triangle of lovers is no more or less legitimate than a couple of them.

But he gave in. I felt it. Something changed in him today. I'm just afraid that he got lost while giving in. That the moment overtook him and he accepted what Alec and I have wanted all along, not because he loves us both equally, but because we were just *there*. That he was a victim of circumstance.

But, the inner optimist inside me counters, *he did give in. And if he gives in once, he can do it again.*

And anyway, Danny Fortnight has never been a victim of anything.

I know I should be thinking about what just happened. About the bullets and the diamond and—

"Holy shit! The diamond! Does one of you have the diamond?"

Alec's eyes meet mine without him turning his head. "Please, nunu. Give me some credit." He reaches into his pocket and pulls out the metal case, then tosses it up in the air. "I believe this belongs to…" He stops to huff out a laugh. "All of us."

Finely honed reflexes snatch it before I can blink. Danny, sitting in the passenger seat, gives me his trademark sidelong smile as he leans into the door, shifting his body slightly away from me.

I know that smile. I remember that smile. And all thoughts about the danger and the risk float away again, leaving behind the doubts I was previously musing about. Did he move away from me because he's still thinking I'm off limits? Or maybe he wanted to see me, and this gives him a better view?

God, this man. I've known him most of my life. As my memories keep coming back, I recognize that I probably still know him better than any other person on the planet, Alec included. He's been there for me every single time without fail. And still he makes me doubt everything between us.

Because he walked out, Christine. And the whole reason he walked out was because you and Alec were pushing him in a direction he didn't want to go. Why can't you be satisfied with what he's offering? Why must you ask for more?

It's a fair question, but wholly unfair at the same time.

A girl is allowed to dream and this—these two men sitting on either side of me basking in the afterglow of death and destruction—they are my dream.

"We need a new vehicle," Danny says. "Take the next right."

"Why?" Alec counters, still leaning out the window.

"Why? Because this one is shot to shit."

"I know why we need a new vehicle," Alec growls. "Why take a right?"

But he takes the right and we enter another abandoned industrial complex. "This left right here," Danny says. Alec takes the left. "Second garage on the left right there. Stop."

Danny is out of the Jeep before we can ask him anything else, punching in a series of numbers on a security system.

"Are you OK?" Alec asks me as we wait.

"Cold," I say, rubbing my hands on my bare thighs to create the heat of friction. "But fine." I look over at him and he's staring at me. "What?"

His hand covers mine on my leg and chills run up my spine. "I—"

Danny whistles to get Alec's attention as the garage door lifts up. "Hey, pull the fuckin' Jeep in."

Alec doesn't finish whatever he was gonna say, just nods at Danny and eases the Jeep forward into darkness, stops when the front bumper is inches away from another car, and the garage door closes behind us.

Lights flick on and then Danny is in motion. Over in another bay of the garage, pulling a cover off a brand-spanking-new Range Rover. "Give me a second to grab some things. Christine. Come with me. I'll find you some clothes."

Putting clothes back on isn't where my mind is right now, but that's stupid. We just lucked our way through a spectacular firefight and we're on the run from someone, so this is no time to be yearning for sex.

"What were you gonna say?" I ask Alec.

"Never mind," he says. "It can wait. Go get dressed. We need to get out of here."

I get out and follow Danny up another metal staircase that looks a lot like the one we just shot our way down less than fifteen minutes ago.

Inside he's already gathering up weapons.

"I left the sniper rifle behind." I say, walking up behind him.

He looks over his shoulder as he hauls guns out of a hidey-hole in the floor. "I got a spare." And then he grins. "It was a birthday gift that year we… you know. I never got a chance to give it to you. But I cleaned it regularly. Just in case."

He offers me one of those smiles. The ones that have melted my heart for years. The ones I looked forward to every day and then longed to see again after he was gone. The ones I remember.

But it feels sad for some reason.

And then he turns back to the job and starts handing me weapons and says, "There's a bag in that closet over there. Get it out and put them inside while I go look for something to cover you up."

Cover me up. I huff at that. Why can't he just accept what I'm offering?

Not the time, Christine.

I know that.

By the time I've got the guns stored in the bag, Alec is coming up the stairs and Danny is coming back with a t-

133

shirt for himself, and a pair of sweats, two pairs of thick socks, a pair of boots, and a navy-blue pea coat for me.

"Sorry," he says, draping the coat over a chair and dropping the socks and boots onto the floor. "This is all I really have."

I recognize the coat. It was the one he used to wear when we first met. And back then I'd be swimming in it, but when I slip it on it fits me perfectly. He's smiling at me when I turn to face him. "Looks better on you than it ever did on me," he says as I hug it close, breathing in his familiar scent.

It's the smell of old days. Of the struggle we went through. Of the love we felt for each other.

"It's perfect," I say, taking the sweats from him and pulling them up my legs. Then I prop my back against the wall and start putting on the socks and boots.

He takes off his leather jacket and I can't help myself. My eyes trace all the finely chiseled muscles of his chest. He sighs, shakes his head, pulls on the t-shirt, and puts his leather back on.

Buttoned up tight again.

That's when we both turn to find Alec looking at us.

"What?" we ask simultaneously.

Alec just smiles. Like he's got a secret. "Nothin'. Let's go." And then he leans down, zips the bag of weapons closed, and hoists the strap up to his shoulder as I finish lacing the boots and take a moment to revel in the newly acquired feeling of warmth.

"Go where?" Danny asks. "And why should we trust you?"

Aw, shit. We're back to that.

"I've got a place, and it's stocked for every eventuality. An impenetrable fortress. So unless you've got one just like it, something with multiple escape routes and—"

"Why would you have a place here?" Danny interrupts, not taking the bait for his implied lack of preparedness.

Alec's gaze falls on me, then tracks back to Danny. "Where don't I have a place, bru? I'm a planner, am I not?"

"Doesn't answer my second question," Danny deadpans.

Alec smiles. Laughs the way he does when he finds something incredible. "Because you know I'd never hurt you two."

"Funny," Danny says. "You'd think that. Because from where I stand that's all you ever did."

"OK, you guys. Can we just get the fuck out of here now? I mean, we're like two blocks away from a bunch of dead bodies that have the name Danny Fortnight written all over them. We can work it out later."

They stare at each other for a few heated seconds. Then Danny looks at me and nods. "She's the reason I'm going along, van den Berg. Not you."

"Noted," Alec says. "Come on, Christine, luv. You're gonna like this place, I promise."

I don't wait for Danny's inevitable huff of frustration and anger. He's protective of me. To the point where it feels a little like ownership.

And I don't mind that one bit.

So I smile as I trek down the metal stairs behind Alec, the cache of weapons in the black bag bouncing against his broad back, and think about everything that just happened.

135

And figure… I'm right where I want to be. Doing the thing I do with the two men I do it best with.

CHAPTER EIGHTEEN

"So how much do you remember now?" I ask Christine, once we're back on the road heading into the dark woods that lead up into the rolling mountains.

Christine just stares out the window. She took shotgun and I'm in the back seat, hand in pocket, finger lying patiently against the barrel of my Sig Sauer. Aiming it at the driver's seat in front of me just in case…

Alec is still the liar I once knew.

Still the weak link in the chain.

Still the asshole he was bred to be.

I'm having a hard time believing… well, pretty much everything that's come out of his mouth since that phone call from out of nowhere.

"Remember?" Alec says, eyes darting to mine in the rearview. "What are you on about?"

Christine looks over her shoulder at me. "I'm fine. Just drop it." Then she turns back to staring out the passenger window.

"She lost her memory, _bru_." I sneer that stupid word. A brew is something you drink. Bro is the word he's looking for and never seems to find. "After that job you sent her on went horribly wrong and she got hit on the head with a blunt object."

"She didn't get hit on the head. And there's nothing wrong with her memory. Seems all in order to me, yeah, Christine?"

Christine's fingers slide up to the back of her head, feeling for the stitched-up gash. "If I didn't get hit on the head, then what did happen?"

"What?" Alec says, taking his eyes off the winding wooded road to stare at her for a second, before returning them to navigate a hairpin switchback turn up the side of the mountain.

I smile. Because the moments when Alec has to admit to himself that he's not some all-knowing, all-seeing god give me pleasure.

"I did lose my memory. Just for a few hours yesterday when I woke up. It's back now, so don't worry," she adds quickly. "But how *did* I get the gash on my head?"

Alec's eyes dart to mine in the rearview again. "We can talk about that later."

"Of course we can," I say. "Later is your favorite time to deal with everything."

"Why are you so hostile, Danny? I saved your ass back there in your quaint little garage."

"Saved my ass?" I laugh. "My ass would've been fine without your help, trust me. And we wouldn't even be in this mess if it wasn't for you. What did you do? Why is Christine fucked right now?"

"I'm fine," Christine insists again.

"You're not fine, Christine." It comes out harsher than it should, but I don't care. We've been out of danger and stuck in this car for almost an hour and the way the two of them just accept that mowing down a half-dozen people in my place of business is part of our normal everyday routine is starting to piss me off. "You've got a pretty spectacular gash on your head, you lost your memory, and just had to shoot your way out of a building wearing nothing but a t-shirt. None of this is fine. And all of this is linked directly back to Alec van den Berg. So I want a fuckin' explanation. And I'm not gonna just sit back here like a good little van den Berg minion and pretend it's all cool. It's not cool. He did this to us. And you always give him a pass. Even though the whole reason we haven't talked in almost four years was all his fault. Everything bad that happened when we were younger is all tied to him. Why can't you see that?"

Alec huffs out a laugh. "I don't recall you complaining when we lived on a yacht off the coast of the Cook Islands."

"See? This is what I'm talking about. You think money fixes everything."

"It does." He laughs again. "That's why they make it. What can't money buy?"

"Me," I snarl.

"Well, that's a new look for you. The Danny Fortnight I knew was a bargain."

Christine sighs. "Do we have to do this now? I have a headache."

"Uh, yeah," I say. "Because he's the whole reason you have a headache."

She turns away from me, shutting me out. Alec reaches over and places a hand on her leg. "Nunu, are the details of what happened fuzzy?"

"A little." She shrugs. "I mean, not like they were yesterday. I was coming off the sedation drugs or something. Somebody sedated me, right?"

"I presume so," Alec says, taking a right turn off the main road. If you can call this narrow path a main road, that is. "You did take a tumble. But we got you fixed up OK, yeah?"

I watch him squeeze her leg, fuming with anger.

"I don't remember what happened. Where was I?"

Alec withdraws his hand and places it back on the steering wheel to navigate the even narrower, even less traveled mountain road.

I watch him formulate his answer in the rearview. His eyes dart to mine, then away just as fast. He's about to lie, but what else is new?

"You know what?" I say. "I'm not in the mood for the fairy tale you're about to spin. So save it. With any luck Christine and I will be on our way soon. Twenty-four hours from now you'll just be a bad taste in our mouths."

"What?" Christine says.

"You can't leave," Alec says. "Not until we're all safe."

"I can take care of Christine."

Alec slams on the brakes, stopping in the middle of the road—pulling on the e-brake for effect—and then turns in his seat to look me in the eyes. "You can't even take care of yourself, Fortnight. You're the reason she's in this mess, not me."

I laugh so loud, Christine turns in her seat too. "No," I say. "This has 'evil Alec van den Berg plan' written all over it. Who did you send her to kill? I want a name."

"I don't know what you're talking about."

"Then how the fuck did you know she needed help? How the fuck did you know to call me to go save her?"

"I didn't need saving," Christine protests. "Jesus Christ. Fucking men."

"You didn't need saving?" I blurt. "Are you fucking kidding me right now?"

"I was fine. I was safe. I was—"

"You didn't even know who you were, Christine!"

"And my memory came back, OK? So drop it."

"I'll drop it when he fills in the missing pieces. Who did she kill, Alec?" And then I make a decision. I take a stand. Because the gun in my pocket is pressed up to Alec's forehead. Right between his eyes. "Who. The fuck. Did you send her to kill?"

"Fucking Danny!" Christine screams.

But I just press the barrel of my gun into his skin harder. "Answer me. Or I'm gonna fuck up the interior of this Range Rover with your bloody brains and then bill your estate for the detailing job it'll need afterward."

"You were always so dramatic, Danny."

"Answer me."

"Fine," he says, pushing the gun away from his head and looking at Christine. "It was an oke named Jimmy, OK? Jimmy Sotoro. He stole from me and—"

"Bullshit," I snarl. "It was Brasil's man David."

"I already told you, I have no clue who this David oke is. Or this Brasil fokker. It was Jimmy Sotoro. He fokked me over and Christine volunteered. Tell him, Christine."

But she can't tell me. For two reasons that he's well aware of now. She doesn't remember and it wasn't Jimmy fucking Sotoro.

"Oh, yeah," Christine says, knocking her knuckles against the side of her head.

"What?"

"Yeah," she says, smiling as she meets my gaze. "Jimmy. I remember now."

"Are you fucking kidding me?"

"Danny, come on. You're making a big deal out of nothing. Jimmy was an asshole. And he stole… from Alec. Right, Alec?"

Are they really teaming up against me?

But I only huff out a laugh at my own silent question.

Because of course they are. He always got her to take his side. I was always the unreasonable one. Because I was always the one talking sense. I was the one who put up a fight every time he roped Christine and me into yet another job to bolster his fortune. I, Danny fuck-up Fortnight, was the voice of reason. That right there should tell you something about how sick this guy is. How power-hungry and self-absorbed.

Christine gets out of the car, slamming the door behind her.

"What the fuck?" I say, already out and walking around the front of the Range Rover before I'm done saying the words. "What are you doing?" I ask, taking her by the arm.

But she shrugs me off and turns her back to me.

"What?" I ask again.

"Come on, Christine." Alec is on the other side of her now. "We'll work it out. This is just us finding our footing again."

I shoot him a look. He sees it but ignores me.

"This is just Danny saying he loves you. He's always so dramatic."

But she bows her head and stares down at her feet. Silent.

It occurs to me that she looks very fucking cute in my clothes. Black sweatpants and boots that are at least two sizes too big. And seeing her wearing my old pea coat, well, it reminds me of better days. Simple days that felt so complicated back before we understood what complicated really means. She was always using it to cover herself back when we were young. The heat never worked right in that shitty motel down on Juniper Avenue. She was forever trying to climb into bed with me, claiming we needed to share body heat. But I always said no. Threw her my coat and told her to sleep in it.

My blood always ran hot so the cold didn't affect me the way it did her.

She was so small back then too. So young. So... fragile. But then again, she was tough like steel. Hard like diamonds. Such an appropriate analogy.

"It wasn't all bad," she finally says in a low whisper. She turns then, looks at us individually for a moment. Then—somehow, I don't really know how—she looks at both of us at once. "Those days we spent in the Cook Islands. It was pretty great, right?"

I sigh, my shoulders slumping a little in defeat.

"Are you joking?" Alec says. "It was wonderful." He smiles at her. Hand still on her arm, squeezing just hard enough to let her know he commiserates with her frustration.

I know I don't hate him, not the way I do other people who I really fucking hate. But I fucking hate him. He always comes off so reasonable. So calm. And I'm the irrational one. The unpredictable one. The one who causes shit and he's the one who cleans things up when I'm done.

But that's not how it is. I'm the voice of reason. I'm the one who tried to do the right thing. I'm the rational, patient, calm one in this little triangle. Not him. Not her. Me.

And yet somehow I play right into his hands. I perpetuate the myth.

I look down at the gun, still in my hand, and tuck it back into my pocket.

"Remember when we spent a whole week on that private island near Aitutaki?" Christine says.

I smile, catch Alec smiling too, but not for the same reason. Not entirely, anyway. If she remembers Aitutaki that's a good sign. And it was fun. It was a fuckin' blast, if I'm being honest.

The Cook Islands were something to behold. White sand and turquoise water. Scuba diving and sleeping on the beach, or the deck of the yacht, or not sleeping at all because we were having too much fun and didn't want to miss a single moment of it.

"I think back on that time and wonder... will it ever be as good again? Will we ever love each other the way we did then?" She allows a small laugh to sneak through her sudden sadness. "Remember that yellow dress I wore like every day?" She guffaws despite herself.

And we laugh with her. Because she did love that stupid dress. And she looked amazing in it. It was right around her sixteenth birthday. And she wasn't the little girl I once knew. She was almost somebody else entirely. And when she put that dress on for the first time, well, that was when I noticed she'd grown up.

I couldn't take my eyes off her. Her body was still very slim, but well-muscled from the hard life we lived. And it was difficult to remember that hard life at the time. Paradise has a way of doing that, ya know? Erasing all the bad things and replacing them with bright sunshine days.

Dinners under the moonlight. Swimming under the stars. Laughing with the only two people who matter.

She was tan, and beautiful, and happy.

What happened to us?

"I want that again," she says. Looking at me, not Alec.

144

I nod. "Yeah," I say. "I know." And I almost say 'me too' but I just can't do it. I can't say it because I don't think it's true.

I don't want us. I don't want the triangle.

I want her. Just her.

CHAPTER NINETEEN

BEFORE

Sydney Harbour glimmers outside the window of the suite. Inside, Christine and Danny glimmer in a different way. Christine shines like the diamonds around her neck. And Danny like the ones in the cufflinks I've convinced him to wear.

He claims to hate wearing a tuxedo, but once he's in it, he really shows it off to its best effect. Christine has never had such reservations about donning an evening gown. If I had her particular genetic endowments, I wouldn't either.

A boozy effervescence suffuses the suite. It is, I imagine, equal parts champagne and endorphins. We came to Australia to visit an old friend of mine. Someone who used to come round and visit, back before my parents died. Someone who, I always suspected, was well aware that the accident that killed my parents two years ago was only an accident by the broadest definition of the word. But I don't know what one calls an automobile accident when there was nothing accidental about it. "An automobile intentional" sounds right stupid.

In any case, my father's old business acquaintance, Roderick, is someone with whom I'd been meaning to have a bit of a Q&A about my parents' death for a while. But life got in the way. And Danny got in the way. Danny's more thorough. More cautious. The voice of reason. I do a fair job of feigning control, but Danny actually possesses the ability to maintain his self-control. And so Danny convinced me that we needed to wait to confront Roderick until all the facts were in.

But once the facts did come in and it was confirmed that dear old Roderick had knowledge of the circumstances that led to my parents' passing before the 'accident' happened, and chose to keep that information to himself... Well. Cautious though Danny may be, once he has his arms around the particulars of a situation, his call to action is loud and swift.

I had almost moved past my need for retribution. Almost. One never really lets go of something like that, I suppose. Anger that is born of pain and betrayal can take root and fester for a lifetime. When one least expects it, the demon can rear its head. I was just-turned-twenty-one when Zander and Yolandi van den Berg were set upon by thieves and run off the N2 Highway just outside Durban, causing their vehicle to crash through a police barricade and careen down the side of a ravine.

The number of things about that story that are fundamentally shit are too numerous to consider, but the resulting effect is that having just turned twenty-one, I was in both the position and of the need to take over my father's business. Gone were the days of flitting about the globe making mischief for mischief's sake. The mischief we got into following my parents' death had to be about maintaining control and power of a highly-tiered, complicatedly-structured organization that is at once obscenely visible and yet necessarily cloaked in shadow.

In other words, it's a fokken balancing act, man.

So, after my initial need to hold Roderick to account for his betrayal had passed, my attention turned to other affairs. But Danny didn't forget. Behind the scenes, he went about confirming Roderick's role in the deaths of the van den Bergs and—after two years—presented me with the opportunity to 'make it right.' As he said.

Because Danny Fortnight believes, above all else, in loyalty. He believes in doing what is right by the people he cares for. One must note that in our world, 'right' and 'wrong' are morally relative terms, but moral relativism aside, Danny lives by a set of ethics by which I have not felt burdened, historically. I've always admired that about him. It's what I suppose has kept him alive. Whereas what has kept me alive is pure luck. And a lot of fokken money. Money is a wondrous thing.

In any event, to celebrate the conclusion of a burdensome chapter in our lives, what with the dismissal of one Mr. Roderick whose services as a human were no longer needed, I thought we should do something special to celebrate.

"Who wants to go to the opera?" I asked.

Neither of them showed much enthusiasm.

But. A production of *Salomé* happened to be having a premiere at the Sydney Opera House, and taking them to see the story of King Herod's feral desire toward his own stepdaughter—a virgin temptress with a taste for blood— just seemed too deliciously on the nose to pass up...

When Christine discovered that it meant getting to dress up in evening wear, her tune changed. She's very likely the toughest person I've ever known, but she is also very much a creature of feminine urges like none other I've met. She'd deny it, probably. Somewhere along the twisted path that led us all to each other, something or someone taught her that feminine equates to fragile. I suppose it was just survival. This world is a cruel place. Frequently more so for women. And Christine is a survivor.

But for about the last year, since she turned eighteen, I've been working diligently to show her that she can be both tough and delicate. An iron fist inside a velvet glove. It suits her, and she's taken to it beautifully, but there are years of conditioning I'll still have to work past to get her to fully embrace both sides.

I would have liked to start earlier, but while I have a loosely calibrated moral compass, I fear that attempting to pluck some petals off Christine's rose before she turned eighteen would have driven Danny past the point of his tolerance. So for the last year, I've been working diligently to strip Christine of a handful of her thorns. Not all. But just enough that it leaves the proper amount of pain when we're together.

Danny hasn't had much to say about it. Which is not because, I don't believe, he doesn't have much to say. I rather more think Danny Fortnight is calculating what his role in our future might be. Deciding if there will be a place for him in our arrangements, long term. If he would simply ask, he would know that the answer will always be 'yes.' But he won't ask. And I'm not inclined to volunteer.

But tonight. Tonight is a special night. Tonight is a celebration of who we are and what we've done. Tonight, I feel, for maybe the first time, like the claim my father made when I was a boy is true.

This world—all of it—is mine.

NOW

"Did you fuckin' hear me?" Danny's voice, next to me in the car. Christine climbed into the back seat when we started driving again. She fell promptly asleep. I'm concerned about letting her sleep knowing now that she's suffered memory loss as a result of her fall, but I suppose, all being equal, that should be the least of my worries.

"I did not. Sorry. What?" He no longer has a gun out and/or pointed at me. Which is what, I imagine, is making it possible for me to reminisce so casually.

"You need to tell me what's going on."

"Bru, I wish I could. I do not know. I got word that Christine was hurt, I did a swift inventory of who was available that I knew I could trust to watch over her, I came up with an incredibly short list, and I called you. That's what I know." *And it has the added benefit of being true, so that's kif.*

"Who was the target?" he asks.

"I told you. Jim—"

"Yeah, Jimmy fuckin' Sotoro. Fine." He looks out the window. After a moment he says, "What kind of shit are you into these days?"

"What do you mean?"

"What I said. Diamond business still holding up?"

"I mean… Yeah. They're diamonds."

"You're not into anything else?"

"Such as?" He's obviously leading me somewhere, but I'm not altogether certain where.

"Nothing. Forget it." And he's looking out the window again. And yet again, after another moment, "How long have you two been back together?" He nods to a sleeping Christine in the back seat.

151

"Back together how?"

"Fuckin'... whatever. How long has it been since you've been doing... whatever together again?"

I can feel my brow furrow a small amount before I glance at him and say, "Bru, we've never been apart."

I put my eyes back on the narrow road ahead of us. We drive in silence for thirty seconds. There's a great lot for us to discuss. But until we can get a better grasp on what exactly it is that's bearing down upon us, it don't matter much.

My mobile rings. I look. It's Lars.

"Hey, man," I answer the call.

"Are you with Christine?" He sounds worried.

"Yeah, bru. I'm with her right now. Why?"

"Because I went by the apartment to check on her and she was gone."

"Fok are you doing going anywhere, man? I told you to leave her there and I'd handle it."

"I know, I just—"

"When I tell you to fokken do something, do it the way I tell you, man. Is that fokken hard for you to process?"

There is a pause on the other end of the line that might compel some in my situation to repeat themselves. For emphasis or the like.

I don't.

Finally, after a healthy, long set of beats, Lars says, "I'm sorry."

"It's all right, man. Don't worry about it. Just... don't worry about it."

I can feel Danny glancing at me. I don't turn my head.

After another beat, Lars says, "So fine. Where are you now?"

"I'm taking Christine somewhere safe."

"Yeah. Where?"

"Hey, did you hire this new laaitie? Solomon?" I don't feel like it's a prudent notion to tell anyone where we're going. Even Lars.

"Did I? No. Who's Solomon?"

It's only just occurring to me to ask. I don't know why I didn't think of it before. And I only asked now in order to change the subject. But suddenly I'm having a very negative set of feelings about the fact that we weighed the diamonds for Wallace before transporting them, but then when he weighed them himself, we were light. I'm having a negative feeling about the fact that at around the same time, Christine was being thrown off a roof whilst on a job that wasn't the job I sent her to. And I'm having a negative feeling that there's a new employee in my organization who wasn't hired by Lars.

I don't know if these individual feelings of negativity amount to something greater or not, and not knowing is causing an altogether unique set of negative feelings.

"Never mind, man. What are we doing to find out who fokken ambushed our girl?"

"We think there may be CCTV footage. We've got a call out to a source inside the local police to try to get hands on it."

"Yeah. Good."

I let it linger for a moment. I debate telling him about the assault at Danny's apartment, but I only know for certain that I can trust two other people right now. And if you ain't in this lorrie, you ain't one of them.

"Call me when you see that footage," I tell him.

"I will. Is there anything else I can—?"

"Ta, bru," I say and hang up.

153

Danny continues looking at me. "Who was that?" he asks.

But I ignore his question as well, because I have to focus on this part very carefully. It's been a long while since I've been here, and it can be tricky.

I approach the end of the road and let the car idle for a moment in front of a towering growth of trees. I'm not certain what kind they are. I'm not a fokken dendrologist. I just know they're big, and daunting, and provide a curtain of safety for what's on the other side.

"What the fuck?" asks Danny.

"Shhh," I say. "I'm trying to remember…"

I count from the left, five massive trunks to the right. I think it's five. Or was it to the right that I was supposed to start and count left? Aw, kak. I'm just going.

"Whoa," says Danny, as I drive past the dead end and into the dominating tangle in front of us. "What are you doing? I thought we were going to some goddamn impenetrable fortress. Where are we?"

"We're there," I tell him, as I motor us forward into the looming blackness.

CHAPTER TWENTY

Christine

"What's going on?" I rub my eyes. "Where am I?" I hate that hazy fog when you wake up and nothing makes sense. I have this weird out-of-body feeling like I'm still dreaming about...

Oh, shit. That was a weird dream. I think it was about—

"Apparently we're here," Danny growls, breaking that last lingering thread of recollection. "Wherever the fuck *that* is." He's holding his phone out the window. Trying to get a GPS signal, I think.

That makes me smile as I sit up and swipe the hanging strands of hair out of my eyes. It throws me into the past and brings me into the present all in the same moment. GPS coordinates were always his security blanket. He has a thing for maps too. When I was a kid I always got him something map-related for his birthday. A little globe made of stone. Or an old book of maps from a garage sale. Once I even got him a button-down shirt with maps all over it.

I laugh, mostly to myself. Because he even wore that ugly thing.

"What's funny back there?" Danny rumbles.

"Nothing," I say, scooting over to the window to see where we are.

It's a forest. A very thick forest. And the road we're traveling on is not a road. It's almost not even a path. It's sorta cleared or we wouldn't be able to get through the thick undergrowth on either side of the massive trees that are so close to the car, I think this Range Rover's paint job is fucked, but there's no dirt or gravel. It's mostly ferns and leafy shrubs that smack up against the grille and drag along the undercarriage.

Danny was always trying to track me back then. Apps on my phone and check-in times. Like a father. Or a big brother. Which pissed me off because I've had a crush on Danny Fortnight since the moment I laid eyes on him and getting him to stop thinking of me as family was a constant battle I fought hard.

But it also felt protective in that other way too.

That way a man has of making a woman feel owned. Or claimed. A possessive way.

And I did like that feeling.

I liked it a lot.

"Here we are," Alec says, pulling the car into a thicket of overhanging trees and turning off the engine.

Danny shoots him a look that requires no words.

"Trust me, bru. Come on."

We get out, Alec shouldering the bag of guns, Danny still holding his stupid phone up trying to get his precious GPS signal, and walk into the trees. I hug the pea coat close to my body because there's almost no sunlight in here. Even in the late morning sunshine. Just darkness that smells like wet earth, and too many plants, and maybe the hint of an approaching storm.

A few minutes later we step out of the woods and into a valley with a choppy lake surrounded by mountains. There's a little bit of misty fog hanging low on the water, making the whole place feel a little surreal.

"Finally," Danny says, mostly to himself.

I guess he got his signal.

"Through here," Alec says. So we follow, end up on a path of smooth pea pebbles, and stand before a large metal door the color of rust.

Alec places his hand on some kind of reader built into the exterior concrete wall, blinks his eyes at a screen, and then there's a flash, and a click, and the door opens just a crack.

"Well, that's not creepy," Danny says.

But it's kinda not. I mean, this is Alec. He's very black and white when it comes to security. Either there's none at all or it's one hundred percent sci-fi military-grade shit.

We're just getting treatment number two right now and after what happened back at Danny's garage, that's OK with me.

We step through, but we don't enter a house. It's more of a… compound. We're on the top of a hill and the lake is just barely visible over the roof of a house down below. Mountains flank us on all sides.

"Wow," I say, the last through. I turn to close the door behind me, but it's already closing on its own accord. "This is some setup."

"Why the fuck is it here?" Danny asks.

Alec shoots him an annoyed look over his shoulder. Just like Danny's earlier, it requires no words.

It's here for us. Obviously.

If there's one thing you can count on when you do business with Alec van den Berg it's that he's got a place for you to go when the job is done. And no, this isn't quite the same. We're not basking in the afterglow of a million-dollar robbery. But it's close enough to that to feel normal.

There's eleventy billion flat stone steps leading down to what ends up being the real front door to this place, and Alec repeats the security procedure.

The door opens a crack and we walk in.

"Holy fucking shit," I whisper.

We've been to some spectacular places in the time we've known Alec. The Cook Islands were just the tip of the iceberg when it comes to fabulous exotic locations. And even though we're probably only a couple hundred miles away from the city, this whole setup feels just as exotic as that beach off Crete where we used to vacation, or the volcanic island hideaway in Fiji where we lay low once after a major heist.

The entire west side of the house is made of glass and through that glass is the choppy lake, and the low-hanging mist, and the conifer-covered mountains all underneath a thick blanket of threatening storm clouds. It's so pretty, in such a dark and foreboding way, I just can't believe it's real.

We walk down a flight of stairs to a large open living room, sparsely furnished with ultra-modern chairs, a slim, armless couch, and a ten-foot-tall stainless steel sculpture in one corner that looks like an ice cream cone, but probably isn't.

All three of us end up standing in front of the window, silent for several moments, as we take in the beauty.

"We're gonna stay here until we figure out what's happening."

"I think we all know what's happening," Danny says.

"I don't," I add.

"We don't," Alec says.

"Specifics aren't necessary. When you're in my life," Danny says, looking at Alec, "everything that happens is because you planned it."

"You're free to leave any time you want, bru," Alec snaps. "But Christine is staying with me."

"Because you've done such a great job taking care of her so far, right?"

"Hello?" I say. "I'm right here."

"Better job than you did," Alec answers, ignoring me. "You walked away. Left her to fend for herself."

"OK," I say, turning to Danny. "Just... can we please just stop this?"

It takes him several long seconds to quit glaring at Alec and finally turn his gaze to me. "He's got us into some shit again, Christine. You have to know that."

"How do you know it's him—"

"It's always him."

"—and not me?"

He blinks. "What?"

"I think the two of you have some catching up to do," Alec says. "So I'm gonna go find the office and see if I can fit all the missing pieces back together."

He disappears by way of a hallway and then Danny and I are alone.

Danny sighs.

"What?" I ask, a little edge in my voice.

"How much do you remember?"

"All of it, I think. Well, most of it."

"Do you remember who he sent you to kill?"

I search for that. Partly because the answer is no—I don't remember this Jimmy Sotoro at all—but also because it feels wrong. Not incredibly wrong, because

Alec has sent me to kill people before. But enough that I can't say for sure that's how I got here. So I answer, "No."

"He said something back in the car while you were asleep. He said…" But Danny stops and kinda shake his head.

"He said what?"

"He said the two of you haven't been apart all these years. Is that true?"

It's a simple question but confusing at the same time. "Would that surprise you?"

"Uh, yeah," he huffs.

"Why?"

"So you've been in contact with him before this?"

"Contact? Danny, we lived together."

"What?"

"Not like that." Not exactly, anyway. I'm just not in the mood to dissect the complicated relationship Alec and I have. "But I've stayed with him a lot over the years. I mean"—I throw up my hands——"where did you think I would go? When you left I had no one but him."

Danny turns away. Faces the glass. Stares out at the lake. "So you've been his personal assassin this whole time?"

I have to laugh at that. "You know what I do. It's not like I can just go get a job, Danny. How was I supposed to live?"

"You have money, you don't need to do that."

"I have money *because* I do that."

He turns and leans back against the glass. Folds his arms across his chest. Takes a deep breath. Lets it out. Glares at me.

"Doesn't work anymore," I say. "That look of disappointment that used to have me begging for forgiveness won't work anymore."

Danny says nothing.

"You left me," I say.

"You gave me no choice."

"Bullshit."

"You wanted him and I—"

"I wanted both of you. And you knew that. I made it very clear. So do not pretend like I was the one who made you leave. You did that all on your own."

Silence as we stare at each other.

"Say something."

But he just shakes his head. "I wanted more for you, Christine. I mean, think about it. Why would I save you from all that horrible shit that happened when you were a kid only to throw you back to the wolves?"

I deflate a little. "Danny—"

"I wanted you to go to school. To college. To be more than this."

"College? Danny, come on. I'm not that kind of smart. College is a death sentence for me. I have one skill, OK?"

"No," he says. Loudly. "No. That's not all you have to offer this world."

"Well, what else is there? It's a real question. I know how to open safes. I know how to shoot. I hit my target. There is literally nothing else I can do. I can't even fucking waitress. I tried. Right after you left. I tried. I tried a million different things. I tried being a housekeeper, I tried being a waitress, I even tried driving a taxi in fucking Johannesburg—"

"So you were in South Africa this whole time?"

"Not the whole time."

161

"When you weren't killing people?"

"Why are you so fucking judgey?"

"Because Christine, the thought of someone blowing your fucking brains out just… fucking…" He exhales. It's his turn to deflate. "I can't. I can't fucking deal with that. It hurts, OK? Being without you all these years hurt, yeah. But I thought you moved on. Found a new life—"

"A new life doing what? This is all I know how to do."

"I never wanted this for you."

"I never wanted this for me either, but—" But that's not true. It's such a lie I can't even finish my sentence. "I just wanted you back, OK? And staying with Alec was as close as I could get to that."

He's frowning. Danny Fortnight is not a frowner. A scowler, almost all the time. He likes to grimace, and sneer, and every once in a while he pulls off a smirk. Danny doesn't do sad. He's always said it was a wasted emotion. But that's what he's wearing right now. Not just disappointment in me, but sadness. For me.

I take a few steps forward, slip my hands inside his leather jacket, place my head on his chest, and sink. "I missed you," I say, listening to his heart beat faster. "I'm glad we're together again."

There's a moment of hesitation. A moment when this could go either way. But then I feel the tension flow out of his body. I feel him relax. And when he finally gives in… when he finally allows himself to put his arms around me and hold me back…

I feel complete.

"Thank you," I whisper.

"What for?" He laughs.

"Finally admitting this is OK."

"It's just a hug, Christine. We've hugged lots of times."

I lean back so I can look up and see his face. But I don't withdraw. If he thinks he can bait me into getting angry with him so we can put this conversation off even longer, he's wrong.

"I'm not taking your bait," I declare.

"What bait?"

"You know, the one where you say things I don't want to hear so you can avoid having the conversation I really want."

"Christine—"

"No," I say, cutting him off. "Your turn to listen to me. I love you. And not like a brother, or a father, or a friend." I have more to say to that. Vulgar things about how I want his cock inside me, and how I want him to fuck me hard, and pull my hair and all that kind of shit. But it's a shock tactic. A headline from a teen-girl magazine.

How to Make an Older Man See You As a Grownup.

That was a real headline in a real magazine that I picked up in a drug store in Auckland when I was sixteen. And the official suggestion went something like this: Just say, "I want your cock," a lot to shock and awe him.

I mean, they didn't say that. They said dirty-talk him to death and then hinted around that he'll get hard and won't be able to control himself because all men are nothing but their primal urges.

Voilà. You're a grownup. And two seconds later he'll be fucking your brains out.

It's stupid. It doesn't work.

I should know, I already tried it when we were in Sydney that one year. I mean, I tried everything that last year we were together. Every. Thing.

And none of it worked. In fact, I think that might've been what finally drove him away. He stopped seeing me as a kid, all right. But I replaced the image of sweet-faced little sister with the image of out-of-control slut.

And this might be my last chance to change things, so I'm not gonna fuck it up.

"Danny." I sigh, placing my face against his chest again, squeezing him tight. "I just... missed you."

I want him, he knows that. Has known that for a very long time. And he knows *how* I want him too. With Alec. And if we don't all want the same thing then this is never going to work. It will always be nothing more than a series of meaningless, uncontrollable, primal urges.

And that's not good enough. I deserve more. He deserves more too. I don't want to trap him, I don't want to lead him into this.

I want him to want it.

And that's not something I can control.

He sighs, releasing yet another level of tension locked up tight inside his body. "I missed you too. I'm glad you're here. Not glad Alec came with you—"

"Why not?" I ask, leaning back again so I can see his face. "Why do you hate him so much?"

"He..." But he stops. Just stares down at me with that scanning look in his eyes like he's trying so hard to read my barcode. Then he smiles. Just a small one. "We tried. It didn't work."

"It worked," I say. "It so worked."

"Look at us, Christine."

"We look pretty fuckin' great! We're not starving anymore. We're not homeless anymore. We're not in survival mode anymore."

Danny smiles, sucks some air in through his teeth, and shakes his head. "We're lying low in a bunker, Christine. Don't let the view fool you. We shot our way through a gang of thugs at my garage and left behind half a dozen dead bodies. And if I didn't make that old Jeep into a tank we'd all have holes in our heads the size of baseballs—"

"I don't need a recap," I say.

"—and I don't know what you call that, but I call it survival mode. Two days ago I'd have agreed with you. Two days ago Alec van den Berg was nothing but a bad memory. And now he's back—"

"And I'm back too."

"But you wouldn't be here without him."

For a second I don't know what that means. It could go one of several ways. I wouldn't be an assassin. True. I wouldn't be alive. Also true. I wouldn't be back with Danny.

"Not true!" I say, deciding the last one is right.

And then I do something stupid. Something ridiculous. I start to cry. And it's not even fake.

"Christine—"

But I can't look at him and I'm too busy wiping my eyes anyway.

"Stop it," he says, grabbing my wrists and pulling them away from my face.

But my instincts kick in and there's a flurry of movements, arms twisting and body turning, and I've broken his hold and there's a loud crack.

Because I just slapped him across the face.

He stands there, hands up kinda half-heartedly defending himself from my attack, and laughs.

So I slap him again.

165

And then his eyes narrow. And his instincts kick in too. He grabs my shoulders, turns me around, and pushes me up against the wall of glass, tight grip on my wrists as he slams them into the window and pins them there so I have a perfect view of paradise as he presses the whole weight of his body into my back.

I hold my breath, unable to see where this might go.

He leans down, his mouth next to the soft, sensitive skin under my ear, and whispers, "I love you. You know I love you."

"Then why are you fighting me?"

"I want you for myself."

"I want you both."

He lets go of my wrists, but I leave them where they are. I stare out at the choppy lake with the blanket of misty fog, and a million things are running through my head.

But then he presses his hips into my back and I realize he's hard.

He kisses me. Just once, right below my ear.

And I hold my breath again.

He does it again and I turn my head to see him, staring into his eyes as I wait.

And when it comes… it's more than I expected. It's hands inside my shirt, and fingertips pinching my nipples, and when his lips touch mine and that kiss finally happens…

It's so perfect I wonder if I'm still sleeping. I wonder if the hazy fog rolling across the lake is the same hazy fog from my dream.

But I don't care either way.

I just sink.

CHAPTER TWENTY-ONE

I should stop. I know I should stop. The word 'stop' is the only thing in my head as I kiss her. But then her tongue is there, pushing against mine. And her lips are soft, and when I pinch her nipples she moans into my mouth.

And I know Alec is here somewhere. Probably watching because when Alec has security, he *has* security.

So yeah, maybe what I do next is for him.

Or maybe it's for her.

But if I'm being honest I know why I do it.

I do it for me.

I pull away and immediately she moans, "No, don't. Please don't."

And I wasn't going to stop anyway, I just want to kiss her other places too. I want to kiss her whole body. I want to strip her naked and fuck her right up against this window.

Her hand reaches behind her, grabbing for my cock through my jeans. She squeezes and that's it for me. All rational thought about what I'm doing and how this should go—it should be special. Our first time should be special—all those thoughts fly far, far away.

I grab her hips, pull her towards me, then press down on her back until she leans forward. Her hand leaves my cock, and I miss that. But only for a second, because she slams her hands back up against the glass and moans.

Her sweatpants are down, the button on my jeans open, zipper released, cock in my hand... all that happens before any more doubts can creep in and ruin this.

I've wanted her. All this time, I've wanted her.

So now I'm just gonna take her.

One hand pumps my cock a few times, the other lifts up the back of the pea coat, and my foot kicks at the inside of her foot and she opens her legs.

It's so fucking hot she moans and I grit my teeth, guide the tip of my cock to her already wet opening, and thrust inside her.

"Oh, shit," she whispers. Her cheek pressed against the window so her breath makes a little circle of fog, which retreats as she sucks in air.

I thrust again. Gripping her hips tight.

"Fuck," she moans. "Yes," she finishes.

With each thrust forward, that's what she says.

"Fuck. Yes. Fuck. Yes. Fuck. *YES!*"

I lean back, hips still pumping, my balls swinging with each back-and-forth movement. She presses back, bracing herself with palms flat on the window, more moans escaping past her lips with each ragged breath.

God, I want her. I want this. And I shouldn't think about that now because she could ask me anything and I'd say yes. I'd kill for her. I'd give her anything she wants to make her mine and keep this going.

Give her to me. I'll do anything.

"Harder," she begs.

Oh, God. If that's all she wants, this is gonna be easy. I smack her ass with one flat hand and she yelps, but when I reach around to play with her clit, she's so wet—so fucking wet, I want to die.

But I don't. I can't. She wants it harder and if that's all it takes, I got this.

I smack her again, thrust harder. So hard all I hear is her groaning to the beat of our fucking and the rhythmic jingling of the zippers on my leather jacket.

But it's not enough. Not for me.

I want to see her face, not just the reflection of it in a window.

So I pull out, she protests with, "Hey," and I immediately say, "Shhhhhhhhh. I just want to see you. Make sure you're real."

I take her hand off the glass, turn her around, and stare into those beautiful hazel eyes of hers until she blushes.

"There you are."

"I didn't go anywhere."

"No," I say. "I did. But I'm not going anywhere now." I walk her backwards two steps, press her back up against the window, and kiss her.

Like… *really* kiss her.

Softly. Because she's soft underneath all the tough assassin exterior. And I like those soft parts. Even when we were together all the time, that part of her was always hard to find.

Then urgently. Because I feel like all this is gonna slip away. Or it's a dream and I'll wake up. And I don't want this to ever end.

She responds, her hands on my face, her palms rubbing the week-old stubble on my cheeks. I reach between her legs, slipping my hands behind her knees, and

169

lift her up. Press my rock-hard cock against her belly. She laughs a little, lifting up the too-big t-shirt with one hand while the other grips the sleeve on my leather jacket to keep herself steady.

I enter her again, only this time slower. Facing her.

Her head falls forward and I press my face into her neck, inhaling the scent of her hair.

How, after all these years, can she smell the same?

I don't know, but she does. She smells like every day we've ever spent together and every night we've been apart at the same time.

I lean back so I can watch her. Memorize everything she does. Her sweatpants are still on, the elastic stretched tight just below her knees so she can't open her legs too far. And I don't know why I find that so hot, but I do.

I inch forward, burying my cock inside her pussy so deep she sucks in air and closes her eyes tight.

"Too much?" I ask, my voice a hoarse growl.

"No," she says, shaking her head. "No, it's just right."

I go slowly after that. Almost painfully slow. But it's the best kind of pain. If only all pain could feel this perfect.

I kiss her mouth. I kiss her neck. I whisper, "Don't ever let me walk out again," into the shell of her ear.

And she responds. She kisses me back. She nips my lip. And she answers, "Never again."

And then there's a moment when she goes still and stiff. And I realize—this. This is what she's like when she comes. And every time I make love to her, from this day forward, I will be looking for this sign.

This signal of utter and total surrender.

I press my whole body against hers. My cock buried as deep inside her as it will go. My chest against her breasts, my hands gripping the outer edge of her upper thighs. And then I close my eyes, bury my face into her so-familiar hair, and I come inside her without giving it a second thought.

And when I open them again, when she has stopped shuddering and our hearts have synchronized in their beats, I see Alec.

Standing outside on the shore of the choppy lake

Hazy mist swirling around his body like a cloak as he stares up at us.

And smiles.

Ten minutes later I find him in his office. I had to wander down a hallway that could be described as either a walled-up glass bridge or a human-sized hamster tube. But there was a small stream filled with smoothly polished river stones running under it, so I guess it's a bridge.

The office is a large room with floating shelves lining one wall. There are no books on them, just… art. Probably priceless art, knowing Alec. And there's a large executive-sized desk made of steel and glass. Fits with the décor, I suppose. And two chairs in front of the desk with a small glass table between them on which sits a bottle of brandy so nice even I've heard of it, and two snifters, both with the appropriate amount of liquor in them.

"Where's your shirt?" He nods to the drink, then the chair and stares unapologetically at my bare chest as I pick up my drink and take a seat. I put my leather back on after I took off the t-shirt. But he still stares.

"I used it to clean up Christine."

"Where's Christine?"

Hmm. So he's got nothing to say about that. I shrug internally. "Taking a bath."

171

We both smile at the same time. It's just so Christine to take baths in the middle of chaos.

"Well, good," he says. "Because we need to talk about what comes next."

I take a sip of the brandy. I don't much care for brandy, but I've had enough of it in the company of Alec to appreciate the taste of this one as it goes down. "What comes next?" I ask. Then answer for him. "The usual, I guess. Hole up here, wait for some information, and move along. That's how it usually goes."

"I don't think it's going that way this time."

"Why not?" I ask, setting my snifter down.

"This is different."

"Different how?"

"We didn't just do a job," Alec says. He's annoyed with me, but I can't tell if it's because he saw Christine and me having sex or if it's something else. "And... I don't know. I can't put my finger on it. Something just feels... off."

"Hmmm," I say. "Could it be... oh, let me take a stab at this... that I just took Christine away from you?"

He smiles. Manages to huff out a laugh. "That's not how I see it."

"Maybe you didn't get a good enough look?"

"Grow up, Fortnight."

I shrug.

"And besides. Nothing has changed. She doesn't want you, she wants us."

And there it is. Didn't take long, did it?

I make a promise to give her everything she wants to keep this going.

And what she wants is the only thing I can't give her.

CHAPTER TWENTY-TWO

He starts to respond, but then stops himself, swallows down the rest of his drink in one gulp, slams his snifter down on the table, and stares at me. I wince. Both because I'm certain he's going to shatter the glass in his hand and the table itself, and because that is simply not how one sips brandy. But I understand. He's aggravated. I am too.

I smile at him, reach for the decanter, and refresh his snifter for him. I take my own drink up and offer him a toast of cheers before taking a sip. Then I take the seat opposite him. Sit for a moment. Feel the air move through my lungs before I speak.

"What happened, man?"

He doesn't respond immediately. Finally, he says, "To what?"

"To us. The three of us. It seemed to me that we were just starting to really thrive. And then…"

"Are you serious?"

"About what?"

"Are you asking me a real question right now? 'What happened?' Are you being this way deliberately or are you honestly stupid? Never mind. I know the answer. You're not stupid. What do you want?"

That is an impressively loaded question whether he realizes it or not.

"Well, Daniel—"

"Fuck you."

"—I suppose the first thing I want is to figure out who has put us in this position." He nods a bit. "And then before I kill them for trying to take our lives—Christine's twice—I want to thank them."

Danny draws his head back, knits his brows together, and takes on an agitated expression. "Thank them?"

"As I said." I sip brandy.

"For what?"

"For bringing us all together."

"The fuck are you talking about?"

"Oh, I realize that whoever-is-doing-whatever-this-is-that-they're-doing is doing it with the intention of somehow wiping the three of us off the planet, but their mistake is that they didn't just attempt to pick us off one by one. Because the three of us? Together? We are, my dearest Danny, an unstoppable force." I take another sip. Not to give Danny a chance to react. I know he won't. I just feel like taking a sip. "The only thing that can undo us," I continue, "is us."

He adjusts himself in his chair. The creak of his leather jacket fills the room. When he settles, he says, "There is no 'us.' There never was."

I smile and shake my head. "You're still a stubborn naaier."

"And you're still a smug asshole who thinks he can get whatever he wants, just because he wants it." He reaches for his own brandy and I place my hand over his, holding it on top of the glass.

He looks down at me holding his hand there. My other hand slides up my thigh. I let it rest on my crotch.

He looks at me holding my cock, then his eyes shift to where my hand is touching his. He swallows. His breathing accelerates. He shifts in his chair again.

"Take. Your. Fucking. Hand. Away." he says.

I don't.

"Alec…"

"You need to get your head around something, bru." The tension filling every muscle in his body is radiating off him. I squeeze my hand around his slightly. I want to make sure I don't grip too tightly too quickly. Not this time. "We need each other."

His jaw tightens. His fist tenses around the glass. I've been lucky so far that nothing has shattered, so I opt not to push my luck further and release my grip on his.

Standing, I remove my jacket, walk around the desk and hang it on the chair behind, and take that seat now instead. Probably best to give a little space for the moment. Then, watching Danny's bare chest move up and down, just like it did in the car earlier, a thought occurs to me. I cock my head at him.

"What?" he asks. I cock my head the other way. "Fucking what?" he asks more emphatically.

"Just… I was just thinking… That's not the first time you and Christine naaied, izit?"

"What? Jesus. Will you just talk—"

"Shagged. Had sex. *Fucked*, man. That wasn't the first time for you two?"

He breathes heavily through his nose. Like an angry bull. His chest rises and falls. Then, "It's none of your fucking business."

"Hawu! No fokken way, man! Really? And I was there to see it? Well, that is just too fokken perfect for words."

He leaps to his feet. For a moment it looks like he's going to bound over the desk and have a run at me. There's a not insignificant part of me that wishes he would. I'd be curious to see if things would go differently than they did in the past. But he restrains himself. Which, to my mind, is really the only flaw Danny has. A willingness to override his instincts.

I suppose if the three of us were to be seen as one person, I'd be our id, consumed with fulfilling my desires and sating my appetites; Christine would be our ego, a realist, looking for ways to satisfy my demands while keeping harm from coming to her or me; and Danny would be our superego, curtailing, when he can, my feral desires, and encouraging Christine toward something greater than merely survival. Something that feels almost like... morality.

Yes. That all sounds about right. Danny... Danny still believes that there is such a thing as good and evil, fair and unjust, right and wrong.

As I say: His lone weakness.

He stares at me angrily once again. What he fails to understand, I think, is that I like it when he does. I enjoy seeing Danny's buttons get pushed. Not because it causes him pain. But because he likes it. He thrives on feeling that heat. That rage. Just as much as I do. And he knows it. We both know he knows it.

"I don't know how fuckin' long we have to stay here," he mumbles out, "but do whatever you gotta do to figure out what the fuck. Because we've already been here too long for my liking."

"I will. I'll get some answers."

"How?"

"However it is I do the things I do. I'm magic, Daniel. Just enjoy the show."

He rolls his eyes at me. Which gives me great pleasure. Because it means he still knows when I'm taking the piss. And he's willing to play along.

I do love him so. I always have. I always will.

He turns and begins to walk out of the office.

"Danny…" I stop him. He spins back around. I smile at him.

"Yeah? What?"

I don't say a word, just unlatch my cufflinks and begin unbuttoning my shirt. He watches me. Also not speaking. I finish unbuttoning, pull the shirttails from inside my trousers, strip the fabric off and throw it on the table, and stare at him. His breathing accelerates, and his eyes narrow in something that's not quite anger.

I turn. My back to him. I stare at the glass wall that's now facing me and can see his reflection floating amongst the trees outside. I speak to the ghost of Danny hovering there on the vitreous partition that gives us the illusion of protection. That, at the moment, is successfully housing us from whatever forces wait for us outside these walls.

"You forgot about it, didn't you?" I ask.

The reflection looks toward the floor and shakes its head.

"No," he says, still staring at the floor. "No. I didn't forget."

And then I watch as he turns his back to my back, stands there for a second, not moving, deciding—I'd like to believe—whether he should go or stay, and finally…

Exits the room.

CHAPTER TWENTY-THREE

Christine

BEFORE

"Dance for me, Salomé! Dance!" Alec exclaims as I twist and turn, moving my hips in front of him and Danny.

It turns out I love going to the opera. Who knew? We're laughing deliriously in the Presidential Suite of the Four Seasons, the lights of Sydney Harbour twinkling at our feet.

I'm drunk. On all of it. The champagne, the adrenaline, the rush of discovering something new, the profoundly erotic pulsing that happens in my body when I take someone's life.

I'm sure that last part is fucked up.

Maybe it is. Maybe it's not. But it's honest.

I don't care if the things we do are right or wrong. I don't even care that Alec is a pretty good liar. Hell, who am I kidding, he's a great liar.

But he won't lie to me. Danny either. So when we started pulling heists, I believed him when he said that no one would get hurt.

And when they did, I believed him that it wasn't my fault.

179

And when it became clear that it was my fault, I believed him that it was for the best.

They were bad people. People who deserved the things they had coming.

I believed him when he said that stealing the diamond from his father would be 'a laugh.'

I believed him when he said that no harm would come from it.

And I kept believing. And I kept believing. And I still believe.

I know that makes me naïve. And I don't care.

Because I also know that I love this life and that it's a whole lot better than the life Danny and I had before.

I love Danny. He's a good person and he deserves to be fed, and warm, and happy.

And underneath it all, Alec is a good person too... Okay, maybe not a good person, but he loves us. I know he does. And I'm grateful for that. Because it makes all this possible.

I don't want it to end.

I just wish Danny felt the same way.

He did for a while. But that was before things got complicated. And not complicated in the way life gets complicated when you're stealing things and killing people. He found ways to be OK with that stuff. Justified it or whatever.

But complicated in the way things have gotten with me and Alec. It was inevitable. Three teenage kids with no accountability to anyone and no one telling us what we can and can't do? What did he think was gonna happen?

Hell, if Danny hadn't been around, I never would have finished boarding school. I barely finished as it was. Danny kept making Alec enroll me somewhere every time we'd land in a new location. I'd last maybe two weeks before some rich Swiss girl, or some rich French girl, or some rich Japanese girl would say something snotty and I'd punch her lights out and get expelled. But Danny kept insisting, and Alec kept buying my way into a new one.

The only one I kinda liked was the last one, in Barcelona. It wasn't that I liked the school so much as they had this incredible music hall. I guess they prided themselves on having cranked out some music prodigy once and decided that they should capitalize on their reputation as the place that produced... whoever. From what I could see, the crazy beautiful music hall hardly ever got used by anyone, so I'd just let myself in and plink out stuff on this hundred-thousand-dollar Steinway they had.

I don't think I'm very good, and I never had a teacher or anything, but I liked playing. It relaxed me. Which is probably why I made it the six final weeks to graduation at that place. Instead of getting into a fight, I'd just go play the piano. Maybe that's why the opera tonight was so amazing. I think it felt calming in the same way.

Anyway, if not for Danny, instead of just pulling 'holiday capers,' as Alec called them, throughout those years, this life we have now would have been my full-time job. This thing between Alec and me would've happened a whole lot sooner.

I know Danny hates it. I just don't know why. I think I made it pretty clear that I wanted him. Wanted to be with him. Needed him. So many times. But he wouldn't take me. I would've begged if I thought it'd have worked.

I mean, for fuck's sake. I didn't even see a cock, much less touch one, until my eighteenth birthday. The same night I had my first kiss.

Does that say something about me?

181

Alec said he had a present for me. And it wasn't the yacht he rented for the party. He pulled me downstairs to the lower deck and gave me the diamond necklace I'm wearing tonight.

I don't even know if he planned on kissing me. I certainly don't think he planned on crying in front of me. His parents had been dead a year and I know he had never cried over it. Not until that night. It came out of nowhere. He placed the diamonds around my neck and burst into tears.

He looked so sweet. Fragile. Broken. Like nothing I'd ever seen him look like before. And it scared me a little. I guess he saw that fear in my eyes because the tears stopped just as quickly as they started.

Then... then his mouth was on mine.

His hand ripping down my bikini bottom.

And everything after happened so fast, I'm not sure I even remember it.

I just know I'm glad it happened.

Except now Danny knows. He's colder. His typical scowl so much deeper. And even though I believe Alec when he says none of that's about me, he's wrong.

It's all about me.

But tonight...

Tonight feels like it used to feel. Before. I wonder if it's because with this Roderick guy gone, Alec feels freer or lighter. Maybe it's just the newness of tonight. The Opera. Or maybe Danny is relaxing. Or...

I don't know. And I don't care. I'm just happy that it's the way it used to be.

So I'm dancing.

Alec and Danny are laughing and have their arms around each other. It makes me so, so, so happy. And I do feel like I'm responsible for this. And that makes me dance harder, faster. And then I trip. And then I fall. Because I'm a terrible dancer.

And they also fall down, laughing. And we're all silly, and giggly, and happy.

This is my life. I can't believe it, but this is my real life.

I guess good things do happen to bad people.

"Stop, stop, stop," Alec says, laughing and standing up. "I want to show you something."

He stumbles to a stand and Danny and I laugh harder. Danny tumbles over and his head lands in my lap. I stroke his hair and he smiles, his laugh turning quiet.

Alec faces the windows and Sydney Harbour beyond. He takes off his jacket and in the reflection in the window we see him begin to unbutton his shirt.

"What are you doing?" I ask.

"Dance for me, Salomé!" Danny giggles out.

Alec finishes unbuttoning his tux shirt and strips it off. And when it hits the floor, we see…

"Holy shit," I say, "When did you…?"

"About a week ago," he answers the question I didn't finish asking.

"Fuck, dude," says Danny.

"It's—" I start, before Alec cuts me off.

"It's us," he says. "Three points, converging, the lines bleeding into each other, making something strong and unbreakable. Like a diamond."

Danny and I stand, slowly, mostly because we're pretty drunk, and we walk over to Alec. I can see his smiling reflection in the window.

The tattoo still looks fresh, the skin around where ink has been injected still tender-looking. I reach out and trace one line of the triangle. Danny does the same with another of the lines. Alec's head drops back, and he breathes in.

"Shit," I say, "does it hurt still?"

"No, man. It's exactly the opposite."

And then a FLASH and a GLOVED HAND and now I'm falling. And I'm falling. And I'm falling! Fuck! Oh, fuck! Who—?

NOW

"Christine!" Danny's voice. His hand, shaking me as I startle awake. I don't know where I am. I look around quickly, taking in everything like I've been taught to do whenever I find myself in a new place. Assessing paths of escape. Assessing points of entry. What can be used as a weapon? What can be used to my advantage?

I'm wearing a bathrobe. A nice one. I could take the belt that wraps it around me and strangle someone to death. I could abandon it in one move if someone grabbed the material and then I'd be gone. Naked and exposed, but also slick and nimble.

I'm on a huge bed. Bigger than a king. Like the robe, it's just a little bit more extravagant than I've seen before. I sit up, sharply, and retreat back on the massive surface, striking at Danny out of instinct. He grabs my arms and stops me from hitting him, wraps me in a hug.

"You're OK. It's OK," he says, his voice pitched low and soothing.

I breathe in and out like I just ran a sprint. Or five.

"What was it?" he asks. "What happened?"

"I dunno. I'm not sure."

"You were kind of smiling when I walked in and then all of a sudden you started screaming."

"I did?" I say. He nods. "I don't... I'm not sure."

It's not even a lie. I really don't know what just happened. My dream from almost seven years ago was so vivid, so lucid, so clear.

And yet... I can't remember shit about what happened a few nights ago.

Fuck.

This whole memory loss bullshit. It's making me edgy. I don't know if I should feel safe, or happy, or scared and sad. But I am hyperaware. Very in the moment. Ready to react to whatever comes next.

I'm feeding myself that story, anyway. Just gonna go with it.

Right now I just need to be here with Danny and let him hold me.

Because... like... how do I even know those memories of us are real? Maybe I made them up? God, if that's what's happening I'm gonna be pissed.

Hell, who knows if this is even happening right now?

"Is this all real?" I ask.

"What?"

"You. Me. Alec. Us. Are we all really here together? Were you and I ... together-together before? Am I in your arms right now?"

He lets out a small huff. "Feels fuckin' real to me."

"Does that mean it is?"

He shrugs. "I'm not a philosopher. I'm just a dude who chops cars and builds bikes and tries to do as little other damage as possible along the way. But I guess... When I walked in here you were in a reality that sure as shit seemed real to you in the moment. But, y'know, you're in this reality now."

He kisses me on the head and I wince because I can feel it in the stitches running down the back of my skull. How did they get there?

God damn it.

"Where's Alec?" I ask.

"Fuckin' knows?"

"Danny?"

"What?"

"I'm sorry."

He pulls back and looks at me, fanning some hair away from my eyes as he does. "For what?"

"For everything that happened. Everything that ripped us apart. I feel like it's my fault."

"It's not your fault. It's his fault."

"But I chose to stay with him."

He nods and chews at the inside of his mouth. "Yeah, well, that's true."

"But you know why, don't you?"

"I mean, I'll go out on a limb and guess 'money.'"

I sigh. Shake my head. "No. Because I didn't think that I'd ever get what I want from you. And so I just decided... I did what I had to do to stay... strong."

"Yeah? Did it work?"

I think about giving him the answer I know I should, but I opt for the truth.

"Yeah. It did. It was the right decision."

I hate seeing him frown.

"But, look, you're here now. And I'm here now. And, I mean, we did fuck a little while ago, so I assume that means you're in a different place about it all than you were before." I bend my head to look at him with a kind of half-joking, searching face that always used to make him laugh.

186

It works. A bit. I go on, "So, whatever. Maybe it all went the way it was supposed to, so that we can be here."

He looks around, "Here? You mean here in this fucking glass box in the middle of who knows where with Alec, who—and don't even get me started on the fuckin' irony that that dude has us living in a glass house—who, I'll bet everything I own, is the whole fucking cause of whatever this is that's happening, but that you can't remember because you cracked your goddamned head open, but the one thing we know for certain is that lots of people with guns and who knows what the hell else are trying to kill all three of us right now?"

That's more of a speech than I'm used to from Danny. Or maybe it isn't. Again, I'm not sure I can trust my memories right now. "Why do you think it's Alec?"

"Who else? I'm not saying he set us up. I don't imagine he'd try to coordinate a hit on himself. But whatever the fuck he's into—and I think I know what it is—he's dragged you into it too, and the result of it all is that we're balls deep in van den Berg again."

I almost laugh at that. "You think you know what he's into? What is it?"

Danny's brow knits and he takes a breath. His lips tighten. Either he's not sure he's right or he just doesn't wanna say it out loud. I'm about to prod him to answer, but I don't get the chance because Alec beats me to it.

"Yeah, Danny. I'm curious, man. What's he into?"

187

I don't see Alec when I look over. I see the silhouette of him. Framed by the doorway, the now-setting sun casting him in shadow. An Alec-shaped phantom.

He's still got his shirt off. Shoes too. Probably doesn't wanna dirty up his fancy glass house. Fuckin' van den Berg.

Wearing only trousers, leaning against the door frame, he looks like he could be on vacation in the Caribbean some goddamn place. Lazing around like he doesn't have a care in the world.

Because he doesn't.

I know he doesn't care if he lives or dies. Or that's not true. He does. We all do. If we didn't, we wouldn't put so much effort into still being here. It's more that as long as he is alive, Alec doesn't have to care at all about what he does or how he does it. Every resource imaginable is available to him. Everything he could ever want is at his fingertips.

It took me a couple of years to figure out why he is the way he is. Why he does the things he does.

I finally figured out that Alec's whole reason for being is to test the world. See how far he can push it before it breaks.

Hell, it would not surprise me if he figured out how to live forever. The only thing that seems like it might be able to end his run...

Is sitting next to me in this room right now.

"Really, bru," he says, entering the bedroom. Christine and I are perched on the bed. "I want to hear. What is it that you think you know?"

"Fuckin' don't, dude."

"I'm not kidding," he says, putting his hands to his chest, feigning innocence. "*I'd* honestly love to know. Because I've been trying to figure out why the fok this is all happening, and I have no good answers."

I glance at Christine. Her eyes show a mixture of curiosity and confusion.

"Brasil Lynch," I say. The look Christine is giving off changes. Now it's something more like a tortured perplexity. Like she knows the name. Maybe she heard it somewhere but can't remember where. It's possible that Alec never told her the name of the people he was having her do a hit on. That's not unlike him. Half the time we were doing shit back in the day, we had no clue who we were doing it to or why.

Interestingly, the look on Alec's face when he says, "Who?" is genuinely oblivious. Not that that means anything. He can put on whatever face he needs to for whatever the occasion calls for.

"Fuckin' Brasil Lynch, dude. The guy I've been working with for the past four years."

"Never heard of him."

"Yeah? He says the same thing about you."

"Well, then, how exactly am I into whatever I'm supposed to be into with him when he and I don't know each other?"

"Because I believe him."

"And you don't believe me?"

"No."

"Shame."

He walks over closer. He swings around me and stands on the side of the bed beside Christine. He strokes her shoulder.

"How you feeling, luv?" he asks. "How's the old brain box?"

"I'm… OK," she says, haltingly. "Alec?"

"Yes, nunu?"

"*Do* you know what happened to me?"

He sighs out through his perfectly shaped, fits-his-stupid-fucking-face-exactly nose, closes his eyes for a moment, and nods, "Some. Maybe." He sits on the bed with us and gently presses his forehead to hers. "Apparently, you were on a roof and someone threw you off. I'm guessing it's one of the same someones who paid us a house call this morning."

"Paid *me* a house call," I say. "It wasn't your fuckin' house."

"Yes, well, do you think it's an accident that they only showed up once all three of us were there together? Because I've always thought you to be dead clever, bru, and if you think it's a coincidence, then I need to reexamine that assessment."

"Go fuck yourself."

"And why exactly did you move her from the apartment where I had her in the first place? Maybe that's the better question to be exploring."

I lean in toward him, because I don't like what he's suggesting. "What are you trying to say?"

191

"I don't know. I asked you to look after her. To keep her safe. And you moved her to an unsecured location."

"Unsecured? Fuck you, dude. We're only alive right now because of me."

"Is that how you see it?"

"You're goddamn right it is."

I don't take my eyes off him. He doesn't blink. He does smirk, however. Which makes me want to knock the simpering look off his face. My fist balls up, but before it can gain any momentum, Christine puts her hand over it. I glance down quickly and see her other hand holding one of Alec's.

"Please, don't." The pleading in her voice takes me by surprise. "Please?" she says again.

There's a neediness in the asking that undoes me a tiny bit. It's so sincere. So fragile. Sincerity and fragility are not qualities that I'm particularly accustomed to. And hearing them come out of the mouth of the person I've known the longest in my life is an unexpected jolt.

My fist loosens, and I let my grip uncurl. I turn my hand over, open up my palm, and allow her hand to cup into mine, our fingers intertwining.

She does the same with Alec, and then she lifts both of our hands to her mouth, pressing our coupled fists together and kissing our knuckles simultaneously.

Then she draws them to her chest and holds us there. Next to her heart.

She looks at Alec, who smiles at her. She looks at me. I'm not sure what expression I should offer in return. So I just stare at her.

Then she leans in, and she kisses me on the mouth.

I don't return the kiss. Not right away. I just let the feel of her lips on mine linger there for a moment. I can't help noticing that she's still holding both of our hands together, and the fact that my fingers are somewhat tangled with both hers and Alec's is distracting me.

But then, after a beat, I kiss her back. I lift my other hand and place it around her throat, holding her here. Or maybe I'm holding myself here. I'm not really sure.

And now, she's let go of Alec's hand and is using her newly freed-up fingers to pull my jacket off my shoulder. She forces it down and I let go of her neck, sliding the leather free from my other arm as well. My eyes are still closed. I don't want to know where Alec is.

But that 'please,' the way she said it… It has me willing myself to stay here and give her what she's asking for even though there's an unknown number of competing emotions urging me to walk out.

It's just that all the voices in my head telling me to move away from here are speaking out for the preservation of *me*. The lone voice encouraging me to stay is entirely about *her*.

She's not a child anymore. That girl is gone and this woman took her place.

And it makes me sad.

Because I missed it.

And I don't just mean these last few years. I mean even when we were all together too.

I had some version of her child-self trapped in the amber in my brain and didn't notice she'd become a new person.

Still the same Christine, but a renewed version.

And so, when I hear that word, 'please,' I don't just hear it being asked now. Being asked so that Alec and I will stop fighting. Being asked so that I will put my lips on hers, my body against hers. Being asked so that I'll move out of my head and into her heart.

I hear it being asked from a place of ancient desire. From a lifetime of want.

Whatever this danger is that's happening to us now isn't about now. It's about before. It's about everything that's led to today. It's about karma. It's about a couple thousand yesterdays of someone else's anger and retribution stockpiling in wait for us to all become unaware, unprepared, and weak.

I don't know if we're going to survive. At least not all of us. I had that feeling back at Brasil's when I decided that I would hand him Alec. I can't prove that Alec is definitely the source of our fresh danger, but even if he isn't, it's time that Christine had a chance at living a normal life. She's twenty-four. In some other life she'd just be getting out of grad school or something. Just beginning her life of climbing the corporate ladder or whatever the fuck people do.

Giving Alec up to Brasil wouldn't be the worst thing that could happen, no matter what. And if Alec is somehow directly involved in the trafficking of human lives now, instead of just the passive way that he's previously been responsible—hell, the way we all have—then it'll be deserved justice. Which is a pretty fucking ironic thing for me to be doling out. Justice. But somebody has to, and I'm just about the only one who can.

But that's all bullshit. Because it's not about Alec. Or justice. Or even saving innocent lives. Because no one is innocent. But Christine was. Once. And because of me, she lost it far too soon. So it's about her. It's about saving her life. And if Alec has to die for that to happen, so be it.

Shit, if I have to… Same thing.

She's on top of me now. Straddling me as I lie back on the bed. I open my eyes and glance left and right to see that Alec seems to be gone. Did he excuse himself out of courtesy so that he wouldn't interrupt this private moment?

Fuckin' *right*.

I lean up to look for him, though. I let my eyes settle on Christine. Her bathrobe is barely held closed by the belt wrapped around her middle. But it's starting to come loose. My eyes track to the edges of her breasts. Bare skin. So soft I want to reach up and touch her.

I don't do that. I avert my eyes and, good fucking God, there's a tantalizing shadow between her legs that makes me want to rip the goddamned bathrobe off completely.

I don't do that either.

Not because I don't want to, just because I'm now thoroughly distracted by what she's doing.

Which is… grinding her pussy back and forth across the denim covering my growing cock.

I lean back and… Fuck it.

I let her grind.

My hands go looking for something. Land on her legs, fingertips clenching into her skin.

And now they're working themselves up, gripping the muscles in her legs, my thumbs massaging the insides of her thighs as they travel forward, pushing the bathrobe aside as they journey up.

She keeps grinding. Left to right. Front to back. And my cock is swollen and throbs more with each move. My hips push up to meet her. Silently asking to be freed from the burden of my pants so that my dick can find a home inside her.

As my hands reach the interior of her upper thighs, warmth radiates out in waves. But I don't stop there yet. I keep pushing, gliding my rough hands up the sides of her hips. Then her ribs. Pushing the bathrobe away with each inch.

The belt is finally loosened. The robe falls away. She shrugs it from her shoulders and her whole, quivering, naked body greets me. My hands land on her breasts. Cupping them from underneath, tracing them, and then finding her nipples and twisting them between my fingers. Her head falls back, and she moans without opening her mouth, the sound rumbling from her throat.

She unfastens my pants and lifts her hips just enough to get the zipper down. Then raises her arms and stretches, extending her hands above her head, pinching her shoulder blades together, and rearing back wide. It is a gesture that says she feels safe enough to be totally exposed and also a gesture that allows me to see every possible millimeter of her, and it makes my dick harder.

The only thing that feels off is…

Her hands are in the air.

And my hands are on her.

So… who the fuck is taking off my pants?

CHAPTER TWENTY-FIVE

Alec

You can call me a lot of things, but I don't want it ever said that I'm not a helper.

I can feel Danny stiffen. Everywhere. His head pivots from around Christine and he and I make eye contact. I try to convey to him a sense of *don't worry, bru. I ain't gonna do nothing.* And he tries to convey a sense of something I can only interpret as worry.

But I don't let it stop me.

I'm knelt down, working his jeans along his legs, and find that in so doing, my face is right by Christine's extraordinary ass. I've had the chance to observe it from every imaginable angle, hundreds of times, but it never ceases to impress.

I pause long enough to give her a tiny kiss on both cheeks and then slide my tongue up along her crack. She giggles and glances ever so briefly over her shoulder. I smile and continue unencumbering Danny from his trousers.

I recognize the risk. But I've always found that old expression, "fortune favors the bold," to be true. I'm of the belief that in this moment, being bold is my best ally. Danny and Christine *fucked* for the first time ever earlier. I know how it feels. I know how fokken good she feels when you're inside her. And Danny is not going to be able to shield himself off from another opportunity to be satisfied.

I look at it in the following way: Christine has now gotten something she's wanted for a long time. And Danny has gotten something he's wanted for a long time as well, even if he'll not admit to it readily. And dear old Alec? Well, dear old Alec should be entitled to get something he wants.

I recognize there is an argument to be made that dear old Alec always gets everything he wants. But that's just life then, ain't it?

As I pull Danny's jeans free from his ankles, he kind of tries to kick at me, but Christine has leaned forward and is kissing his chest while still rubbing her wet clit along his shaft. He may not want me here. He may want to fokken kill me. But there's no way he doesn't want her more.

Watching her writhe against him; watching her back rise and fall as she kisses him and sucks at his nipples; watching her tease his cock as it slides back and forth between her legs, almost sliding inside her but then her pulling away...

What it's doing to my own cock is providing a clear answer to the age-old question, 'What is there in the world that's harder than a diamond?'

I want to touch her. To touch him. I want to join them. Complete the triangle. But it's not right. Not yet. I pushed too hard too soon the last time and it was the beginning of the end. So I will just have to satisfy myself for now with continuing to watch.

That's fine. I can wait. But just because I'm waiting doesn't mean I have to feel unfulfilled. I can still share in this. I can be part of it. I am part of it. As are they a part of me.

Fokken hell, man. When I was killing Wallace and his men just the other day, I didn't imagine that I'd find myself here. Now. Life's funny that way.

I unfasten my trousers and let them fall to the floor. Kicking them off along with my boxers, I look down the length of my body. I've never felt my cock so full. So engorged. So thick and pulsing with the blood pumping through my veins.

It's the equivalent of what happens to my other limbs when I'm threatened or under assault. I can feel my skin expanding. I can feel my chest expanding. I can feel my heart pounding in my cock. Sex and violence. Best mates.

I reach down and take myself in my hand right at the moment Christine finally releases Danny from his torment and lets him slide inside her. He moans out and it's like it's happening to me. My breath catches in my throat and my fist tightens around the shaft.

She begins riding him and I stroke myself in time. I close my eyes for a moment and listen to the sound of her groaning. Straining. I imagine myself under her. Between her and Danny. And I stroke myself harder.

Before I know it, I'm walking toward them. I don't mean to. My body just pulls me in their direction. From where I stand, I can see that Danny has his eyes closed. I move around to the side of the bed, facing their undulating forms.

Christine glances over and sees me there. Danny still has his eyes closed. She smiles at me. I fist myself harder as she rocks back and forth, allowing Danny's cock to be stroked and massaged inside the walls of her pussy.

And then Danny opens his eyes.

"What the fuck, dude?"

Christine reaches down and turns his chin to face her again.

"Shhh," she chastens, "Stay here. With me. Just look at me," she says.

He shakes his head a bit in resistance, but when she drops her hips low, driving her ass backwards and pushing him as deep into her as she can drive him, he relents.

"Oh, God," he moans out. "Oh, Jesus Christ."

He closes his eyes again, and now he turns his head away from where I'm standing. I know the expression he has on. It's that of a person trying to will themselves to stay lost in a moment. Not to give over to whatever anxieties they have or cautions their brain is telling them to listen to.

Good.

Christine is sliding back and forth now. Pushing and pulling on him. Working to milk him dry. And looking at me.

She bows her head in my direction and I move forward, stroking more slowly as I approach. I'm about, oh, I'd say *ten inches* away from her when she lifts a hand, takes my cock in her grip, and begins stroking for me.

My neck twists and my shoulder blades pull together. I'm leaning back while pressing my hips forward. She leads me to her, closer, closer, closer, riding Danny hard the whole time. I'm right beside her now. Danny's still looking the other way, moaning and thrusting his hips into her deeper and deeper.

I know he can feel my body heat. I know he knows I'm here. It gets me even harder, which I didn't think was possible. I want so desperately to straddle him and let her take my cock in her mouth. But I feel like I'd be pushing

200

my luck if he looked up to see my ass in his face. Maybe that will be something that can happen just now, but not now now. Maybe if we make it to tomorrow.

Maybe.

But I do notice that Christine is doing a lot of work and I feel like I should lend her a hand. Mine, specifically.

I step in further so that she can get a full grip around the whole of me. And also so that I can touch her. I want to feel her swollen and wet.

I reach my hand to her belly and slide my fingers down so they're resting on her clit. I know I've hit it because she jolts a bit. The jolt makes Danny jolt too, but he keeps his eyes closed and his hands clench the sheets.

I'm rubbing with two fingers, as careful as I can be not to rub my hand against Danny. I want to. I very much want to. But right now, we are perfect, and that's all I need. Perfection.

The touch of my fingers on her tumescent pussy makes her wail. She's moaning, shrieking, grunting, fucking Danny more and more angrily as she hammers her hand on my own inflamed cock. Danny's grunting as well. He's still refusing to look, but he's close. I can see him. His face is contorted, and his knuckles are whitening with his grip on the sheets.

My fingers on Christine are frantic. Miniature jackhammers vibrating against her beautiful, needy blessing. I'm willing myself not to come all over Danny. That feels like it would be ill advised. And it is fortunate for all involved that my will is a thing of legend.

And now...

Her grip around me tightens more and her back shoots up erect. Her knees crash into Danny's hips and she stills, shaking from within.

Danny yells, "Oh, fuck!" It's half release, half surprise.

They are coming at the same time and standing above them, I feel as might the savior himself. An amatory messiah standing holy over the degeneracy of his deviant flock.

Christine shivers, spasms, twists, turns, and finally falls to the side of Danny.

And when she does...

She takes me, unexpectedly, into her mouth as she crashes off. She wraps her lips around me, fisting the base and at once sucking violently. And now I have no idea what Danny is doing. Because I can no longer see. My eyes are still open, but I go blind as I spray into her throat, hot and unceasing. It's all I can do not to fall face forward right across Danny's chest.

I come, and come, and come until I can come no more. And then I come more. And she takes it all. She keeps drinking me down until I am spent and useless and broken.

And I do mean spent. I can no longer stand here. My legs betray me. And I fall forward. I collapse, hard, right across Danny's stomach. He jolts.

But he doesn't say anything. I'm expecting him to yell, *Get the fuck off me, asshole!* Or something of the like. But he doesn't. He just breathes in jagged bursts. Like he's trying to take in air, but his lungs have forgotten for a moment how they're intended to work and so they shudder and start, like an engine trying to turn over.

Christine crawls around to the other side of him. And me. She positions herself at the point between where our heads lie. She stretches one hand out to place in Danny's hair. The other arm straightens to reach the top of my head. She massages her strong fingers into my scalp. I assume she's doing the same with Danny. Trying to knead us into shape with one another.

My arm involuntarily slides down Danny's legs. I allow my fingertips to stroke the muscles in his calf. Again, his breathing darts out of him in tiny bursts, but Christine whispering, "Shhh," seems to calm him enough.

I nuzzle my head into Christine's hand. I turn my neck to spy the geometric way we are positioned together. Christine, one point, me and Danny, the other two.

The automation in the house has turned the lights on, and the golden glow in the room casts warm shadows. The lights embedded into the base boards along the wall form long, arcing columns of radiance. Out of the corner of my eye, I see the pattern we appear to be forming on the ceiling, and I smile. Unplanned, I grunt out a couple of tiny laughs.

"What?" Christine asks. "What is it?"

I don't say anything. Just twist my neck further and cast my eyes ceilingward, gesturing with my chin for her to look up as well.

She does. And she sniffs a laugh out as well.

And finally, Danny opens his eyes also. I can't read him as he sees what we see, but his breathing changes to a more normal pace. And as the three of us stare up at the contours of us painted on the room above us, I try to decide from the image I see…

Is it a scalene? All sides are different.

Is it an isosceles? Two sides are equal. One is out of proportion.

Or. Is it equilateral? All sides are equal.

I want very much to believe it is the last one.

CHAPTER TWENTY-SIX

I lie there breathing hard for a few seconds. Trying to wrap my head around what we're doing. What I just said yes to. How this is all gonna play out and how it's all gonna go to shit. Because nothing is making sense to me right now.

After you have sex with your girl you turn in bed and wrap your arms around her. You lean into her. Let her lean into you. Kinda play it all back in your head as your rapidly beating heart calms down and your muscles relax.

But this isn't what's happening now.

All three of us are on the bed. All three of us staring up at the ceiling. And I don't know what they're feeling but as the seconds tick off and turn into minutes I'm starting to get a better idea of what I'm feeling.

This... was a mistake.

I'm here to protect Christine and keep Alec in my sights so I can turn him over to Brasil in exchange for a fresh start.

Sex can't change that. Won't change that.

The dude is as selfish as they come. He's always looking for more. More power, more money, more excitement. And I don't give a fuck what he says, that's all we are to him. A means to an end.

His end, not ours.

We're not going down with this guy.

So yeah, the fucking was fun—but that's all it was

Fucking. Fun.

I swing my legs over the bed, grab my jeans, pull them up—

"What are you doing now, then?" Alec asks, almost annoyed.

I don't answer.

"Get back here," Christine sighs, clearly tired and spent.

I don't answer her either. She's not gonna listen to me. Not in the afterglow of what we just did. I just pull up my zipper and walk out into the glass-walled hamster-tube of a hallway.

"Oh, fok you, man," Alec calls after me.

No we already did that.

I hear a thump of feet landing on the hardwood floor of the bedroom, then the soft thud of footsteps as he follows me out.

Naked.

Figures.

I turn, my gaze absently clocking all the beauty surrounding me on the other side of the glass. The small stream running beneath my feet. The choppy lake. The low-hanging mist. And I think about how exposed we are. How I hate that. How I should just grab Christine and leave right now. Get her somewhere safe. Somewhere away from Alec and all his fucking baggage that will surely come crashing down soon.

Alec grabs my upper arm, turning me towards him.

I allow this because we *are* gonna have this talk.

"Come on, man."

I stare into those lying amber eyes and he recoils. Just a little. Just his head as he takes in the change of mood.

"What now?" He opts for ignorance. Figures.

I just shake my head at him. "Nope."

"No, what?"

I realize he's still gripping my arm. I shrug him off, getting angrier by the second.

"Danny—"

"Shut up."

He does. Fucking miracle, that.

He stares back at me, gaze changing from satisfied to cautious as I breathe through the hot anger building up inside me.

He shrugs as I try to keep cool. "This again?"

"Meaning what?" I say. My heart is beating fast like it was, then wasn't, and now is again. But for wholly different reasons than it was a few minutes ago.

"You're going to run away because we had a little fun?"

"Fun? Is that what this is to you? Just another spontaneous moment of adventure?"

"Danny—" Christine is leaning against the doorjamb. Naked. "Just come back to bed. We can figure shit out tomorrow and—"

"No," I say. "There's nothing to figure out." And then I look back at Alec. "You should've kept the sexual tension going a little longer, eh?" I mimic his stupid accent. "Then I'd still be caught up in the game and not thinking with a clear head."

"What are you on about?"

"This," I say, pointing my finger at him, then Christine, "isn't happening."

"It just did, bru." And he has the nerve to snicker at me. Like this is some fantastic joke.

My fist hits his jaw and wipes that smirk right off his fucking face.

And then I lose track of everything. He hits me back. Christine is yelling something. Time blurs. Seconds meld into each other. There's a sharp pain in the side of my head, my knuckles splitting open as I connect with his ear. Taste of blood in my mouth as I'm pushed up against the glass. I hit it so hard I wait for the inevitable shattering that never comes. And there's no time to think about that because Alec is on me. The way he was on Curtis that day at the gym.

But I'm not Curtis and I have no plans of going down like him, either.

He swings, I block with my left and connect again. His lip splits and he bends over. Then rams me in the stomach with his head, crashing me against the window again. His arms wrap around my waist and he presses himself into me. Almost hugging me.

"Get the fuck off me," I growl.

"Stop it!" Christine is still yelling. She's tugging on him, and me, and her fucking breasts are swinging—so goddamned distracting I pause, giving Alec the break he needs to twist my arm around my back, forcing me to turn into the window.

He holds me like that. Just enough pressure on my arm to make the threat of a dislocated shoulder real. Then a jerk—pain shoots up my arm—to hammer that home.

"You know what your problem is, man?" he growls, his words low and angry right up against my ear.

"You," I growl back.

He gives me another jerk, and as the shooting pain runs up my arm, I decide… fuck Brasil. I'm gonna finish this job myself. I turn, weight on my left leg as my right leg sweeps behind him, hooks his ankle and as he goes down, I wrap both arms around his legs, taking away the major threat.

But I'm in control for less than a second. Even after all these years apart, Alec is as familiar with my moves as I am with his. His forearm catches me under the chin as he pushes my head to the side, and quick as that—he's out from under me, getting to his feet.

I'm on my feet too, and we circle each other. Half crouched. His cock—slightly hard from the sex we just had, or maybe the fight turns him on, who the fuck knows—swings back and forth.

"I might be biased," Alec says, spitting blood onto the floor. "but I agree that it's perfect. Feel free to stare, my boet."

"You guys!" Christine shouts. "Enough!"

"Not yet, nunu," Alec says. "We're just getting started. But don't worry, Danny'll be back in the old bed as soon as he gets it all out of his system."

"I will, but you won't," I snarl back.

"Why are you so goddamn uptight, Fortnight? Jesus Christ. Your hang-ups are starting to bore me."

"Is that what you think this is?" We continue to circle each other. Eyes locked. Hands in front of us, fingers spread wide, each waiting for an opening. "Shame?" I laugh, then lunge, hitting him in the chest the way he got me. He goes reeling backwards down the stupid hamster-tube hallway, but doesn't lose his footing.

I probably should've anticipated the position this would put me in a little bit better… because I get a good

209

long look at his cock and then a slap, as it swings up to hit me in the chin.

Alec laughs. "Don't bite now, Danny. That's a rule I have no matter who has their head between my legs."

I push harder. He pushes back. For two eternal moments we're immovable forces. Equal and opposite in every way. And then…

He gives in and we go reeling—me forward, him backwards. His back crashes into the floor and I crash into him. Instantly his leg wraps around me, his hard cock pressing into the muscles that line my waist, and we trade positions.

The next thing I know I'm face down, in a head lock, and he's got his lips pressed up against my ear. His breath flows into me with his words. "Why don't you ever believe me, Danny?"

"OK, that's enough!" Christine is yelling. I think she's been saying shit like that on repeat since we started fighting, but I lost track of sound so I'm not really sure.

"Because nothing you tell me is true," I hiss back, barely able to get the words past the pressure of his forearm against my throat.

"Everything I say is true."

"Ha," is all I can manage. I might be blacking out.

He eases up and the blood begins to flow to my brain. The fuzzy feeling fades as Alec lifts his body up off mine, allowing me to turn over so I'm no longer pressed face first into the floor. Just as quick, he leans down again. Pressing his chest against mine as he grabs my hair with both hands and gives me a shake. "What do you want from me? A ring? A wedding? Do you need a dress and a cake and dancing under the stars?"

"What the fuck are you talking about? And get the fuck off me, asshole."

"Not until you answer."

"Answer what? Your stupid jokes?"

"It ain't a joke, man. Just... tell me what I need to do to convince you I'm real. Yeah? Can you do that? Give me a hint, maybe? So we can come to terms and get back to fucking? Because that was preferable."

"I don't even know what you're trying to say."

"Oh, my fucking God!" Christine screams. "He's trying to tell you he fucking loves you!"

I actually laugh.

"That's funny, izit?" Alec asks.

"Yes." I'm still laughing.

But then I stop laughing. Because... he's kissing me.

For a second I don't know what to do. Punch him in the face because this fight isn't over? Or just...

Give in.

I give in.

Because Christine is kneeling behind me. My head between her open legs. Scent of her pussy infiltrating my nose. Everything forgotten as both her hands cover Alec's, which are still gripping my hair as his tongue pushes its way past my lips and slips inside my mouth.

Christine's long hair brushes against the side of my cheeks as her lips flutter against the corner of my mouth, wanting to complete our triangle.

I lean into her. Ready for more of that. But Alec isn't about to let me forget he's here too. His cock is practically stabbing me now. So hard. So ready.

Christine's hands slide down my face and reach over my chest, fingers splayed open like her legs. Her tits dangle like ripe fruit over my mouth and I reach for them, twisting and kneading them until she begins to moan.

Alec lets got of my hair, lifts himself off me until he's sitting on my thighs. I don't miss his kiss. I still have Christine and she's the only one I want.

Until... until Alec's fingers drag my zipper down and pull my own rock-hard cock out.

I grit my teeth and close my eyes.

"Fok that," Alec says. "Open your fokken eyes this time. Coward."

I do. Mostly because the venom in his voice doesn't match what he's doing with his hands. Which is slowly pumping my cock with a firm grip. "What?" I ask, my voice rough and throaty.

"No more sticking your head in the sand. No more pretending. No more bullshit. We. Were meant. To be together. The three of us. It's perfect. Our love triangle. And I'm not going to let you lie your way through it again. You will make a decision. Now. Get up and walk out forever. Or stay and commit to us. To what you know is right."

CHAPTER TWENTY-SEVEN

Christine

It's one of those do-or-die moments. A defining moment.

And I refuse to leave it up to Danny. Because he's always worrying about tomorrow. He's never satisfied to just take the prize and run. Always has to overthink things. Always dwelling on the stupid consequences.

We don't have time for consequences. We could die tomorrow and then who the fuck cares, right? We might not even make it to tomorrow.

I feel guilty for even thinking like this. Because I know that, truthfully, if Danny wasn't Danny I'd probably be dead right now. I sure as fuck wouldn't be in a love triangle with the unofficial forty-fourth richest man in the world and a car-chopping mastermind—

Wait. *What?*

The memory of what Danny really does for a living comes crashing back to me like a hammer to the head. It actually hurts. A pain shoots through my brain and then... then... it's gone. The foggy haze that mimics the mist outside receding, the missing parts of my life—did I know there were still missing parts?—rush back in as the black-out pressure is released like a dam breaking.

"If I leave," Danny says, bringing me back into the moment, "I'm taking her with me."

Her. *Me.* He means me.

"No," I say. "No." I look down at Danny and frown. "If you leave, Danny, you leave alone. If you walk out on him, you walk out on me."

"Christine—"

"No," I say again. "No. I'm done."

"Done how? What do you mean?"

"I'm not gonna let you ruin everything, Danny. Not again."

"Again!" He chokes on his incredulous laugh.

"You were the one who couldn't commit. You were the one who divided us. You were the one who walked away. Not us."

He cringes at the word 'us.' But I don't care.

"Oh, yeah," I continue. "There's an us." The hurt on his face is automatic. And I feel it like it's mine. I'm not trying to hurt him. I don't want to hurt him. But he needs to see the truth and this needs to happen now. "Alec didn't walk away from me."

"Christine, I only ever wanted what's best for you."

"I know that, but you never stopped to ask me what I wanted."

There's several moment of awkward silence. My tits are dangling in his face. My hands splayed out on his chest. Alec is naked, still sitting on Danny's thighs, still gripping Danny's cock, slowly and automatically pumping it up and down as he locks eyes with me.

Keep going, his eyes say. *Tell him. Make him listen. Make him stay.*

There's a lot going on in my head right now. And the seventeen stitches are just the beginning. What do I know? What's true? What's missing?

"Christine," Danny says, jerking me back to the present. "He's not good for us. He's not—"

"Stop it," I say. "Just stop it. I mean, come on, Danny. Everything good that's happened to us is because Alec was there."

Danny shakes his head. "How can you even say that?"

"Because it's true."

"We're criminals, Christine. Because of him."

He has to know that's not true, so now he's just lying. And that pisses me off. "You were a criminal long before Alec van den Berg came along. Or have you forgotten all those years we spent together? Alone. I saw you, Danny. I saw what you did. I know who you are. And that guy was inside you long before you appointed yourself my knight."

"He taught you to *kill*, Christine!"

"Thank God he did, right? Or you'd be dead right now."

This shuts him up.

Alec sighs. And when I glance at him, notice that he's *still* giving Danny a hand job, I want to laugh. Because he makes me happy. Because I love him. And I know that Danny loves him too. It's just... complicated. And I get that. I do.

So I lean down and kiss Danny. And when his lips part to receive my offering, I whisper, "We love you, Danny," into his mouth.

His head tips back, his eyes on mine. Scanning me the way he does. Searching for the mysteries inside me.

But there's no mystery. "It's just love in there," I say. "That's it. That's all. Just love."

"No," he says, one hand coming up to rest on my cheek. "You're pretty inside. It's blue in there."

I sigh. Long, and low, and softly. "It's blue in you too."

"I can be blue," Alec says. "Just tell me what it means and I'm every shade of blue you like. Light blue, navy blue, cerulean blue. I'll even be turquoise."

When I look at him he's smiling like the fucking Cheshire cat. "Don't gloat," I say. "Be gracious."

"He doesn't get to be gracious. He didn't win."

"And you," I say, leaning back down to bite Danny's lip. He hisses at me. "Be honest."

"With what?"

"Oh, for fok's sake," Alec sighs. He's about to swing his leg over and dismount Danny's thighs when I reach out and place a hand on his shoulder.

But I don't say anything. Not to him. Instead I look at Danny. "This is it, OK? Your last chance. If you want to walk away from him, go. But I'm staying. And if you stay, it better not be for me. It better be for us."

Danny's eyes dart to Alec.

Alec shrugs. "I'll get us all rings. How many carats do you need to feel loved and cherished, Danny?"

Danny smiles. Then he laughs. "Fuck you."

"I mean, you do realize that diamonds have nothing to do with forever, yeah? They're just a made-up token invented by the mining industry."

"Fuck off."

"But I have connections. I can make you feel special."

And then... that defining moment is back. Because that last part comes out different. It's not a joke. He's not making a joke. He's serious. And slowly, so slowly, Alec lowers his head down to Danny's stomach and begins to kiss him. His eyes looking up Danny's chest. Wide open.

"I don't even have to try hard," Alec says, pausing to kiss his way up Danny's abs. "Because it's always been true. I wanted you first, you know."

I'm so close to Danny I hear him swallow.

"I went to that boxing club to get your attention."

"Fuck off."

"No, it's true, man. It is. I was fighting for you that day."

Alec is still holding Danny's cock. His fist tightens around his shaft, making Danny suck in a breath and hold it.

"Christine. She was…" And now Alec's eyes lift up to mine, just as his face hovers over Danny's. "A little bonus. And yeah, nunu, I fell in love with you that day too. I mean not nearly the way I am now, but it was love. There was something. It was real."

Alec starts grinding his hips against Danny's cock. Slowly. Back and forth. So slowly.

None of us dare move. There is only the sound of our breath. And this time, when he leans down to kiss Danny, it's different.

Danny responds and I stay absolutely still as I watch their lips meld together. I am mesmerized by their contrasting jawlines. Danny's week-old stubble. Alec's just a few days' worth. I get glimpses of tongues, and teeth. And when they groan and growl, I moan with them.

Alec pulls back, his hand taking mine as he sits up and eases me forward over Danny's face.

"There you go," he says. "Yes, just like that," as he places my hips directly over Danny's eager tongue and pushes down on my lower back.

"Oh… fuck," I whisper, as the first swipe tickles past my opening. And when he flicks it against my clit I can't stop myself. I press into him. Sinking down on his face. Seeking out the rough edges of his jaw. Loving the way the stubble feels against the soft, tender skin between my legs.

Alec, ever the facilitator, pushes my head down towards Danny's rock-hard cock and my hands automatically reach forward to grab his shaft.

I'm fully bent over now. Danny's finger finds its way inside me. And then his large hand spreads my cheeks so his thumb can massage the tight pucker of my ass.

Alec, still balanced over top of Danny's thighs, says, "I get it, man."

Danny pauses. His mouth still against my dripping wet pussy.

"I gave you so many reasons not to trust me. I showed you who I was, after all. The real me. So I don't blame you for being cautious or wanting some grand gesture of commitment. So how about I give you something better than a ring, yeah?"

Alec pushes me aside and takes Danny's cock from my hands. He says, "Stay close, nunu. I've got something for you too." And then his mouth covers the head of Danny's cock.

"Motherfucker," Danny says, lifting his hips up to thrust deeper inside Alec. He squeezes my ass cheeks, then slaps them, making me grunt from the sharp sting. But he's too distracted to keep licking me. And I don't mind that one bit. I want him to have that needy ache for us the way we have it for him.

So I rise up on my knees, Grab Alec's shoulders, digging my fingernails into his hard flesh, and settle my clit against Danny's chin so I can fuck his face.

I grind on him. Just as Danny grinds on Alec. And poor Alec. No one has his cock in their hands, or their mouth.

I want to fix that. I want all the sides of this triangle to be equal. So I duck under Alec's muscled arm, reach for his cock, and begin to stroke him.

"Oh, yes," he breathes out around Danny's swollen tip. "I like that very much, thank you."

I want to suck him. I want to suck them both. I want them to be inside me at the same time. I want all of them...

And just when I think there's no possible way to feel more...

Danny begins to lick me again. His fingers bang inside me. One, then two, then... Oh, Jesus Christ, that's exactly what I've been waiting for. I grind harder on his face. My clit bumping up against his chin. Everything is wet. I feel like I'm dripping. My fingertips slide between my legs, scoop it up, and then grab Alec's cock again so I can share it with him.

My hand slides effortlessly up and down his shaft. Alec's sucking noises are driving me crazy. Danny's fingers, and his chin, and my hips, and his hips, and...

I come.

Moaning and writhing. And the second the release escapes, I want more.

More of them. More of us. More of everything.

CHAPTER TWENTY-EIGHT

Danny

I don't know what the fuck is happening. All I know is… it feels like… I can't even describe it. Alec is sucking my cock like he worships it. And he's right, it's better than a ring. Tells me way more than a ring ever could. More than words ever could.

Christine's come is all over my face. Her body went stiff, just like before. The perfect little tell. I like the way her legs trembled when she climaxed. I like the way her pussy quivered and clamped around my fingers and I want that to be my cock. I want to be inside her and… and I want Alec to be inside her too. I want to feel him fuck her as I fuck her. I want to feel his balls tighten against mine as we come inside her.

I push Christine forward and she slumps over onto my chest, her breath hot against my sweat-slicked stomach.

"Turn around," I say. "And put me inside you."

"Oh, my God," she whispers. But she does it. And Alec helps her.

His eyes meet mine when he sits up, and he smiles. His hand is still working my dick. Like if there's any possible chance I'll soften before Christine lowers her pussy over me, he's gonna be there to save the moment.

There is no chance of that.

JA HUSS & J McCLAIN

Christine is facing me now. Her hips hovering over mine. Her hand grasping my cock, guiding it to her deliciously wet pussy. And the moment I enter her is one I will remember for the rest of my life.

It is pure bliss. It is everything I've ever wanted. Better than the first time. Better than the second time. Because this time I'm hers. And I give in. I'm his too.

Being all in makes a difference. It changes everything.

"Stop thinking so hard, my boet," Alec says. "Enjoy it, man."

"I am," I moan out. "It can't get any better than this."

He mumbles something like, "Give me a little credit."

And then Alec pushes Christine forward so her face is tucked up against my neck. I hug her around the waist as Alec thrusts his hips forward.

I expect him to take her in the ass. But that's not what he has in mind.

The tip of his cock presses along my shaft, his fingers wrapped tightly around it as he pushes…

Christine squeals as I imagine the lips of her pussy stretching to accommodate his considerable girth. She tries to sit up and ease the pain, but I hold her tight and whisper, "I love you," over and over into her ear.

Then the tension breaks and he's inside her. We're *both* inside her.

"Oh. My fucking. God!" Christine says.

"Too much?" I ask, pushing the hair away from her face.

She responds by thrusting her hips back. Forcing us both to go deeper inside her.

Alec leans over her back, his arms braced, palms flat on the floor on either side of my shoulders. Our eyes meet and… and we smile.

His eyes say, *I told you so.*

Mine say, *Fuck off.*

We are slick with sweat as we slide into a rhythm. Christine rebels against my tight hold on her, so I ease my grip and allow her to sit up a little. Her hair hangs down, brushing against her tits, and my chest, and my face.

She leans over, kisses my mouth, and begins to moan again.

And that's when Alec sits back up, smacks both her ass cheeks, then grips them tightly as he pounds her from behind. Just. Pounds her.

Us.

Her.

Us.

Her.

The friction of our dicks inside Christine's pussy is overwhelming, but in all the right ways. I don't know how it feels for her—judging from the way she's now screaming. "Oh, God, yes! Yes! Oh, my God! Yes!" I'm gonna go out on a limb and say fantastic—but it's a million times better *with* him than *without* him.

"Shit," Alec moans. "Fuck."

I think he's gonna come. I get irrationally proud that I can outlast him, even when were in the middle of the best sex I've ever had.

And just when I think victory is mine, he grabs my hair, forces me up into a sitting position, still fucking the shit out of us as Christine slumps against my chest, fully spent, and kisses me on the mouth.

I explode.

And two seconds later, so does he.

223

CHAPTER TWENTY-NINE

BEFORE

The feeling of their hands on my back as they trace the lines of my new tattoo is making me hard. This is the moment I've been waiting for. For years.

From the first time I saw Danny, I knew I needed him. He possessed something naturally that I had to condition myself to attain.

Grit.

Grit is indefinable. But it is something that says you will not be cowed. You will not be broken. You will stare down the oncoming torrent and whisper in its face, "I am the storm," and all that.

That is who Danny is. Organically. In his bones. I had to learn to be that way. And I learned it, in no small measure, from him.

For that, and for so many other things too innumerable to mention, I have loved him.

And somewhere along the way, that love became desire. Yes, of course, it's sexual. Danny's just fokken sexy. There would be something wrong with me if I didn't feel that way about him. But it is more than that.

It is that by joining with Danny, fully, entirely, perhaps I can become part of him and he can become part of me. And we will become greater than the sum of those parts.

I already feel stronger, more resilient, since Christine and I have formed our union. I want so much for Danny to be a part of it with us. I want him to know the euphoric serenity that comes of feeling absolute. Of feeling whole.

And tonight is the night that happens.

"Jesus, man," Danny mutters. "That's a hell of a piece for your first one."

"Well," I say, "as you always tell me, 'Go big or go fok yourself.'"

Danny and Christine laugh.

What I don't tell him is that I *wanted* him to be impressed. I *wanted* him to have this reaction. Every piece of ink on his body reflects something he's experienced. Something he's endured and survived. Something that has meaning for him.

Nothing has more meaning for me than him and Christine. Nothing ever has. Nothing ever will. And if I'm only going to do this once, I wanted to make it count.

I turn to face them, and their hands stay on my torso as I pivot around. They are both touching my chest. This is the moment I've been holding onto in my imagination. I smile at Christine. She smiles back. She leans in to kiss me. Our lips touch. And having Danny's hand on my chest at the same time feels like... Nomathemba.

"*Hope.*"

But then, tragically, the hope fades away. Along with Danny's hand. I grab for his wrist and pull him back into us. Christine turns her kiss from me and places it on Danny's mouth instead.

He resists, but I hold them together. Then he pushes me away, pushes her away, and steps back, saying, "No. No. No," over and over again. To himself as much as to the two of us.

"What?" Christine asks. "Danny, come on…" She moves toward him, and he retreats further.

"Fuck off," he says, pointing a warning finger. "I mean it."

"Come on, bru," I tell him, moving in his direction. He has his fists up now. "Danny. Don't, man. It's all right," I implore a bit, advancing further, my hands up in a gesture that's intended to look non-threatening.

But all it really does is expose my midsection to the shot that hits my stomach.

"Fok, bru!"

"Jesus! Danny, stop!" Christine shouts as she runs over to tend to me.

"God damn it!" Danny shouts, punching at the sides of his head like he's trying to jostle his brains into a new space.

"Danny, Danny, stop. Come on. What is it?" Christine asks, moving to him now. Trying to calm him somehow.

"We can't!" he shouts.

"Can't what?" she asks. "Can't what? We *can*, Danny. We can do anything. We can *have* anything. We can. It's OK."

He shakes his head. "We can't!" he shouts again. "It isn't fucking real, goddamn it!"

"What isn't?" She's pleading with him now. Just moments ago, everything was perfection. Which is all I want. And now everything is shit. Cocked up and dangling by threads of almost-was.

Part of me wants to hit him back. Part of me wants to just pound some goddamn sense into him. Or pound some goddamn resistance out of him. Either way.

But I know that the second I lay a fist on Danny in anger... we will be done.

So instead, I just slump to the floor and sit there as Danny pulls away from Christine and retreats into another part of the suite. She chases after him. Leaving me there alone. The lights of Sydney twinkling in the distance.

Fok, man.

I couldn't have been more goddamn wrong.

Shit.

I guess tonight is not the night.

NOW

"Fuck is this?" Danny asks.

"Rooibos," I say, placing the steaming mug in front of him. "You don't like rooibos? Everyone likes rooibos."

"I don't," he says.

"Fine. I also have chamomile, hibiscus, peppermint—"

"Yeah, you got a fuckin' beer?"

I smile and chuckle at him. "Sure, bru. I got you a brew." I say the second part in my tragically inept American accent.

He laughs a little bit and shakes his head as I open the fridge and pull out a bottle of cold beer for my old friend. From where he sits at the kitchen island, he glances over his shoulder and says, "Fuckin' incredible, huh?"

I look at where he's observing Christine curled up in an oversized, tufted lounge chair. Fast asleep. "Yes, it is. Never known anything like it. I envy her."

"Being able to sleep anywhere?" he asks.

"Being able to sleep at all."

I pop the cap and hand him the bottle. He offers me a 'cheers' and takes a sip. I sit across from him, sipping my tea. After a moment, I break the silence.

"So, Danny—"

"How long you had this place?" he interrupts.

"Oh, I don't know. A while."

"Yeah?" he says, taking another sip from the bottle. "Why'd you get it? You don't have enough places?"

"There will never be enough places," I tell him.

He laughs a bit. Sort of a half-resigned, half-contemptuous laugh.

"Danny?" I say.

He waits, as if I'm being rhetorical. I'm not. I genuinely want his permission to go on before saying more.

Finally, he says, "Yeah?"

"I think about you every day, man." He eyes me cautiously. "I mean it. I don't say your name out loud because... Because I don't. But I think about you all the time. Wondering if you're doing all right."

He nods. Licks at his lips. Says, "Are you waiting on me to tell you that I think about you all the time too?"

"No."

"Because I don't."

"OK."

"I'm serious."

"I believe you."

That hangs in the room as I sip my tea and he picks at the label on his beer bottle. Then, quite unexpectedly if I'm being honest, he says, "You know why, right?"

"Why what?"

"Why I don't. Why I can't. Why I couldn't. Before."

While I don't think he's being rhetorical, I don't prompt a response. I just sit and wait for him to decide if he feels like baring himself further.

He does.

"It's because of the cost," he says.

I cock my head to the side. "Which cost? Sorry, man. You'll have to explain. You know I rarely take cost into consideration."

He rolls his eyes and shakes his head. "Couple things, I guess." He takes another drink before putting the bottle down and saying, "With Christine... well, I mean, shit. With her. She was a kid. Y'know. Seen her grow up. Watched every fucking minute. Just felt. I dunno."

I nod. I do understand him. Were I saddled with a conscience, I likely would have felt the same.

"But then add you... you *and* her..." He breathes in deeply, letting it out in a long sigh through his nose. "The way I survive... the way I've always survived and been able to keep going... is by never letting myself believe that I care about or... *love*... anything enough to be beholden to it. You know what I'm saying?"

I take a moment and nod. "I believe I do."

"If you don't love anything... if you can walk away from anything at any time... they can't hurt you. They can't get to you. You know that shit you said earlier about us being stronger together than apart or whatever?"

I nod again.

"Yeah. I don't see it that way. I felt like if I ever gave over... if I let myself really fuckin' give in to my feelings and shit... that'd be like fuckin' kryptonite to me. Because then I'd have something in my life that would be too precious to lose. And if I did lose it, I wouldn't be able to bounce back."

He tips his head back and says, "You two always saw me as the conscience or the fuckin' cautious one or whatever."

He looks down at the island in front of where he sits. Shakes his head a tiny bit. Scrunches the corners of his eyes like he's deciding how to say what it is that he wants to say and then starts with, "Shit isn't morals, man."

Then he pauses. Picks at the label on the beer bottle once again. He pushes the bottle away, sits back, and says…

"It's self-preservation."

That hangs in the air as we keep eye contact. It takes a long, long while before whatever this odd lump is that has formed in my throat diminishes enough that I can try to speak.

I'm just about to respond when I hear a sound from across the room. A yawning sound. A tiny squeaking yawn that makes my heart fill with yearning.

Christine stretches out like a cat, blinks her eyes open, and says, "Did I fall asleep?"

231

CHAPTER THIRTY

Christine

"You could fall asleep in the middle of a goddamned hurricane," Danny says, answering my fake question.

"She did that once," Alec says. And then he sorta laughs. "Typhoon Hopea."

"In my defense," I say, getting up from the chair and walking into the kitchen to search for food, "we weren't anywhere near that thing." We were lying low in the Shengsi Islands, which wasn't in the direct path of the storm, but it was still intense enough to shut the local villages down for a day.

Danny grins at me as he takes a draw of his beer.

"What? I can't help it. Storms relax me."

I *was* sleeping. To answer my own question. At first, anyway. I can sleep anywhere, pretty much any time, through everything you can imagine. I mean, I'm not narcoleptic. I don't nod off during a fight. And when I'm in assassin mode I'm all in. But after, when shit calms down, I shut down. It's almost like I have an off button.

Comes in handy in lots of ways. Means I'm always fresh when the next bit of bullshit comes up. Also means I hear things that aren't always meant for me.

Like this conversation Alec and Danny were having.

I have a lot of opinions about this topic. Danny and his morals. Danny and his self-preservation.

Look, I get it. He's a tough guy. He's big, bad Danny Fortnight. Tatted-up monster. Mastermind criminal. Beholden to no one and nothing. Blah, blah, blah.

But it's a front.

If there's a good guy in this little triangle, it's him.

It's sure the fuck not Alec. I love him but he's the most selfish, entitled, power-hungry person I've ever met and I've been around the block a dozen or so times, so that's saying something.

And it's definitely not me. If I ever had a moral compass it fell out of my pocket a long time ago.

Danny will weigh things before he makes a decision. He will ask himself one question. *Can I live with myself after?* And if the answer is yes, he does the thing he's weighing. If the answer is no, he doesn't.

On that level he's very simple. Everything is black and white. With Danny, you always know where you stand. Which is probably why Alec is trying to have this conversation with him right now. He has no idea where he stands with Danny and that's not a good thing.

For most people indecision is weakness, but indecision makes Danny stronger. Some kind of instinct kicks in. Some small voice inside him, maybe? Telling him to take a stand?

This makes the people he's undecided about uncomfortable. Because he could swing either way, and once that happens, his mind is made up.

Oh, we all know where *I* stand. Danny is always on my side. But a couple rounds of hot sex isn't enough footing for Alec to feel comfortable.

On the other hand, Danny isn't punching him in the face and he hasn't walked out.

So… progress.

But not enough. Not for Alec. Not for me either. Because Danny just lied and I'm gonna call him on it. "It's not true," I say, pouring myself a cup of tea. Mostly just because it's there, but also because this house gives me the chills. All the glass feels cold. Like there's nothing between us and the wilderness outside.

"What's that?" Alec says.

I look at Danny. "I'm the one thing in your life that's too precious to lose."

He huffs. "I let you go, didn't I?"

"And yet here we are."

"You came to me."

"Not exactly," I say.

Danny shoots a quick glare at Alec, which makes him recoil. Not like he's afraid of him. More of a *what'd I do now?* way.

"Calm down, monster," I say, reaching over to pat Danny on the chest. "Yes, Alec sent you to get me. But the important point here is… you did it. He called. You answered. He asked. You said yes."

In other words, he did make a decision. He chose me and in doing that, he chose us.

I just need to remind him of that.

Danny smiles at me. It's not a big one. No teeth. No dimples pop out of their secret hiding places. But it's a smile all the same.

"So stop it already, OK? You love us—"

Now he laughs.

"—and that's all we need to know. Right, Alec?"

Alec manages a smile. But it's pretty weak and Danny doesn't miss that fact.

They stare at each other. Gazes steady.

But Danny's not glaring, and Alec's not smirking so... progress.

My hand is still on Danny's bare chest. I sweep the tips of my fingernails across his pectoral muscles and his skin prickles up like I give him the chills. "You love me," I say, pausing to wait for him to meet my gaze.

"I do," he says, his rough voice low.

"And you love Alec too."

His gaze wanders back to his declared nemesis.

"In your own way," I say, turning my body to face Danny. He looks down at me again, his blue eyes solemn and maybe a little sad.

"I don't trust him," Danny says.

"He doesn't trust you either."

"Fair enough."

I look over at Alec, who might be holding his breath. Because he's still and silent. Like he knows this moment counts for something. Finally, after several painful seconds, he lets out the breath and says, "I'm here for *you*. Both of you. What other possible reason? Just... this is all I want, bru. The three of us. That's it. You asked why I have this place?"

Danny nods.

"Because I've been waiting for you. I never forgot what you are. What you mean to me. I got a safe place to be ready for the moment you realized... well, that you made a mistake. Because I believed you *would* realize it. That's all there is to it."

I feel Danny's heart beat faster under my palm. And for a moment I wonder if telling Danny Fortnight he was wrong was the best way to proceed.

Then he sighs. "Fine. I might've... could've... maybe I... just... *fine*. I overreacted, OK? It's been known to happen."

I have to shake my head and stifle the giggle.

"Hundreds!" Alec says. "Now, was that so hard?"

"Fuck you," Danny says. He takes another drink, but only to hide his smile.

"Can we be on the same page now, eh? Like old times?"

Danny offers up half a nod. Still wavering on the whole *us* thing, I can tell. And I want this moment to be in the past. I want this talk to be over with. I want this hesitation to be history.

I want us to be committed again. Like we were, but different.

I want Danny to love Alec as much as he loves me. The way we love him. And sure, he gave in already, but I need to make him see that this world just isn't the same unless all three of us are in it. In the same place. At the same time.

So I reach for Alec's hand and bring it to my breast. He squeezes without prompting, but I don't stop there. I hook my finger into the waistband of his pants and tug. Make him take a step forward. And place his other hand on Danny's chest next to mine.

I look at Danny to gauge his reaction, but he's calm. Looking at Alec, not me. "It's not how I thought we'd end up," he says.

Alec just… shrugs. Slides his hand along Danny's chest until he's got it cupped over his shoulder. "Why do we have to end up anywhere?"

Danny just huffs.

"Why can't we just keep traveling?"

I know why. I see both sides.

Traveling—for Danny, anyway—is being lost. Because he's been adrift his whole life. He needs a home base. He craves stability. He wants… *normal*.

And it's just never gonna happen.

So I say, "Some people get boring office jobs." They both look down at me. "And some become international jewel thieves. And I'm not knocking the boring office job. But it's just not for us. We are these three people." I turn Alec a little so I can point to the tattoo on his back. "We are these lines. This," I say, "is the shape of our love."

CHAPTER THIRTY-ONE

The shape of our love.

I'm looking at Alec when these words echo in my head. He's looking back at me like... like he _needs_ something. He's always had that look. I've always felt that need. "Back in the gym that first day we met," I say.

"Yeah?"

"You said you were there for me."

"I was."

"Why?" I say. "What the fuck did you ever need from me?"

His eyes narrow a little. "Let's start with what I didn't need, yeah?"

"Whatever."

"I didn't need your help," he says. "Not the way you thought. I certainly didn't need anyone's help stealing diamonds. Hell, I didn't need to steal diamonds at all. That's not why I wanted you around. And I definitely didn't need a fourteen-year-old girl hanging about. No offense," he says, eyes meeting Christine's briefly before returning to me.

"Then what the fuck was all that about? Just the thrill? The danger? What?"

"A bit of that, I guess. But why can't it just be about you, man? Why do you find that so hard to believe?"

"So you wanted to fuck me?"

"Everyone wants to fuck you, Danny."

Christine laughs.

"You're bleeding hot, bru. You've got everything going for you."

"Shit," I say.

"You do. More than I ever had. Not money. Obviously. I'm talking about... this... self-possession. Even before I knew you, I saw it. You walked around with a goddamn invisible sign on your chest that said, *Take it or leave it*. I wanted that."

"So you wanted me?"

He shrugs. "What can I tell you? It's not fokken rocket science. It's just... attraction. Which is more of an earth science." He winks.

And in the moment I take to process this, his hand slides up to my neck. His fingers wrap around and grip. Just enough to make me lean forward into his space.

I know what's coming. And it's not our first, so my heart shouldn't be beating so fast.

But it is.

Because when his mouth finds mine I do something different.

I don't give in, I don't give up, I don't resist, and I don't complain.

I just... kiss him back.

The way he wants me to. The way I'd kiss Christine if it was her, not him.

Open mouth. Pliant lips. Probing tongue.

Long, deep breaths in those fractional seconds when we change position. Inhaling, and exhaling. Christine's body between us. Her arms around us, hands wandering, fingertips encouraging.

We've been here before. Hell, the past two days we've gotten past this point a few times.

But it *feels* different.

It feels intentional. This kiss is no accident. Not a heat-of-the-moment reaction.

It's deliberate, and passionate, and real.

Christine takes off her shirt. Presses her bare skin up to ours. We lean into her. Accepting her offer. And in doing that we lean into each other too. Growing closer—still kissing—growing in other ways too.

My cock is hard when Christine's hand finds it beneath the fabric of my jeans. She lowers herself between us and in one of those long, deep breaths I realize she's gripping Alec's cock through his pants too. Nimble fingers unbutton, unzip and then she pulls us both out and begins to pump her hands up and down our shafts.

And this is when things change for me. This is when I finally see what they've been trying to show me all these years.

We are a triangle. Alec one side. Me the other. And Christine, holding us all together.

Her mouth covers the tip of my cock and I respond. Not to her, but to him. I kiss him harder, the adrenaline pumping through my body releasing the last of my irrational inhibitions.

Everything about Alec becomes urgent in that moment. And I allow myself to experience it. To feel it. To take it all in and burn it into my memory.

"Like that," he says, hands reaching up to grip the sides of my head. "Just like that."

Christine responds by giving his cock her full attention. I miss her mouth on me, but...

I laugh into Alec and feel him smile. Hear the unasked question. *What's funny, bru?*

Nothing's funny.

"I just... maybe sharing isn't so bad."

Christine's hand grips my cock tight. Urging me to step a little bit closer. And when I do, I realize she's sending the same signal to Alec. Because our bodies angle just so, and we become the sides of the shape we make when Christine's lips suck both of us at the same time.

I can't not look down. So I break away from the kiss and angle my eyes to watch.

Her eyes are closed, but they open suddenly. Like she felt my gaze. And she stares up at me. Locked in on me, then Alec, as both cocks slide in and out of her mouth. Slick with her spit and swollen with her sucking. It's too beautiful. Too perfect.

I place my hand on the back of her head and push, encouraging her to take a little bit more of us. But I have an urge for more. So I pull back a little, letting Alec's cock fill her mouth, and I make her take him deep. Push her into him. Push him into her. He kisses me again, forcing his tongue inside me, bites my lip in a sudden moment of aggressive possession.

Or maybe he's just trying to thank me.

I keep Christine in place, refusing to let her back away. Making her throat muscles contract around his dick as her fist squeezes my shaft.

Alec growls something into our kiss. Something rough that I can't make out. But Christine moans. And that... that right there... that's all I need. All I want—all I've ever wanted—was to make her happy. Satisfy her the way she has always satisfied me.

I pull out of the kiss and Alec bends down to her, withdrawing his cock from her mouth. He wraps his hand around hers and they both jerk me off.

"Take these off," Alec says, referring to her panties.

"No," I say, making them both look up at me. "Just pull them aside. Show me her pussy."

"Fuck," Alec moans. But he does it. His hand slips between her legs, pulls her panties aside and bares her wet, glistening pussy.

I'm watching Alec's fingers play with her clit when his tongue swipes across the tip of my cock. Little flicks, back and forth. Like my cock is a substitute for her pussy. Like he's sucking me off and eating her out at the same time.

I get chills. Chills like... like something special is happening.

I reach for Christine. I want to be inside her *right now*. I pull her up and make her face me. Alec's hand is still between her legs when I reach down. We meet in the middle, our fingers slick with her juice, sliding inside her at the same time.

But it's not enough. And my free hand reaches down behind her knee and lifts. Opening her up so I can find her opening.

Alec is there to help me. Guiding me inside her. Pressing his chest up to her back, pushing her close to me.

We surround her now. And the minute I'm truly inside, Alec lifts up her other leg, allowing her to wrap herself around my middle and slide even deeper inside.

"Over there," Alec says, pointing to the wall of glass that overlooks the lake outside. He grips my upper arm tight, leading me.

243

Another time I'd take offense to that. But not right now. Right now... I like it.

He's desperate for her. For me. For us.

When we reach the window he turns me around, pressing me up against the glass. It's cold against my bare back but there's so much heat between us, I don't feel the chill.

Alec looks me in the eye as he pumps his cock a few times. And then he smiles—a smile I don't even think I recognize—as his hand dips between her legs, presses along the side of my shaft, and drags her wet desire over her asshole.

I smile back because he's gonna take her ass this time.

We are gonna fill her up.

Christine sucks in a deep breath and I know he's already there. Pushing on her, squishing her beautiful tits into my chest. I hold her in position, bracing my back against the window, hips thrust forward a little to give him better access.

She bucks her back, hisses out something mean, but then... then she grits her teeth and leans her head on my shoulder.

He's inside her. Not all the way, but I can feel him. My balls tighten with the new sensation and when he gives one more small push... "Oh, fuck yeah," I growl. "Fuck yeah."

Alec is grinning. Almost laughing as we begin the double penetration dance. His hips go forward when mine go back. Mine thrust forward when he retreats.

And it's perfect. A goddamned ballet of fucking.

Christine's fingernails dig into my back. Dragging and scraping as we move back and forth. We take her from both ends. We fill her up completely.

I watch Alec's face. Get off on his grunts. On his grimaces. And he stares past me. Outside at the choppy lake, and low-hanging mist, and the full moon that bathes his face in a ghostly glow.

It's too good to last. Too perfect. Too beautiful.

Too much.

I feel our collective climax building as we writhe together. I feel the energy we create. I feel him, and her, and me. All three sides to make the triangle of us.

And then it happens. Christine goes stiff. Her back straight but arched at the same time. Like she's reaching for Heaven as she gets ready for the release. Her fingernails biting into my flesh like teeth. Her pussy contracts around my dick. Alec moans from behind, and just as I shoot my come inside her, he pulls out and spills his come all over her ass.

This, I decide.

This is the shape of our love.

CHAPTER THIRTY-TWO

Blue is the color of the heart.

That's something I heard once. Believe my mother told me. It's not true, mind you. After doing some research, I discovered that she was either wrong or simply lying. Which would be all right. I wouldn't have cared. Everyone lies.

But no. Inside the body, the heart is a dark, dark red that *resembles* blue because it's covered by tissue and isn't as oxygenated as the blood in one's arteries. Once ripped outside a body, however, the heart looks bright red.

That I can personally verify.

But I suppose the sentiment behind "blue is the color of the heart" is a nice one. It's visually appealing and it sounds good.

This has popped into my thoughts in a sudden wave of memory as I walk along, staring up at the bracing blue sky above.

The sun is starting to set on the day. This day that I have waited for for so long. This day that I always believed would come.

This day, if it's the last day I ever have, will have been worth it.

The lone sound I hear—that of brittle leaves crunching under my feet—reminds me how secluded we are. I've only ever been here once before, when it was summer. I came to see the finished product. I was struck by how lush and green the area around the house was. Now it's gold. Brown. Rust.

Not unlike me, Danny, and Christine.

We started out fresh, green, new. Once upon a time. We must have. I'm sure we did.

But over the years we've become stained. Stained by the passage of time. Stained by the blood of those whose blue hearts we've taken from them. Stained by the lives we've lived. And now we are rust. We are brittle. But we are still beautiful.

Or at least we are to each other. And that's all I really care about.

More memories tumble through my head as I continue walking, feeling the sharp sting of the late afternoon air filling my lungs.

Speaking of memory…

"Hey," Christine's voice comes from behind.

I turn around to see her half-skipping toward me through the kaleidoscope of leaves on the ground. I grin. She's done that ever since I've known her. Even when in the midst of a moment freighted with danger, she's always maintained a bouncing lope in her gait. It's in her bones. Embedded deep into her DNA, I suppose. That buoyancy. That life.

Fokken hell, I love her so.

"Hey," I say back.

"Where are you going?"

"I need to make a call. There's no reception in the house."

"By design?"

"Yes and no. It's ballistic, wire-mesh glass. Which no one bothered to mention would play havoc with mobile reception. Shame. But you rarely get one thing you want in this world without sacrificing another."

A puff of frosty breath leaves her lungs. She's wearing the same clothes she had on when we arrived. She hugs Danny's pea coat to her body and her shoulders tense up in the direction of her ears. Her hair is still a bit damp. I stroke a strand of it from her cheek.

"You should go back in. You'll catch cold."

"I want to walk with you. Can I?"

"Where's Danny?"

"Shower." She nods over her shoulder back toward the house.

I look at my glass castle. One of approximately seventy homes around the world that I currently own. Right now, it is by far my favorite. All the others could disappear with the wave of a magic wand and I wouldn't care. In fact, everything I own in this world could disappear right now and I don't think I would care.

Which is the first time in my life I have ever thought something even remotely resembling that. And suddenly, a notion occurs to me. An idea. A fantasy. One that makes me laugh.

"What's funny?" she asks, also smiling.

"Nothing. Yes, let's walk. I want to show you something. You should see this."

She takes me by the crook of the arm as I stick my hands in the pockets of my topcoat and we amble off in the direction I was heading. To see us now, one might think we were simply two lovers out for a stroll. I am reminded of a time I sat on a bench in the Central Park

Mall in autumn and watched people walk along, amidst the falling leaves, carefree and content with their understanding of the world.

I recollect thinking how nice it must be to live a small life. Not 'small' in a pejorative sense. 'Small' in the way of easy. Worry-free. Simple. A life that wasn't about chasing the rush of adrenaline that comes of escaping barely alive.

I imagine that this... now.... walking along with Christine's hand on my arm, and Danny inside, taking his morning ablutions... feels like that.

If you take away the added element of the gun in my pocket.

And the bullet hole in my topcoat.

And the borrowed clothes Christine is wearing that we retrieved as we made our escape from a military-style tactical assault on the three of us launched by an as-yet-unknown enemy.

And the seventeen stitches in Christine's head.

"Nunu?"

"Hmm?" she replies.

"Talk to me about what you remember."

She breathes out through her nose and says, "I remember pretty much everything, I think."

"Do you?"

She nods. "Yes. You. Danny. I remember."

"Yes. But do you remember what caused this?" I reach and touch, gently, the stitches on her skull.

She champs at her lower lip and says, "I was doing the job—"

"The Jimmy Sotoro job?"

She stares at me for a second, "Yeah. The Jimmy Sotoro job."

250

Gaan naai 'n boom. Either she's lying to me or she still doesn't recall what happened. Lars made it plain that she was off on some other endeavor. And Danny is convinced that it has something to do with some oke called David.

Although I suppose it's entirely possible that either one of them could be lying as well. Fokken hell, man.

"OK, yeah, and then what happened?" I ask.

She looks pained. It's a look that lets me know one thing, at least. She's not lying to me by choice. She's not voluntarily trying to mislead me. She doesn't know. Christine is a good enough liar that she has no tells when obfuscation is called for. Her skill at lying is, in fact, unparalleled.

Except by me. Which is appropriate. As I'm the one who taught her how to do it.

She shakes her head and says, "Someone... pushed me."

"That part seems clear, luv." I smile, trying to put her at ease. "Any idea who?"

She looks at me again with a face I've seen once or twice before. It's a face she takes on when she doesn't want to disappoint me. It breaks my otherwise unbreakable heart.

"It's all right," I say as I kiss her almost dry hair. "It's all right. We'll figure it all out. Over here. We're almost there." I speed up my step and she follows suit, the sound leading us in the direction we're headed growing louder as we approach.

"What is that?" she asks.

And then she sees.

As we round the edge of a grove of trees, the earth falls away and in front of us looms endless, boundless horizon. The ground disappears and drops into a seemingly bottomless gorge hundreds of feet below. The sound she heard is that of a waterfall. Emanating from a mountain stream off to our left, it cascades down the side of the sheer rock wall, crashing to the depths below with exquisite, pulverizing power.

Her breath catches in her throat and I feel the tug of her hand on my arm as her knees go weak. It is an apt reaction to witnessing the majesty of nature's force.

"Wow," she says.

"Indeed."

"Do you own all this?" she asks, moving her head around to suggest the breadth of the panorama before us. "Is all this yours?"

"No, my sweet," I say, withdrawing her hand from my arm and turning to face her. "All of this is ours."

She tilts her head as though she doesn't understand.

"All of this," I continue, fanning my hands out, "*all* of this. This world. All of it. Is *ours*. Yours, mine, and Danny's. It is if we want it to be."

"I don't—"

"I'm saying that we can stay. If we want."

"What? Stay where? Here?"

"Yes. Here. No one knows where we are. No one can find us. We can stay here. Our own universe. Our own ecosystem. We can escape all the bullshit that's out there, beyond, and we can have a utopia here. We can stop the chase and just… be."

Her eyes get watery. She blinks. She swallows.

"What do you think, nunu? Would you like that?"

Her chin quivers and then she starts laughing hysterically.

"You," she says, "want to stop the chase. You, Alec van den Berg, want to just… be."

"I—"

"Sweetheart," she says, taking my face in her hands like I'm a daft five-year-old, "I fuckin' adore you, but there is no way in *a million years* that you will ever be satisfied just 'being.'"

For some reason that I can't quite put my finger on, I am reminded of being slapped by my father when I was a boy.

I start, "But what I'm saying is—"

"And how would we eat?" she asks. "How would we get food? Supplies? Get them brought in from somewhere? Kind of defeats the idea of escaping and being hidden away from everything, doesn't it?"

She looks at me earnestly. Like she can't believe what a dullard I am.

She's right.

Of course, she's right. And of course, it was a foolish thing to think, much less say aloud. But I've never before felt the way I feel this morning and I don't quite know how to engage with it. My father instilled in me the value of strength and the cost of vulnerability to such a degree that I don't even know if what I'm experiencing is actually the sensation of being vulnerable, but it's most definitely unwelcome.

"I was just making a metaphor, Christine." It is the best, and maybe only, response I can think of that will quash this moment of shameful weakness I have just displayed, and right our bearings.

"Oh," she says, nodding.

I kiss her again on the head. "Just go sit over there for a second and let me make this call, yeah?"

She keeps nodding. "Who are you calling?"

"Lars. Since we're clearly not going to stay here forever"—I wink, back on form—"we need to decipher exactly what might be waiting for us when we depart."

I can't grasp a handle on her expression. It's not quite disappointment. Not entirely sorrow. Maybe confusion? I can't be sure.

I take her around the waist, press my lips to hers, and then allow my tongue to slip into her mouth. She breathes into the kiss, her hands sliding under my coat to grab for my belt. I laugh and pull back, kissing her on the forehead as I do.

"You'll catch cold," I say.

"It'll be worth it," she responds, reaching for me again.

I continue laughing as I attempt to compel her to keep her hands to herself. Although I don't particularly want to.

"As soon as we get back inside," I say. "We'll warm up. Maybe we'll get lucky and Danny'll still be in the shower. We can get clean together."

"I don't wanna get clean," she says.

"Another metaphor, luv."

"I know." She draws out the words and sticks her tongue out at me.

Fok, man. I know it's not real, not possible, and can't happen that we could all just fade away into our own, private world…

But it certainly would be nice.

She turns her back on me, sassily shoving her hip toward me as she walks away, giving me a moment's distraction, thinking about her ass, and perhaps she's right. Maybe it would be worth the pneumonia. Oh, it most definitely would, but the world keeps spinning whether I want it to or not. And I have to try to keep us all a part of it.

As she plants herself on a bit of rock, I pull out my mobile and check to see if I have a signal. Enough. I make the call.

"Lars," I say, as he answers.

"Fok, man. Where are you? I've tried to call and can't get through."

"Did you get that camera footage?" I ask, ignoring his question.

"Yeah, we have it."

"And?"

"Can't make it out, bru. Too grainy."

"Fok do you mean, 'too grainy,' man?" I'm trying to keep my voice low, but the frustration of the things I want to know not being supplied to me in an expedient fashion is starting to weigh.

"I'll show you directly. Where are you? Maybe if we get together, we can—"

"No, man. No. Here's what I need you to do. You ever hear of an oke called Brasil Lynch?"

There's a pause as though he's mulling it over. "No. Why? Who is he?"

"That's what I want to know, bru. Find out who he is. What he's all about. And find out who a fokker called David is too."

"David?"

"Yeah."

"David who?"

"Fok if I know, man."

"Just some oke called David?"

"Fok, man!" I whisper-yell to the best of my ability. "Some naaier called David who has something to do with this Brasil fokker. Start with the one, work to the next. Christ, man, this isn't that hard!"

255

There's silence on the other end of the line. But, as usual, I'll not be the one to fokken speak next.

Finally, "Yeah. OK. And what do I do when I find them? How do I call you?"

"I'll call you," I say, and tab end.

Shoving the mobile back into my pocket, I turn to see Christine. She looks like a portrait, sitting there, the glory of creation behind her, the water crashing down below her perch. I wish I had a talent like painting. If I did, I'd paint this. I'd call it something like "The Edge of Always."

Which is fokken terrible, but I ain't got a talent for poetry either.

I'm really only good at one thing in this world. And that's making sure I come out ahead. Seeing to it that my hand is the one that's raised in the middle of the ring when the fight is done.

But today… when I look at her and I think about Danny, and how much I feel about them… for the first time in my blessed, foolish life, I might—*might*—be willing to come in second.

CHAPTER THIRTY-THREE

Christine

Back inside Alec disappears into the office and I follow him, but don't enter. Just lean against the doorjamb for a moment, watching him take off his coat and unbutton his shirtsleeves, thinking as I stare down at my feet.

Something feels off and I can't put my finger on it. Like I'm still very much missing something.

Which I know is true because I do not remember what happened that night I got hurt. I know parts of it. I was sent to kill someone, but it wasn't Jimmy Sotoro because I have no idea who this Jimmy guy is.

At least I don't remember him right now.

God, am I insane? What's wrong with me?

You got pushed off a building, Christine. Hit your head, went unconscious, seventeen stitches.

My hand goes up to feel them again. Like there are answers underneath the skin and the sutures are holding them hostage.

Alec lets out a long sigh and when I look up at him, he's facing me, holding the little metal box. His eyes meet mine as he snaps open the lid and turns it in his hand so I can see the diamond.

Funny thing about diamonds. The more carats they have the heavier they get. But they don't get proportionally bigger in size. So this seven-carat diamond could conceivably be mounted in a ring or a pendant and not look much bigger than one that's four carats.

To be sure, four carats set in a ring is pretentious. Unless you're married to a billionaire or an actual reigning monarch, no one will believe it's real.

"When?" Alec asks.

I shrug. "Right after you hid it away."

"How come?"

"I dunno." I say automatically, but I actually don't know. "Ask Danny."

"Because you don't remember?" Alec asks.

"I... I guess not," I admit.

"Do you remember why?"

I do. Very clearly. "No," I lie.

"Nunu," he says, snapping the lid closed. My eyes track to the etched triangle on the lid. Funny thing about triangles. They always have three sides, but they are not always equal. Yet the interior angles always add up to the same one hundred and eighty degrees, no matter what.

They can be balanced, but small changes throw the whole dynamic out of equilibrium.

A circle is always three hundred and sixty degrees, so you think, well, that adds up to something predictable too. True. But there's no sides in a circle unless you cut it up into triangles. And a square has angles, and sides, and all those angles are always ninety degrees. And even though a square can never be a circle, the parts always equal the whole three hundred and sixty degrees.

A triangle is only ever one half of the whole. It's inherently *missing* something.

"What?" I say.

It's a question begging to be answered. An emptiness begging to be filled.

"Are you keeping something from me?"

Yes.

"No," I say.

I just don't know what it is.

"Are you sure?" Alec asks, setting the box down on the desk and walking towards me.

No.

"Yes," I say.

I'm not really sure about anything right now.

"Because you look troubled. Are you troubled?"

I huff out a laugh. He takes both my hands in his and looks down on me with a small smile.

"I was born troubled."

His smile grows a little bigger. "Yes, weren't we all? But that's not what I'm asking."

"What's going on?"

We both turn to find Danny coming down the glass hallway towards us. Wearing jeans, but shirtless. Skull tattoos on his chest still glistening with random drops of water. His blond hair wet and dark, making his blue eyes that much bluer.

"I think Christine needs to see a doctor."

"What?" Danny and I say at the same time.

"What's wrong? Are you OK?" Now Danny is worried. And when he reaches me his hands stretch out and pull me into him.

"I'm fine," I say, wriggling a little in his embrace. Because Alec is still holding my hands and the whole moment suddenly feels... stifling.

"She's still missing memories," Alec says.

259

Danny looks up at Alec, frowns, then back down at me.

"I'm fine," I insist. "I swear. I mean, shit. I just woke up from a major head injury a couple days ago. And most of my memory is back, it's totally normal for parts to still be missing."

But inside I know this is wrong. I feel like the triangle. The sides are unequal, the dynamic is out of equilibrium. There are questions begging to be answered, and an emptiness begging to be filled.

And with this revelation I feel tired. And my head really begins to pound. "I just have a headache, that's all." At last I have something to say that's true.

"I'm going to ring a doctor," Alec says.

"No," I say, pulling away from them both. "No, I just need to lie down. And take some aspirin. Rest," I say. "That's all I need. It's been a crazy couple of days."

"And food," Danny says, going with it. "You go lie down. We'll make a meal and call you when it's ready."

"Yeah," I say. "I think I'll do that."

I turn away from them, acutely aware that they are still watching me. I don't even know where I'm going or which bedroom I should sleep in. Danny came from the other direction but it's too late now, I'm headed this way across the glass hallway that thinks it's a bridge and I have this overpowering desire to get away for some reason. So I don't turn back, I just keep going.

There are windowless steps at the end of the glass hallway. Just half a flight that takes me up to another level of the house. One side is a wall filled with black and white nature photographs. Aspen trees and snow-capped mountains. The other is a wall of windows looking out over the lake, but with a slightly more elevated view than the one down in the great room.

I think about what Alec said outside earlier. About staying here. It confused me. He's really not the kind of guy who hides away. Or lives in a secluded mountain compound protected by a wall. But there was something in his voice. Longing, maybe?

Maybe I was rude? Maybe I was too quick to dismiss the idea? Maybe we could make a fresh start out here in the middle of nowhere?

I stop and look over my shoulder. Should I go back and tell him that?

But I hear the familiar sound of cupboards being opened and closed as they search for food. A low rumble of male conversation.

No. They need some time together. Just the two of them. Danny has come a long way in a very short period of time, but I know him so well, I can sense some underlying hesitation. They need to come to some sort of understanding if we're all going to be together.

I turn back and keep walking across the narrow room, which I now realize is an art gallery, and climb yet another half-flight of stairs that leads to another hallway, this time windowless.

What a weird house.

The sounds behind me fade quickly once I reach this level. And the hallway makes an abrupt ninety-degree turn. I end up at the bottom of another flight of stairs and I suddenly realize—I have no clue what this place is. I'm incapable of forming a mental map of it in my mind.

It's a very large tree house maze made of glass and concrete.

So strange, so odd, so... intriguing.

261

At the top of the stairs is a massive room. Like a ballroom, maybe. I don't know how one would hold a party out here, so why this is necessary, I have no clue. But who can predict the whims of the über-rich, right?

In the corner is a concert grand piano.

I stop. Take a breath. And think about it for a moment.

My head still hurts, I haven't found the bedrooms—if any exist on this side of the house to begin with—and I have an overwhelming urge to touch those keys.

So I walk over to it, take a seat, catch my breath as I look out at the view of the lake and surrounding mountains, and place my fingers on the keys.

I don't know a lot of songs. Just three. And I'm not any kind of professional musician. But the ones I do know I practiced relentlessly and a moment later the sweet sound of Schumann's *Scenes from Childhood* fills the room.

I like this piece for three reasons.

One. You can play it softly. It's a soft song to begin with, but it's very easy to adjust the pressure of your fingertips to make it even softer. Like a warm blanket that wants to cover you on a cold autumn evening.

Two. Because the scenes I remember best from my childhood are all filled with Danny. The later ones have Alec too, but I wasn't a child anymore when Alec joined our family. Those years Danny and I were together are all I have left of the little girl I once was.

And three... it's happy even when I try my best to make it sad.

I play it very soft now. I need that blanket.

Because something is terribly wrong here.

"*What's down that way?*" I ask Alec. We both watch Christine disappear through the glass hallway.

"I have no clue, friend. But the kitchen's this way. And I think making a meal with what we have is going to be challenging."

"Typical," I say.

"How so?"

I follow Alec down the hallway the opposite direction of where Christine disappeared and get an overwhelming feeling of dread.

And I know that the anxiety I'm feeling is mostly due to the whole turning-Alec-over-to-Brasil plan I came up with and am now regretting.

But there's something else too.

Something with Christine.

"You know," I say, sighing, "we always had a few hundred thousand dollars of diamonds on us, and we'd be on our way to a luxury yacht that would take us to paradise, but we'd have to hitchhike to get to the marina."

"It's called improvising, bru. And besides, we always made it."

"Yeah, but I like a plan."

"Like that plan you had back at your garage? The extra escape route?" He laughs. It's not a mean taunt. Just a true one.

"Yeah, well. I had the guns. And the Jeep."

"That you did," Alec says, opening up the pantry door. "And we made it. Which is the only thing that matters." I join him in the opening and we both stare at the shelves. "Assuming we have pots," he says. "I guess we'll be eating pasta."

"I guess we will," I say. Because aside from some condiments and baking supplies, that's all that's on the shelf.

He backs away, walks over to the Sub-Zero fridge-freezer, and opens the stainless-steel doors. "Well, shit."

I almost laugh. "I guess we're hitchhiking?"

"We could go out to eat. Might be nice to get out of the house."

"We've only been here a day. You already itching to move on?"

He sighs. "We could go grocery shopping. Planning a grocery list feels very domestic."

"Maybe we should just find the nearest Super Target? That way we can eat hot dogs and Slurpees at the snack bar and pick up some clothes too."

He shoots me with his finger. "Yes, we should. Target is so... *provincial*. I'll have to go outside to get a signal and find the closest one, but—why are you laughing at me?"

"Because you're so stupid." He leans against the fridge and scrunches up his eyebrows. I lean against the stove opposite him and cross my arms over my chest. "We're not playing house here. People are after us."

And, I don't add, *Brasil is probably out of his mind pissed off that I've disappeared. He's probably got people looking for me.*

Alec doesn't answer right away. Just stares at me. Which gives me ample time to study him. It's been a while since I took a good long look at Alec van den Berg.

He's tall. Lean. Ropey. He's well-muscled, but he's not yoked, ya know? Not like I am.

"We're safe here."

"Are we?" I ask.

Alec takes a step forward, a sly grin creeping up his face. I get this weird feeling in my gut as he crosses the few feet between us, unbuttoning his shirt and discarding it as he approaches, and then slides his hand along the muscles of my waist.

"What the fuck are you doing?"

He leans in, his hand sliding behind my back in a gesture I find possessive. Like I might try to duck out of this encounter and he's thinking three steps ahead. "We're safe," he says, breathing the words into my neck as he begins to kiss me.

I have about six million conflicting thoughts, but first and foremost, should he be touching me without Christine?

"Stop," I say, pushing him back. But even I have to admit, my rebuke is half-hearted. So I'm not the least bit surprised when he pays absolutely no attention to my command.

"You have to make a choice," he says, his other hand sliding across my stomach.

I grit my teeth. Because I can't help it. I respond to his touch. I don't turn my head and kiss him back or anything. But that feeling in my gut has sunk down to my cock and... yeah. That's how I respond.

"I want you as much as I want her, Danny."

265

I hold my breath for a moment. And this is so stupid, but the way he says my name... "Fuck," I say.

"And I'd like to know," he says, still kissing my neck, "if you feel the same."

"Of course," I say, my breath heavier now. My eyes slightly closed.

"You say that like it's obvious. And it's not."

"Jesus, Alec. What do you want? A fucking ring? How many carats does it take to make you feel special?"

"Seven," he whispers.

I turn my head to look at him. Because my comment was just a way to get his hand around my dick so we can stop all the talk about how I'm *feeling*. But now... now I feel like we've jumped worlds and his response was an accusation. "What's that mean?"

He backs up. Not a lot. Not enough to make that feeling in my gut go away. Just a few inches of space. "Means whatever you want it to mean."

"You got a problem with what we did?"

"Knowing what it means? What it represents? I have a big problem with it, yes. I would have given you anything you wanted, Danny. You just had to ask."

Just my fucking luck. I don't want to talk about my feelings for him so I bring up diamonds. And I want to talk about diamonds—specifically *that* diamond—even less than I do my feelings. Hell, maybe they're the same thing.

So... choices. Choices.

I guess feelings win the day.

"You know that day in the gym?"

He smiles. "One of the best days of my life."

"Yeah," I say. "Mine too." And that's not even a lie. Not today, not last week when he was the last thing on my mind. Not even when the whole fucking thing blew up and the three of us fell apart.

Well, the two of us, I guess.

"Go on," he says.

BEFORE

"You there," the kid in the ring says. He slithers through the ropes like a snake. Sleek with sweat that glistens on his perfect physique of a body. Tanned in a way he shouldn't be. And even though he's only said two words to me, there's no way to miss his… *foreignness.*

He doesn't belong here.

"You mind, bru?"

"What?"

"Hand me my shirt, yeah?"

I look down at the pile of clothes at my feet. The blue blazer with the embroidered private school emblem. The expensive shoes. Then I reach down and pick up the white shirt, thrusting it at him.

"Thank you…"

"Danny," I say. He smiles at me. Which just makes me squint. "You live around here?"

"What do you think?"

"You have a beef with Curtis or something?" I ask.

The kid looks over his shoulder at Curtis, who has been helped to his feet by a few of the other guys. "Is that his name?" And then he smiles at me. "No. I just wandered in and felt like beating the shit out of someone. He was just the first one who said yes to my offer."

"Oh," I say. "Cool." Because I've had days like that myself.

267

"Alec," he says, shouldering into his shirt and extending one bloody hand in my direction.

NOW

I'm not really a hand-shaker, but I shook. Our hands touched and he was hot. Blood trickled down his knuckles. And when I pulled away some of it was on me.

It wasn't the way he looked. Not really. I mean, he was—*is*—a very nice-looking guy. But it wasn't his looks. Or his stupid accent. Or that he didn't belong. Or the fact that Curtis just got his ass kicked because he was the first person who took him up on an offer for an ass-kicking.

"It was the blood," I say.

"What?" Alec laughs.

"That day at the gym. You had blood on your hand. And when we shook some of it got on me."

"Oh," Alec says, thinking about that for a second.

"You're..." God, why is this so hard to say? Why can't I just tell him?

"I'm... what?"

I uncross my arms, grip the countertop with both hands, and lean back. This makes him smile. Because the whole gesture is one of opening up. "You're..."

"Danny," he grunts. "Come on, bru. Just say it. It'll feel good when you get it out."

I want to hit him right now. But I want to touch him too. "We're in this together," I blurt.

"No," Alec says, shaking his head. Enjoying how uncomfortable this moment is for me. "Not good enough."

"I got your back," I add quickly.

"Danny. Bru—"

"And when the time comes I'll choose you, OK? I'll choose you."

That shuts him up.

"We good?"

He tilts his head a little. Trying to read between my lines. Opens his mouth to reply but then stops. Because somewhere in this house, someone is playing the piano.

"Well, that's quite nice," Alec says. "When did she get so good? I thought the only thing she could play was Chopsticks."

"You're asking me?" I say. "You're the one who's had her all these years."

He shoots me a look that says, *Don't*.

And if I were in a fighting mood I'd shoot him one back. One that says, *Try to make me*. But I'm not in a fighting mood. Not at all.

"Should we go find her?" I ask.

He's still very close to me, his hand still on my back. "Yes, but first... answer me this, OK?"

"What?"

"Will you always need her to have me?"

I don't even hesitate. "Yes."

"Fair enough." He sighs. And then he withdraws his hand and walks off in the direction of the music.

CHAPTER THIRTY-FIVE

Schumann leads us toward her. Like a snake charmer calling for serpents.

Entering the room from behind, neither of us make a sound to disturb her playing, and she doesn't turn to see us.

Kinderszenen. "Scenes from Childhood." Schumann's Opus Number Fifteen. Thirteen movements that call to mind a young person at play. At times giddy, at times somewhat more melancholic, it was the first piece of music I ever remember hearing as a boy. My mother played it for me when she was trying to get me to sleep.

I have no idea how in the world Christine would know that.

Moreover, I had no idea Christine could play like this. Jesus Christ, man. For all the things I've seen and done in my life, it warms my spirit to know that I still have the capacity to be surprised.

The piece is almost twenty minutes long, and for almost twenty minutes, Danny and I stand behind her. Listening. The movement of her head, her neck, her shoulders, suggest that she's lost in the music. Bathed in euphonic bliss.

I wish I could see her eyes. I feel certain they're closed. The way she's giving herself over to her playing, there's no way she can be thinking about it. She's unconscious, and it's mesmerizing.

She comes to the conclusion of the piece and she strikes the final. Three. Notes. With a languid precision. Methodical in their delivery, but insouciant in their execution. It is, quite honestly, a perfect performance. And only Danny and I get to hear it.

I begin my clap slow and soft, so as not to startle her, but startle her it does nonetheless. She jumps and spins around.

"Shit! You fucking scared me."

I continue my applause. The small smile on my face is mixed with something akin to wonderment. Danny's head is cocked to the side, and after a moment, he shakes it a bit and begins clapping as well.

"What?" she asks. "What? Why are you doing that? Stop it."

It is annoyance underpinned by insecurity. Feeling exposed can induce that in a person. Instead of stopping, we both applaud more vigorously.

"Fuck, stop, goddamn it! Seriously. Don't make fuckin' fun of me."

I start shouting, "Brava! Brava! Encore!" Danny does the same. In his own way. His choice of words is, "No fuckin' way! That was fuckin' incredible!"

"You guys are assholes," she says, attempting to motor past us. Danny stops her, grabbing her by the arm.

"Hey, whoa. Slow down," he says. "We're not fucking with you. That was... When did you learn to play like that?"

"Like what?"

272

"Like flippin' Yuja Wang," I say.

"Fuck is Yuja Wang?" she asks.

"Trust me, it's a compliment," I tell her. "But as Danny asked... Oh," I say, having a sudden dawning. "Is this one of those situations where someone takes a bump on the head and it unlocks some prodigious ability that they never knew they had?"

She looks at me with exasperation. "No," she says, "I just, y'know, practiced."

Fair enough.

"Well, it paid off. Color me impressed," I say.

She steps back from the two of us, looks at us standing there shirtless and somewhat awestruck at the discovery of our Christine's freshly unearthed talent, and says, "Yeah. I guess we're all learning a whole lot about each other recently, huh?"

I have no idea if she's aware of the fact that she's being dead clever with her couldn't-be-more-right observation, but I choose to take it as such.

"Yes, my dear, we are." And pressing toward her, I reach to my side and take Danny by the wrist as well.

"Fuck are you doing?" he asks.

"Christine here's not the only one who can make sweet music."

It is, of course, an awkward attempt at seduction, but I'm far less interested in being witty than I am in seeing both of them naked and writhing in about thirty seconds.

Christine bows her head, looking up at me through her eyelashes as I press my body into her and walk her backward, dragging Danny with me as I go. Danny's not galloping along, per se, but he's not exactly resisting either. We might not be able to live here forever and escape the dangers of the great, wide world beyond, but we are here now, and that's all that rightly matters.

The backs of her knees hit the piano bench and she drops into a sit. "Do you even play the piano?" she asks me.

"No. Why?" I respond, sliding her top off over her head in the process.

"Because this is like a hundred-thousand-dollar Steinway sitting in a glass box in the middle of nowhere."

"I told the designer to think liberally," I tell her as I now lift her shirt from her head and drop to my knees to emancipate her from the bondage of her sweatpants.

She presses her palms onto the bench, lifting her hips, and aids me in sliding her bottoms off. It is notable that she is not wearing any underwear. Braless, panty-less, her white skin in graphic contrast to the polished ebony of the piano bench. Like one, lone, ivory key waiting to be played.

But as I lean down between her legs and start to deliver my opus, she tightens her knees around my head and stops me.

"Problem?" I ask from within my seductive vise.

She fists my hair, pulls my head up, looks from me to Danny, and says, "You first."

"We first, what?" Danny asks.

"I want to watch."

"Watch what?" Danny repeats.

I find this whole interaction unendingly amusing.

"I want to watch you kiss. Will you kiss for me? Please? For me?"

I look up over my shoulder at Danny, his mouth tight and his glare narrow. He tilts his neck back and shakes his head at the celling. I wait, patiently. Then he looks down at me, grabs my arm, pulls me up, and yanks me into a kiss.

It is forceful. Dominating. Establishing himself as the one in control. That's fine. It's exhausting being in control all the time. Let someone else take charge for a change.

My hands reach for his trousers as he presses his rough mouth against my own. I fiddle with the buttons and the pants drop to the floor. We've been on the run, and we haven't really eaten anything, and I assume, like me, Danny has retained his athletic metabolism all these years, so it's possible he's shed a couple of pounds and his jeans no longer have the same purchase they did before.

It's also possible that they've now come off so many times that they're simply used to being on the floor.

He steps out of the denim, and when I push my body forward, I feel the tension in his huge cock as it presses against my exposed abdomen. Reaching down with one hand, I take him up and begin a halting, violent jerk on his shaft. His breath catches in his throat and he bites my lower lip. My lower lip that pulls away from his teeth as my emerging smile stretches it wide.

I turn my head to see Christine. Her legs are spread wide, heels pressed against the legs of the piano bench. With one hand, she rubs her breasts and pinches her nipples, and with the other hand, she pushes her fingers in and out of her pussy, alternating with rubbing frantically at her clit. "Keep going," she gasps out.

I turn my face back to Danny and press my mouth again to his, never letting go of my hold on his cock. It's not a long, lazy stroke that I'm using to pull on him, but a strong, punishing yank. I can feel the muscles in my forearms tensing with my grip. The veins bulging as I strain his dick. The grunting sounds he makes are those of a person in mild pain, but are filled with an affirmation, encouraging me to keep doing what I'm doing.

I do.

And now Danny fumbles with the button of my trousers. But he's having trouble getting them unclasped, presumably because I'm attempting to virtually rip a river of come from somewhere inside him, and so I let my grasp free and step back.

"No, don't stop," Christine whines, continuing to finger herself and grind her hips back and forth on the piano bench.

The sight of her grinding there, the sight of Danny's red, swollen cock pulsing with blood, well... loop naai, I just about rip my pants in half, taking them down my legs. The Hulk has come to fuck.

Grabbing Danny's wrist again, I drag him over to Christine. He and I stand above her, watching as she looks up at us shyly, still rubbing at herself. I try to imagine what she sees and how it must feel. Two monstrous men— murderers, thieves, angels of destruction—naked, hard cocks fully engorged, ready to take her and each other, towering over her. Harbingers of lust, announcing their arrival into the fragile temple of her familiar body.

It must look terrifying. And it must feel like the most exquisite anticipation a person can know.

She need not anticipate further.

I grab her up by the arms, pull her forward, and then I sit down on the bench behind her. My elbows bang the piano keys as I land, plunking out a discordant song of seduction.

She glances over her shoulder back at me, and I reach my hand out, turning her cheek gently to face ahead of her. Toward Danny.

Placing both hands on her ass, I push her in his direction. He walks forward and, taking her by the face with his hands, guides her mouth around his cock. He moans in beautiful agony and she swallows him whole.

I guide her. With both hands on her hips, I slide her back and forth. Back and forth. She braces herself with her own hands on Danny's hips, and widens her stance so that she is anchored to the floor like the bottom of a pyramid.

I slide my hands inward along her ass, pull her apart, and spit into her asshole. Looking around the spartanly appointed room, I see nothing that would work as an adequate lubricant, so we'll have to make do. I massage my spittle into her backside with one hand and spit into my other hand, rubbing the hot saliva all over my cock as well. The sound of her breathing around Danny's cock and the sound of Danny's needy groans have me pulling on myself so aggressively that I think I might come right this very moment.

Which would be a shame.

So I slow things down. I want this to last. This moment. Now. I want it to last.

Because there is a reality to face.

We are probably not going to survive.

At least not all of us will.

One or more of us will die. Soon. It is the price of doing business in the way we have for as long as we have. The assault on Danny's apartment was timed to happen when all of us were together. As one. It is not a coincidence.

Whatever it is that has happened out there in the world beyond our forest-walled fortress, it is waiting. It will not abate. It will wait for us to emerge from our hiding place and will make its presence known with force.

I'm not scared. I'm not sad. I don't know that I'm capable of feeling those emotions. But when I think of losing Danny and Christine, I am disconsolate.

I wasn't before. Not the night in Prague when everything fell apart. Because I knew it wasn't the end. It couldn't be. Our story wasn't done being written. There was more for us to know about each other.

That was not the end because the triangle had not yet been completed. The lines were so very close to being fused and finished, but we hadn't yet fulfilled our destiny.

Now we have.

And maybe what Danny said to me is true. Maybe the coming together of us as one does somehow weaken us rather than make us stronger. Because, after all, he is right. When you love something so much that it will cost you dearly to lose it, it gives your enemies something to target. The one place on poor old Achilles where the armoring waters did not fully bathe him. A point of entry where someone can come in and steal your blue, blue heart.

I'm not maudlin and I'm not macabre. I'm simply realistic. And the reality is that I don't know how many more chances we'll have to be together as we are right now. And so, I'm in no great hurry to let this moment pass.

I push Christine and Danny forward and drop off the bench onto my knees. Christine keeps working Danny's hard cock and he digs his hands into her shoulders.

Now, on my knees behind her, I spread her ass open once more, wanting to ensure that when I place my cock inside it, she'll be ready.

My tongue laps its way into her asshole and swirls about as with my hand, I cup her from underneath and slide one, two, three fingers inside the walls of her pussy. Her knees shudder, and just when I think I couldn't possibly get a fourth digit inside her as well, my hand presses upward involuntarily and my pinky slides inside her too.

A muffled yelp from her. She slams her head forward and back around Danny even harder now, and I massage her insides, feeling her saturating wetness spill all around my fingers, across my palm, and down my wrist.

As I told Danny before, when dealing with a situation in which one finds oneself without the appropriate resources, one must find ways to improvise. The improvised lubricant Christine, Danny, and I just created feels like it will help us hitchhike all the way to our destination.

I pull my fingers out, smearing her sex all over her own ass and all over my throbbing dick. Standing up, I draw her back into my hips, spreading her ass cheeks as I do and slowly, but firmly, slide my cock deep inside her asshole. She freezes, tensing up all over, but then, after a moment, she relaxes and begins grinding.

I pull her back, she pulls Danny back, and I lower myself once again onto the bench. And also once again, an odd, some might almost say orgasmic tune gets hammered out by my shoulder blades on the keys.

And as Christine takes all of me deep inside her, and also takes all of Danny deep inside her, I close my eyes and what I hear in my head isn't an atonal cacophony of notes getting mashed about by the grinding of our bodies.

It's a fugue.

It's an opera.

It is a symphony written by the three of

CHAPTER THIRTY-SIX

Christine

We've had a lot of sex today. And all of it has been good. The kind of sex you only have when time is running out. Desperate, reckless sex.

But this isn't sex.

This is what I've been waiting for since the very first moment I fell in love with them.

This is the love we found. The years we shared, the years we didn't, and the longing we've felt growing between us for the past ten years.

This is the shape of our love.

The perfect equilateral triangle.

My hands grip Danny's cock as I suck and lick him into a state of bliss. His hands have a tight hold of my hair and every time I take him deep into my throat he clenches his fists, the hair-pulling sting sending a chill through my whole body.

And my ass. Jesus. Alec's thick, long cock is fully inside me. And even though Alec and I have been together in many ways, many times, over the past several years—this is more than I could've ever hoped for.

The whole thing feels… *right*.

We are perfection in a state of lust.

Or lust in a state of perfection.

Either way, it's paradise and we're just getting started.

I let myself drift a little. Let myself dream about all the months, and years, and yes, *decades* that we will share. There will be a house somewhere. A tropical paradise, or a mountain retreat, or a farmhouse tucked away in a valley. I picture all of them. Every possible version of the happily ever after I never thought I'd get. Never thought I deserved.

We will be three forever. We'll get rings heavy with diamonds. And have a ceremony. And a honeymoon that probably looks a lot like this moment in time right now. Wild fucking in a glass house, or on a yacht anchored in a sea of unreal blue-green water, or on the most perfect white-sand beach.

Danny lets go of my hair and pulls me out of my childish fantasy. His fingers rest on my chin, making me tilt my head up to look at him. I meet his gaze and picture what I look like from his point of view.

My long, auburn hair mussed and crazy from his fists. My mouth open, lips wrapped around the shaft of his cock. Cheeks puffed out, eyes watering—tears forming in the corners from the effort, and the longing, and…

And the deep-rooted fear that someone is about to come rip it all away from me. Laugh in my face and say, "You don't get the fairy-tale ending, kid."

I force those irrational feelings down. Swallow them as I push my face forward to take even more of Danny's cock.

He smiles at me, but backs away. I grip his hip, trying to force him to stay.

But he just says, "Shhhhh," as he bends down and kisses my mouth. Breathing his soft reassurances into me.

And I swallow them down. Believe them. That everything is fine. This perfect moment can last forever.

I kiss him back, more desperate than ever to keep him close.

Don't leave me, I want to say. And then I do. I say it. "Don't ever leave me again."

He smiles into our kiss and whispers back, "Never again. Now let's see how far we can take this tonight."

I don't know what he means. But before I can think about that further, he grabs my shoulders and gently eases me up.

Alec is breathing hard behind me. Slowly pumping his dick back and forth into my ass. His arms wrap around my waist as Danny positions me fully into Alec's lap and we crawl backwards, up onto the keys, and then, as Alec slaps away the bar holding the lid up, onto the top of the piano. And once we're there, Alec still deep inside my ass, Danny grips my knees, spreads me open, and slides his body forward.

I look down between my legs and watch. I watch as the thick, swollen head of his cock bumps back and forth against my wet pussy. Teasing me until I'm moaning, my hand gripping his forearms, and then finally slides inside and everything disappears… because I close my eyes tight and just experience the completion of *us*.

CHAPTER THIRTY-SEVEN

Danny

I moan. We all moan. It's a single, guttural, satisfied moan. Like this is where we're supposed to be. Like we've been working up to this moment for an eternity of lifetimes.

I want Christine to open her eyes. I want her to see me. I want her to watch as I fuck her. I want her to look down at my cock sliding effortlessly in and out of her pussy.

But I want to just enjoy it too. And besides, there's Alec. Staring right at me. Our eyes meeting, holding each other in a single, shared, heated moment.

He smiles, grimaces as I thrust forward, making Christine's whole body push against his chest.

Somehow the day has gotten away from us. The dusk has turned dark since Alec and I found Christine here at the piano. A blanket of moonlight shines through the wall of glass, bathing us in an unearthly glow the color of dust.

I feel Alec just as much as I feel Christine. Our cocks, separated by mere millimeters of skin, slide back and forth against each other inside her. We are synced up. In perfect rhythm. Connected at three points, on three sides.

It's this moment I will remember forever. A single tick of time that adds up to everything I've ever wanted. And even though, before today, I had no idea I needed Alec in order to fully have Christine—I understand that now.

There is no her without him. No me without them.

Alec breathes out. Our eyes still locked. Like he's reading my mind and he's enjoying this tick of time too. It's relief, I think. A respite from the stress of losing the shape we made and unmade, over and over again. And a satisfaction at the same time. That we made it. That we've connected again. That this time, we all know what we want and where we belong.

I slow down. My thrusts softer. My eyes half closed as I grab her tit with one hand and slide the other one up to her throat. I don't squeeze. Not because I don't think it's hot or that she wouldn't love to feel that little uncertain rush of adrenaline.

I don't squeeze because I want her to know I'd never hurt her. Ever. I have dedicated my life to Christine Keene. I changed the course of everything that day she wanted to poke the blue out of that bug.

I made her a promise over ice cream.

We are a team.

And later, Alec made her that same promise too.

For that alone, I love him.

I stop fucking and lean forward, my hand still on her tit squeezing hard as I bring her nipple up to my lips and suck. I look up, past her shoulder, to Alec.

And that's when I know what I have to do.

I kiss my way up her collarbone, stop to nip the tender skin of her neck, and then... because it has to be done, because I want to do it...

I kiss Alec. Full on the mouth. Tongues twisting.

And I fuck him as I fuck her.

Only Christine's small, soft body separates us. I lean down on her, pressing myself as close to Alec as I can get, and we make love.

To her. To each other. To the idea that the triangle is real. It's not some elusive pot of gold at the end of a rainbow, it exists. And we found it.

"Come," Alec commands.

And I'm not sure if he's talking to me or Christine, but she begins to push back. Asking me to go faster with her hips.

I obey. Her, or him, or who the fuck cares who I'm obeying. I do it.

I fuck her deep. And hard. And fast.

Her body stiffens. The tell-tale sign that she's close. And then Alec says it again. "Come."

So we do.

She goes rigid underneath me, her head falling backward into the crook of Alec's neck.

And I grit my teeth as the pressure inside me builds and then explodes in a rush of relief.

Alec goes completely still. I want to look at him. See the expression on his face. I want to look at Christine too. But I can't bring myself to open my eyes.

I want to enjoy this one moment. This one tick of time that has suddenly stopped so I can feel the pleasure of what we are. So I can accept the shape of what we've become.

The triangle.

Then I snap out of it. Realizing Alec hasn't had his turn yet. So I pull Christine forward, letting Alec's cock slip out of her ass, and hold her. Wrap her up in my arms as I meet Alec's intense, longing-filled gaze, and say, "Come."

287

He does.

He shoots himself all over her back with grunts and groans of supreme satisfaction.

And that's when the alarm begins to scream.

That's when the bullets come crashing through the wall of glass, shattering the dream and pulling the dust-colored moonlight blanket off us in a single sweep.

CHAPTER THIRTY-EIGHT

Danny shrouds Christine in a protective embrace and rolls them off the piano and onto the floor. This makes them no less vulnerable to the penetrating gunfire than they were on top, it just makes them vulnerable and also now on the ground.

Lying on my back, on top of a Steinway concert grand piano, spent from the rigors of our gymnastic sex, my wilting dick in my hands… It seems like the perfect way to die. It doesn't mean that I'm not going to work like hell to avoid dying just now, but if it must happen, I reckon I'll be fine with it.

Fokken kak, man. This has been a shit week. But it's also been a fokken brilliant week. We're about to find out which one will triumph. The sun or the shitstorm.

"What the fuck?" Christine yells, as I roll off the piano top and land beside them.

"How'd they fuckin' find us, Alec?" Danny shouts.

"Fokked if I know, man!"

Jesus, the gunfire is loud. I've seen war before. Seen it up close. I've been in some proper warzones and also some hostile environments that look like warzones, just without a formal declaration of war. And this is exactly that. Someone isn't just trying to kill us. Someone has declared war.

I know this because not all gunfire sounds alike. I cannot explain how such a thing is possible, but it is. Some gunfire sounds clinical, unemotional. And some gunfire is filled with rage and blistering passion.

This gunfire feels very much like the second one.

"I thought the glass was bulletproof!" Christine shouts over the maelstrom of metal.

"It is!" I return.

"Yeah?" hollers Danny. "Doesn't fuckin' look that way, does it?"

"It's not made of fokken unicorn dicks, man! It ain't magic! It has its limits!"

Spying our discarded clothes on the floor, I crawl out from under the piano and retrieve my and Danny's trousers and Christine's sweatpants and t-shirt. My still-leaking cock sliding across the cold floor makes me a tiny bit wistful. Moments ago, it was so goddamn warm and happy. *Gaan naai 'n fokken koei*, man. Go fuck a fuckin' cow. Kak.

I grind back under our sorry excuse for cover and parcel out our paltry outfits. As we slide clothes on Danny yells, "Guns!"

"No shit, bru!"

"No, motherfucker! Do you have any?"

"Ah. Right! Yeah, man. Of course! I have a whole fokken cache of them!"

A streaming river of automatic weapons fire comes flowing into the piano. Right where the three of us were enjoined in libidinous congress just moments before. It makes a horrific sound.

A lullaby for a nightmare.

"Where are they?" Christine shouts.

"What?"

"The guns, Alec! Where are the guns?"

I'm so distracted right now. Violence and death have been a part of my life for so long that I don't process it like other people, I suppose. When you're born into conflict, it just becomes part of your routine. Like those videos of befok soldiers you see in war zones. Those jas naaiers who just smoke cigarettes while bombs are going off all around them. It's a conditioning. We are all animals. And we can be trained.

I have been trained to accept death as a necessary end to all. It's where that Hulk fokker comes from. He swells and expands and makes the confrontations I'm in less appalling to deal with. He will be making himself known shortly, I imagine.

So it stands to reason that as much as I'm not chuffed to have this foolishness unfolding all about us three, I'm just as much lost in pleasure at the notion of it being us three who are stuck in the middle now. I look from Danny to Christine and back again. And I can feel myself smiling.

"Fuck are you smiling about?" Danny asks.

I love you both, I think. *I'm so glad you're here.*

"Guns, Alec!" Christine again.

Oh, right.

"They're on the other side!"

"The other side of what?" growls Danny.

"The house, bru!"

Danny's eyes close tightly, and he says, "I'm an asshole for not having an escape route, but you only have guns on the other side of the fucking glass house?"

Fair point he makes.

291

"They're really good guns, bru! We just have to get them!"

He shakes his head and Christine asks, "Fuckin' fine! How do we get to them?"

Tipping my chin, I say, "Down the hall."

Their faces drop.

"The exposed glass hallway?" Christine asks.

"I'm sorry, luv. The house was designed for privacy and seduction and all that. It wasn't intended to be used as a goddamn bunker!"

Danny looks at me, grinds his teeth, then gets a tiny smile and in what is a clear imitation of me says, "Shame."

"All right!" Christine yells. "Let's go fuckin' get 'em!"

She starts to leap out from under the piano, but I hold her back. I take Danny with my other hand. I pull the three of us toward each other until all of our heads touch. Then I close my eyes and breathe.

I let my lungs fill. This time not just with my own breath, but with the breath of all three of us. We breathe into each other. I take from them, I give back, and I feel myself growing in my body to thrice my usual size.

When I open my eyes and sit back, they are looking at me. They don't say anything. I squint at them with a tight-lipped grin on my lips and then give a tiny nod.

And at that, we scurry out from underneath our nominal cover, like the proverbial rats fleeing the proverbial ship, and we clear our harmonic canopy just as a ribbon of small-arms fire lacerates the legs, and the strings and keys comes hammering to the floor in a kind of screeching death knell.

CHAPTER THIRTY-NINE

Christine

"Glass house. Fuckin' ridiculous." I'm whispering that under my breath like a mantra as Alec, Danny, and I make a break for an interior concrete wall. Bullets chase us. The spray shatters the concrete floor in the exact place the soles of my feet were less than a moment before.

This is a serious fucking ambush.

But I don't have time to think about that. I don't have time to think about anything. Not even the hopeless nature of this stupid plan that isn't a plan. Because a fresh round of automatic fire comes bursting through the window, making Alec duck back.

He looks at Danny. Small hand movements. Eye gestures. Danny moves his head in a way that tells me he's disagreeing with Alec's proposal. But then a shoulder shrug.

Whatever. We're dead anyway, that's what that shoulder shrug says.

We're not really in stealth mode. I mean, shit. There is only one reason for that platoon of fucking people to be outside the house shooting at us.

They know we're here.

But the silent shorthand language of gestures feels right for some reason.

JA HUSS & J McCLAIN

Danny lifts up his hand, flicks his fingers at me, and the second the fire lets up, we break for the interior stairwell that will take us down to the art gallery—I mean, death trap. Because that's what it is.

But those are details that can be worked out later. And by later I mean ten seconds from now. Because the only thing that matters in this moment is that we make it to the concrete tube of a stairwell that will act as a shield.

I run. Oblivious to the thousands of pieces of shattered glass under the bare soles of my feet. And when we duck into the stairwell and realize none of us were hit, we lean back and smile.

It's sick, the way we smile when we're in the middle of shit.

But it's familiar too. And comforting.

"OK," Alec says in the eerie silence. "We're good for a bit. The hallways and stairs are concrete. So now we've just got to go through the gallery and the glass hallway."

"Is that all?" Danny growls.

"Why did they stop shooting?" I ask, trying to peer ahead. It's pointless though. There's nothing but stairs leading down into the hallway that will take us directly into the art gallery. "Do you think they're inside?"

All three of us simultaneously look back where we came from.

"No," Alec says. "That room is too high up off the ground. Unless one of them is a parkour prodigy or they brought grappling equipment, they're not gonna get in that way."

Now we all look at each other. Because there was a team of people we knew once. A team of people who were the kind of enemy who *could* get into a tree house like this without the aid of equipment.

294

"It's not them," Alec says.

"No, can't be them," Danny agrees. "When we last saw them we were even."

Shit.

"Focus," Alec says. "We got this."

Sure we do. But we focus. Because that's the only choice we have.

A second later we're at the bottom of the stairs, easing our way along to where it makes that sharp ninety-degree turn back into the gallery.

The shooting has stopped and that worries me more than if the attack was still happening.

"Why did they stop?" I hiss a second time, ducking under Danny's arm. A barricade to keep me behind him. Alec has stopped at the corner, badly wanting to peek around to see what's waiting for us. But I get there first, crouch down on my knees, and cautiously peer around the edge of the wall.

I duck back immediately. "Shit."

"What?" Danny asks.

"Laser sights. Like a dozen of them, darting back and forth across the gallery."

"They're looking for us," Alec says. "Which means they're not familiar with the house."

"Neither are we." Danny huffs.

I pop my head out again. The lasers are fewer now, like some of them have moved on. They're either wearing radio headsets or employing a secret hand-gesture language like we do. Because outside, it's silent.

Doesn't matter. Either way, a team like this has professional written all over it. The exact opposite of those dumb fucks who came in like blundering bulls at Danny's garage this morning.

I watch, Danny and Alec waiting patiently for me to give a sit rep.

A few seconds later I whisper, "No more lasers. Must've moved on. Let's go." I make to go first, but Alec tugs on my shirt and pushes me behind him. Danny does the same, and I end up last again.

Fucking men and their fucking hero complexes.

CHAPTER FORTY

"Stay behind me," I whisper to Christine. I know she's capable of taking care of herself. Hell, she's saved my ass many times in fights like this. But there's no way I'm gonna let her go first into the death trap that's waiting ahead.

She can bitch at me about it later. I can't wait for her to do that. Because it'll mean we made it out alive and she's still around to throw one of her I'm-just-as-tough-as-you-two-assholes tantrums.

Alec flashes us a hand signal. *Crawl*, that gesture says.

Maybe they have moved on. Maybe no one is waiting for us to make the walk of death down that long, narrow hallway lined with glass on one side.

Then again, maybe not.

So we crawl. And every inch we move forward I wait for it. I wait for the bullets to rip through my body. Or worse, Christine's.

But it doesn't happen. And if I didn't just live through a hailstorm of automatic gunfire, if there wasn't a whole room behind us ripped to shreds from bullets, and a piano reduced to shards of wood, I'd think there was nothing happening here at all. It's that quiet.

We make it to the next stairwell, get back on our feet, and wait. All crammed into a six-by-six-foot landing space that leads down into the glass hallway.

"OK," Alec whispers. "Decision time."

I want to laugh at that. Because Alec's not typically in a democratic mood when it comes to war zones.

But he knows we could all die here. We could be dead in seconds if we walk into that hallway and they're waiting for us.

But if we don't walk into that hallway and get to those guns, we're dead anyway. So what the fuck.

"Let's do it," I say.

"Go," Christine says. "Just run."

Just run.

Her words echo through my head as Alec steps out into the hallway like he's invincible. He's running, so not quite Mr. Invincible. But it's one of those fuck-it moments.

We die. We don't die. We can't really control that right now.

But if we get to the other side. If we get to the guns…

Yeah. It goes like that through my head as I take off after him. I want to look over my shoulder, make sure Christine is behind me, but that's when a stream of bullets slaps against the glass.

Thoop. Thoop, thoop, thoop.

Unlike last time, it's not a barrage. Just one guy, probably. Just one guy left behind.

And the reinforced glass holds. For like two whole seconds I think, *Fuckin' hell. We're gonna make it. We're really gonna make it.*

I'm about halfway across when that thought hangs there in my head.

And that's when the barrage comes.

That's when they open up. Not one guy, but the whole fuckin' team.

I just run. I run the fuck out of that hallway. And when I crash into Alec on the other side and see his face, I know.

Christine didn't make it.

CHAPTER FORTY-ONE

Christine is ducking her head forward and then pulling it back. Ducking forward and pulling back. Like one of those plastic birds they sell to tourists at the ocean. The kind that are weighted to dip their heads into a glass of water and then spring back, making it appear that a fokken plastic bird is drinking from your tumbler.

The glass walls have lost their battle against the gunfire and sit defeated and shattered on the floor of the hallway. It is not, however, the decking of tiny glass daggers that is keeping Christine from running down to join us. It is the unrelenting wave of hot metal pouring in that is keeping her pinned down.

The fire will abate for a moment, but then it commences again the moment Christine ducks around to see if she can make it. The laser sights, which betray their owners' positions and indicate that the shooters can't see what they think they can as well as they'd like, disappear and reappear every time Christine disappears and reemerges. The fact that I don't respect their flippin' lasers doesn't make the after-effects of using them any less deadly.

And in the blink of a gnat's eye, Danny steps out into the hallway, ready to dart back in the direction from which we just ran. I grab him and pull him back.

"Fok are you going, man?" I shout to him, sotto voce for some reason. It's loud, we've already been found, and quieting my voice now won't give any cover or prevent us from being shot to ribbons, but I do it anyway. Habit.

"Christine!" he screams to her, not nearly so self-conscious.

"We can't get to her, man. We have to go forward," I tell him, with quite a bit more disappointment and regret than I'd like to be feeling.

"Fuck you," he says, pushing me off.

For so, so many years Danny was Christine's protector. Her lodestar. But Christine is graduated well past the point of needing him in that way. She's well past the point of needing anyone in that way. And it's that almost superheroic self-sufficiency she possesses that I'm counting on to save her now.

"She'll figure it out, bru. You can't help her none if you're dead on the fokken ground. We need guns, man."

He looks at me, a tortured anger in his eyes. I feel his frustration. But he knows I'm right. It's a miserable feeling to be relegated to the last option rather than the best option, but that's where we find ourselves.

"Stay down!" he shouts to her. "Don't try to run this way until we've neutralized some shit!"

Danny has never served in the military. I don't know where he inherited all of his military speak. Movies and television, probably.

Americans, man.

"Yeah," Christine calls back, her voice dripping with sarcasm. "Thanks," she adds.

Dear Christine. Same as she ever was.

She's going to be fine.

I hope. I deeply and desperately do. We'll find out soon enough.

"Let's go," I say, dragging Danny with me in the opposite direction as we watch Christine disappear from our view.

CHAPTER FORTY-TWO

Christine

I'm not a complainer. I'm really not. I'm a total go-with-the-flow kinda girl. You have to be in my business. So when the hellfire cuts me off from the guys, I deal. I do. In fact, I think Danny takes this the hardest.

I do not wince, either. I'm not a wincer. But as I run through the shattered glass house, back the way we came, back through all that chaos that we just crept our way out of—I feel like I deserve some complaining and wincing time.

Because my feet are bare. And I'm running through glass shards. And my partners in crime are together and I'm not with them. And there's this small army after me, and I'm stuck in this weird maze house, and I have no gun.

So thirty seconds to... you know, *process* this bullshit would be nice.

What the fuck is happening?

I'm past the gallery. I kinda just ran straight through it without stopping because I figure, fuck it, right? They're either there or they're not and I certainly can't stay in that tiny hallway just hoping for a rescue.

So now I'm at the top of the stairs, peeking out in the great room where the piano is—was. I mean, it's still there but like, three legs have been blown off with automatic

305

weapon fire and that hundred-thousand-dollar Steinway might as well be firewood at this point.

And I can see them out there. Skulking in the moonlight between trees. Every once in a while, I catch sight of a laser cutting through the branches.

Who the fuck uses a laser sight in stealth mode, anyway?

No one professional.

Or they're not actually in stealth mode.

Because they're here to scare us.

Except they did just try to kill us, so just what the fuck is happening?

I wait there in the stairwell for thirty eternal seconds, watching them. And then I make a decision. And I step out. Feet crunching over the glass shards. Eyes locked on the forest, waiting for one of them to see me. The other side of the room so far away.

They don't see me. They don't even look my way. They think this part of the house is secure and what they're mostly doing is regrouping and heading down the hill towards the lake.

Did they come in by boat? Swim in like a SEAL team?

Sneaky, sneaky fuckers. Because that's how I'd have come. And I knew that. Every single time I looked out at that lake and marveled at the low-hanging mist. The choppy water. The walls of mountain surrounding it on three sides.

I knew that's how they'd come.

I get to the other side of the house, the part I never made it to, and end up in another concrete hallway. Which I traverse quickly, and without much caution. I turn into the first room, a bedroom with a wall of glass, and almost shit myself when I realize this is ground level now and there's a soldier ten feet away on the other side of the window.

He looks at me. Perhaps catching my movement in some stray moonbeam. Perhaps not.

He's wearing a faceplate so I can't see him. But he can sure as fuck see me. Because I can feel his gaze like heat when it lands on me. I can feel his stare behind that plate.

And then he turns away. Starts walking. His gaze scanning the forest as he stalks along the side of the house.

Or can he? See me? Maybe...

The tactical side of my brain processes this and comes up with two possibilities.

One. That faceplate is hiding infrared gear. I'm behind glass, which hides a heat signature because it's reflective.

Two. He's not after me.

I back out of the bedroom and creep along the hallway—no glass shards here so it's a nice reprieve—and follow him. Looking into doorways as I pass bedroom after bedroom. Catching sight of his dark figure outside as he walks the perimeter of the house.

We end up in a small living area. Three sides encased in glass, one of which is a door. One of those foldaway window doors that open up to an expansive deck.

He's coming up the stairs to the deck landing when I enter, so I scramble down to the floor and crawl, sniper-style, over to the couch. Just in case he can see me and we're in the middle of a secret meeting or something.

What? Christine, this isn't a game, bitch. This guy is here to kill you.

He opens the door and I hold my breath, my heart pounding so fast, so loud. For sure he can hear that.

But he just steps inside, assault rifle at low ready.

Which makes me pause.

307

And then a tinny voice through the faceplate speaker says, "Christine."

You know that feeling in your gut when shit just got real? Well, I get that. I get that feeling so hard, so bad, I want to vomit.

"Christine," he hisses again.

No.

I swallow down the sick and shake my head.

No.

"*Christine*," he repeats. This time louder. More urgency. "Jesus Christ. Where did you go?"

I am *not* the reason this is happening.

"Christine." He traverses the room, out of sight for a few seconds as I silently scramble along the couch to keep us on opposite ends. And when I peek around the edge of the arm, his back is to me. He's looking down the hallway, head tilted like a curious dog.

I *am* the reason this is happening.

Some part of me understands this. Knows this to be true.

I just don't remember it.

But just because he's not here to kill me doesn't mean I'm not here to kill him.

I position my bare feet on the smooth concrete floor, angle my body like an Olympic runner getting ready for a race, and don't even think twice when I launch forward— feet slapping on the floor, arms reaching for his rifle—and I knock into him with the full weight of my body.

He's turning when this happens, so I hit him in the hip. His rifle does not leave his tight grip and I know, right then, this was a mistake. I'm not going to get that weapon. And the only way I get out now is if I run.

So that's what I do.

I run.

The whole time I'm darting through the door and out onto the deck. The whole time I'm running down the stairs, thump of tactical boots right behind me. The whole time I wait for the rifle to cut me in half. The whole time I wait for the bullets to the back.

Because I deserve that. I deserve to go out this way.

I am the traitor. I am the reason these people are here.

I am the only thing that could pull Danny Fortnight and Alec van den Berg together again.

And now that I have, I will be the weapon that takes them down.

CHAPTER FORTY-THREE

Danny

The room where Alec has his weapons stored looks like the hideout for a James Bond villain or some shit. There's no secret entryway to get in, it's just a door with a lock. A biometric retinal scan and fingerprint pad lock, but still. Just a door and a lock. I dunno why that's something I notice. But I do.

Inside, it's laid out like a showroom. Guns and weapons of various shapes and sizes strapped to the walls. Machine guns. Handguns. Shotguns. Sniper rifles. And…

"Is that a fuckin' RPG?" I ask.

"I believe it is, yes," he says.

I believe it is. Leave it to fucking Alec to have so much shit lying around that he doesn't even know what all he owns.

He runs over to the wall and pulls down a couple automatic rifles. As he reaches up, the muscles in his bare back and shoulders tense and expand. It's not something I should be noticing, I suppose, and I'm sure it's just my imagination, but he looks bigger. Bigger than I think of him. Bigger than he appeared even a few minutes ago when we were together. It's almost like he's found a way to fill the space around him so that he can become more than he was.

Or else my mind is playing tricks on me. Either way wouldn't shock me.

He tosses me one of the guns and then grabs a duffle, starts loading it with spare clips, and chucks that over to me that as well. I sling it over my shoulder, feeling the tug of the canvas strap against my naked back.

I want to ask him… If this house was built as a secure haven, a place where he could stay close to me, a paradise manufactured for the purposes of giving the three of us a refuge one day—even if he wasn't sure that day would come—then why did he build a room to store enough firepower to wage an invasion?

But then I realize that I know the answer.

Because this is our life. This is the life Alec brought us into. He's a fucking diamond smuggler and thief. And so are Christine and I. The possibility that a war will be fought has always been just around the corner for us. None of us recognized it while it was happening, I don't think, but everything we ever did just propelled us further and faster in the direction of this moment. This moment where the monster we've been feeding over the years has grown too big for us to control and now we have to put it down or be devoured.

Our world is a beast and we no longer hold its fuckin' leash.

"Grab the RPG," I say.

"Yeah?" he asks, skeptically for some reason.

"Yeah, dude!" I shout. We don't have time for this shit. "There's however the fuck many of them and there's two of us! A fuckin' rocket-propelled grenade could come in handy!"

He stares at me for less than a second and then says, "Three."

"What? Fuck are you saying?"

"There's three of us," he says.

My mouth tightens, I blink the emotions out of my eyes, and nod my head.

"Yeah," I say. "Three." Then I grab the RPG and add, "Let's fuckin' go."

CHAPTER FORTY-FOUR

Unlike Danny, I do have a secondary escape route. Wouldn't make a lot of sense to have an artillery bastion without a way to maneuver forth from it without being seen.

The biggest problem right now is that I haven't actually spent much time here. So, when it comes to knowing all the particulars of this compound, I'm less well equipped than I would prefer. The only thing I feel I can count on is that I still know it better than does whoever is here for us.

And that's when a cold chill skitters down my unshirted back. Do I? Do I know it better? The fact is that someone *does* know we're here. And there are a very precious few people who even know this place exists. So that we've been discovered…

But before I can think about it any further, Danny stops short. We've made it out of the back exit of the house and are well hidden by the copse in which we now find ourselves.

"What?" I ask, almost bumping into him.

"There," he says.

Up ahead I count at least a dozen armed men. Maybe fifteen to twenty. A fokken lot, that's all I can be sure of.

They are all wearing proper tactical gear. A fully organized, military-style assault.

This morning at Danny's apartment was nothing compared to this. This morning was a pinprick compared to this. My instinct tells me that the morning was something akin to a fact-finding mission. If they could have killed us then, so much the better. But ultimately it was a test balloon. Getting us out here where no one will find us and where we can just be… disappeared from the planet. This is preferable.

I only know one person who checks all the boxes necessary to make something like what's happening now happen.

But why?

Several more of our attackers are now venturing into the house through the broken glass. Scouting. Seeking. Laser sights flashing about in the now-dark forest.

There are a handful of lights still on inside, and there is a bright, harvest-like moon overhead. Just enough illumination to make out the figures as they continue on their hunt. They are all wearing faceplates. I don't reckon so much to shield their identities as to try to keep a bullet from piercing their fokken eyeballs.

There's little possibility that our shooting at them now is going to help our situation. Christine is somewhere we don't know, and we are outnumbered and under-armed. All shooting will do is give away our position and invite them to kill us quicker. I'm trying to consider our options when Danny mounts the RPG on his shoulder.

"Fok are you doing, bru?"

"You have a better fuckin' idea right now?"

It's as if he was reading my bloomin' mind.

"No, man. I don't. Fokken shoot, I reckon."

316

He turns around, faces the murder of assailants now exploring the property and conferring about where to look for us, fiddles with the locks and safeties and triggers for a moment—one must assume that Danny has never actually shot an RPG before—and then when he's got it all sorted out, he pulls a firing trigger.

The *thwomp* sound calls to mind for me someone blowing on a didgeridoo. The sound of the explosive landing in the middle of the circle of unknown enemies and blowing them to smithereens is somewhat less quaint.

The blast knocks Danny back about three feet. We still do not know how many men—or women; impossible to tell with their faces covered—are left alive, but we simultaneously decide that the prudent move is not to wait to find out. We take off on the run, maneuvering out and around where a small handful of still-mobile attackers is charging to find us.

And as we flee the area, I glance over my shoulder to my right and I see…

Christine.

Running.

She's made it out of the house and is, coincidentally, charging in the direction Danny and I are headed right now.

Aweh, man! I cannot believe that we are going to fokken get out of this kak! We are! We're going to make it! All three of us! Ayoba, man!

That is the thought that *should* be running through my head at present. It should be. But it is not.

Because running behind her is another masked figure. Someone who was not hit by the blast. Someone who seems hell-bent on catching her. *Catching* her. Not killing her. Not shooting her in the back. Why?

317

Someone who has a familiar gait. Whose graceful, galloping stride is recognizable to me instantly. Someone whose body moves in a way that I know well.

Well known because his stride, his gait, his movement, his manner…

They are also mine.

CHAPTER FORTY-FIVE

Christine

The thwomp of an RPG leaving a rocket launcher is a sound you never forget. You hear it once and that's all it takes. One time and it's burned into your memory for lifetimes to come.

So when I heard it, I dropped. It's just instinct. I dropped to the muddy ground and thought, *Welp. I had a good run.*

And then the explosion happened. And I was still alive.

But my attacker—my... friend? Partner? Who the fuck is this guy?—behind me. He didn't drop. He used those precious seconds to catch up.

God, I really suck at this job. I might need to hone my typing skills and work in that office after all.

He grabbed my ankle while I was still cowering. Gripped it tight. Like I was a prize he'd never let go of.

I kicked him hard. *Hard.* But the faceplate. The body armor. It didn't do much. It just did enough.

He let go and I ran.

I run.

I run so hard, my panic so big, my breaths so desperate, my lungs and throat are burning like the hell I suddenly find myself in.

We are all gonna die today.

No. Not you, Christine.

Them.

Alec will die. Danny will die.

But somehow, I know I will live through this. This is not hell around me. Hell is waiting on the other side of tonight.

And then I see them. Danny, RPG rocket launcher mounted on his shoulder. Alec, staring at me like I'm a ghost in the mist.

And I hear the others behind us. The tinny voice in the faceplate yelling, "Here! Over here!"

And boots. I hear boots. I hear screams. I smell fire, and flesh, and chemicals.

And Danny yelling, "Say hello to my little friend!"

I smile at that. I smile all the way through the next *thwomp.*

Rational thought reemerges. I am not the weapon that will take them down.

We. Will not. Go down tonight.

The second explosion is closer. Just down the hill.

The boots stop. The screams grow louder.

I scramble, one last push to reach Alec. His arm extended thirty feet away. His hand outstretched. Like if I would just reach out now, he'd cover that distance and pull me into the safety of his arms.

So I do. I believe him. I reach.

And I stumble.

Face first into the mud.

My attacker is gripping my ankle. Crawling up my body. Head in the crook of my neck like a lover. Faceplate up, or gone, or whatever, because I can feel his breath when he says, "Christine."

Then Alec. Poor, poor Alec.

Because I know who this is now. I know this man. I know him.

"Lars?" Alec says.

CHAPTER FORTY-SIX

I don't know what makes me reach for the phone in my jeans pocket. Maybe I'm looking for a gun? Not sure. I just find that I now have a phone in my hand. And as Lars tackles Christine, I bring it out. Don't look at it. No time to look at it.

But I don't need to look at it.

I caused this. I brought these people here. Me and my stupid obsession with GPS coordinates.

They tracked me through my phone. Because of course they did.

They are Lars. Alec's brother. The only person on this planet he trusts outside of our triangle.

I stuff the phone back in my pocket, pick up a rocket, load it into the launcher and feel... pretty fucking ridiculous because who the fuck am I gonna save with this thing?

Christine is thirty feet away. On the ground, face covered in mud as Lars kneels on her back and points his pistol at her head. "Don't do it," he says.

"Do it!" Christine screams. It's a wild scream. A little bit of hysteria in that scream. My gut clenches at the sound of her fear.

Lars yells, "Don't do it, Fortnight. Don't fokken do it. I'll shoot her in the fokken head before you can pull that bleeding trigger!"

He's on his feet. He's got Christine up too. Pistol still flat against her temple.

"Do it!" Christine screams again. "Fuckin' *do it!*"

"Lars!" Alec yells. "What the fok—"

"He sold you out, you know?" Lars cuts him off.

I look at Alec. I shouldn't. Because Lars could kill me in that moment of shame.

"Him! Your precious fokken Danny! He sold you out to Brasil Lynch. Oh, yeah, bru, I do know who Brasil Lynch is, by the way. Sorry. I lied. Danny's only with you to take you in. Hand you over. He fokked you, man!"

"What the fok is happening right now, bru?" Alec yells at me.

I keep staring at Alec. I look back at Lars. I look around at the destroyed house, the blown-apart forest, the screaming and burning bodies around us. How the fuck did we wind up here? I drop the rocket launcher on the ground.

Lars smiles.

And I make a decision. One I will probably regret. But I make it anyway. I honor Christine's request. Kind of. I dive to the ground, retrieving a weapon from the clutches of some poor, dead asshole, and lay down fire aimed directly at Alec's little brother.

Lars shoots back. Empties his fucking magazine as he retreats. And as he runs, one thing strikes me as especially strange.

He doesn't hold Christine in front of him like a shield in the way I would expect. He pushes her behind him.

He shields her.

Christ.

My stomach sinks. He was never going to kill Christine. Because they're together. They're *together*. And again, I ask myself: How the fuck did we wind up here?

The realization has me laying off the trigger. Stunned. And suddenly… More gunfire. Not from Lars' gun, from another weapon's barrel. One of Lars' gunmen is still alive. He's not wearing a mask for some reason. Young guy. A goddamn baby. Dark skin and scared eyes.

Lars pushes Christine in his direction and yells, "Go!" The young guy drags her along. She resists initially, but then Lars yells at her, "Christine! Go!" And she does. Confusion plastered all over her face.

"Solomon!" Alec shouts. The young kid dragging Christine along looks back. He hesitates. He looks torn about what he should do.

They know each other. Alec knows him. One of his men. Or one of what Alec thought was his men.

Christine set us up? Christine set us up. She and Lars. Why? And why did she—?

"Solomon!" Alec screams it now, holding his own weapon up and aiming it. But he doesn't pull the trigger. He doesn't shoot. He just holds it there, screaming the kid's name over and over again.

Fuck it. If he's not going to shoot somebody, I will. But before I can, a fresh round of bullets has both me and Alec darting for cover. Lars again. Reloaded. Our uncharacteristic hesitancy has us pinned down once more.

"Lars!" Alec bellows.

Lars doesn't respond. Just keeps firing at the tree behind which Alec has hidden himself. I poke my head around the side of my own sorry excuse for cover, seeing if I can get a shot. But Lars is backing up, firing wildly, and then he turns and starts running in the direction of the kid and Christine.

I could nail him. Could shoot him right in the back. But I don't. Because when I look at him, I see Alec. I mean I see Alec reflected in him, but I also literally see Alec. He's crouched down, hugging his body and rocking back and forth. I've never seen him like this.

"Fok!" he lets out, still rocking back and forth. "Fok, fok, fok!"

And so I hesitate. I don't fire. Just one more mistake to add to the long list I'm writing. Because I want to go after Christine. I want to save her. Be her knight. Be her hero.

And I can't. Because...

Because Alec.

I want to save him too. Be his hero.

And by the time I sort *that* all out, everyone is gone.

Christine is gone. Lars is gone. Alec is holding his head in his hands and I'm not sure if he was hit, or he's just as confused as I am.

Dead bodies are scattered around us.

We are in the middle of nowhere, miles and miles from hope.

I'm left alone with Alec. Alec who I was going to betray.

Lars has Christine. Christine, who may have betrayed us both.

We are not a triangle. If we ever were. I don't know anything anymore. Except that we are not joined in some deep way. Not now. Now, we are just three broken lines scattered by the fucking wind. As helpless and lost as the fallen leaves blowing in aimlessly through the shattered glass of the shelter where just moments before, Christine, Alec and I thought we had maybe found a home.

CHAPTER FORTY-SEVEN

In a semi-meditative state, the world slows. In a semi-meditative state, events become clearer, less confusing, more precise. In a semi-meditative state, one maintains control even as life spins out.

I am not in a semi-meditative state.

The events whirl around me in a stumbling jumble. We are nowhere. Everywhere is somewhere, but in a much more significant way, we are nowhere right now.

Lars…

I've never known my younger brother all that well. I was already well on my way to becoming the sociopathic deviant I pride myself on being when Lars was born. I was eight. It always struck me that Lars wasn't actually an accident. I think Mom and Dad looked into my eyes, saw a terrible goddamn mistake and figured, "Let's try again."

Lars was thirteen when they died. I was twenty-one. I didn't know shit about how to raise a child. I was proper stunned when I discovered that I had been left as Lars' legal guardian. I have to assume it was some paperwork mistake that never got sorted.

I did my best. I made sure that he stayed in school. Made sure he had caretakers looking after him. Made sure that I saw him at least once a year, on Christmas. But I had no idea who he was becoming. Who he was turning into.

Some would call it selfish, yeah? I suppose. I might argue in return that because I saw no place for him in the world that was mine, Danny's, and Christine's, that I was being righteous by keeping him at a distance.

It wasn't until a few years later when Lars kept getting kicked out of upper school after upper school that it began dawning on me that nature is perhaps more powerful than nurture. That you can try to protect a child, shield them from the evils of the world, but—at the end of the long day—they are who they are.

Maybe it's because our bloodline traces back to our great-grandfather and great-grandmother. Two fearless people who followed their hearts. Hearts that had to be filled with so much passion that they spit directly in the world's face and said, "Ek gie nie 'n fok nie." I don't give a fuck. Fok your rules. Fok your system. Fok your world. We will do as we like.

Maybe it's because our father was a heartless naaier who left a trail of hurt and pain wherever he went on his way to achieving his own brand of power.

And that's what birthed us. That combination of passion and ruthlessness is bred into us.

Or maybe we're just fokken insane.

It's probably a mixture of all of it.

Regardless, after a while it became clear that Lars wasn't meant for civil society. So I brought him along with me. I am Captain Hook, after all. Collecting lost boys—and girls—and helping them learn to be pirates. Like that laaitie, Solomon. Dear Solomon, who seemed so nervous and grateful when he approached me on the plane. Dear Solomon, whose life I saved back in the warehouse in

Cape Town. Dear Solomon, who seems to have picked the wrong side in this fight and who I'm going to take great pleasure in watching die.

Eish. That's just rage talking. Izit? Probably. No place for rage. No time for it. One must assume that he was just following orders. I feel quite confident that Lars, whatever this plan of his is, didn't tell anyone the details. Didn't tell them *who* they were being dispatched to handle. As my number two, Lars is expected to be listened to when I'm not around.

To be clear, the distance between number one and number two in my organization is a great length to travel indeed. But still… Lars is the rightful heir. Looks like maybe my bae bru has grown tired of waiting his turn though.

But that still doesn't explain a few things.

Things like: Christine. The tumble she took. The shot she took. Why she's been taken rather than killed.

Although I assume I know the last one. And it makes me sick to my fokken stomach.

What is also unexplained though is: *Why?* I know power is intoxicating. I understand that better than most. But these are some extraordinary fokken lengths, man. This is an awfully elaborate set of circumstances into which one must put one's energy just to seize something like *power*.

There has to be another reason that this is playing out the way it is. There must be.

The only thing I'm sure of is that this is my fault. I did this. I started this all in motion. Not when I arrived here. Not even when I called Danny. I set it in motion a decade ago when I pummeled that unfortunate naaier in that boxing club. When I decided that I wanted Danny Fortnight to love me.

I have all the money anyone could ever need, but none of it could've bought me the glimpse into the future that I needed to keep this nightmare from happening.

This is my fault.

"Let's fuckin' go!" Danny's voice. Shaking me from my stupor.

He stands above me, bare chest sweaty and glistening in the chilly moonlit night. He's reaching down for me. I stare at it a moment before ignoring his reach and standing. We're looking each other in the eye.

"What?" he says. "Let's fuckin' move!" I keep staring. "Dude, come on!" he shouts. "What?" he asks again when I don't respond. "Fuckin' what? The Brasil thing? Fuck. It's not... I wasn't going to... I'll explain it later, but we gotta fuckin' go!"

I don't know who to believe. Who not to believe. Ironic, since I'm usually the one not to believe. Maybe I've just told so many lies that I can't keep track anymore. Maybe some of these lies are mine and, like Christine, I just don't remember.

Danny was setting me up. Christine was setting both of us up. Or not. It don't matter. Only one thing matters right now.

I lift my gun and point it in Danny's direction.

He flinches, shock on his face, and he ducks as he lifts his weapon in return. Which is helpful, because it leaves me an open shot to take out the remaining naaier who had his stupid fokken laser sight pointed at the back of Danny's head.

You don't need a laser sight if you know how to aim well.

A spray of blood from a lanced jugular vein arcs up into the black night as my bullet finds the lone exposed bit of flesh on the gunman's neck. His faceplate comes flying off and I realize I recognize him.

Gerry.

Gerry who had an unsecured mobile as I was flying here to wander unknowingly into something resembling End of Days. Ah, well. As I thought when he loaned me his phone, normally an infraction like having an unsecured mobile would be grounds for dismissal. This is a much greater disregard for the rules. Much greater.

So… *You're dismissed, Gerry, my china.*

Danny looks behind him at Gerry's fallen body, a startled expression in his eyes.

I lower my gun. Danny turns back to look at me. I nod.

"Sure, bru. Let's fokken go."

CHAPTER FORTY-EIGHT

Danny

Alec van den Berg doesn't scare me.

We have... *done things* together. And at no point while doing any of those things did he ever act like anyone other than who he is.

A self-absorbed asshole who thinks he owns the world.

A guy who has no fear of anyone or anything, and that kind of shit is contagious when you're on the same side.

He's not afraid of me. I'm not afraid of him.

We have no fear of anyone.

But the truth is—Alec and I have never been on opposite sides. Not really. I left, did my thing. He stayed, did his thing. Paths didn't cross again. So I've never actually seen him the way I see him now.

He stares at the man on the ground behind me. The glint of confidence and occasional mischief that usually lights his eyes is gone. They are hollow and dead.

In this moment I am afraid for less than a second. It actually takes a beat of my heart to remember we're on the same side.

"Brasil Lynch, then, eh?" he says, still not looking at me.

And then I remember... we're actually not.

I run my fingers through my hair, giving myself a moment to practice picking my way through the minefield I'm gonna cross. "Yes, I sold you out. But *bru*"—and I smile here. Not to disarm him or anything, just to be a dick—"it was a half-hearted attempt. Trust me. There was no scenario where I actually took you back to that asshole."

He turns to glare at me finally. Nostrils flaring. Amber eyes not as hollow as I thought. They're actually burning with hate.

And in that moment, I know how other people see him. People who are not me. Not Christine.

But the way I know him is just... the way I know him. So that version fades, if it was ever there to begin with.

"This really how you wanna spend this time?"

Another beat of hate as he continues to glare. And I know him so well, have seen him in every scenario imaginable, that I can read his mind.

He's ticked off ten ways to kill me. Maybe three ways to torture me before that happens. Where he'll leave my body, what curse he'll mutter as he stands over me, how he'll justify it to Christine, how he'll go on when it's over.

And then he's back.

Just Alec.

I shrug again. Consider all the things I should probably say to him. Things like... *I knew you'd come. I just needed a way out of Brasil's office so I could get back to Christine and be there when you did. I love you, you know I fucking love you.* Shit like that. True shit.

"We can dissect it later. But right now..."

"They're gone, man," he says, looking around at the carnage. "Lost in the forest like fokken Red Riding Hood."

"Yeah, but…" I kinda laugh. It's so inappropriate, but I can't help it. I'm just Danny. And then I dig into my pocket, pull out my phone again, and tab an icon. "I know where she is, *bru*." I wave the phone at him. "Do you think I was worried about the fucking GPS signal the whole drive up here because my Boy Scout sensibilities were being violated? No. Asshole. I have a tracker on her."

There's a long moment before he says, "Say again?"

"The sweatpants she has on. I have a beacon tacked into the leg."

He looks at me like I'm crazy. That's fair.

"Why?" he asks.

"Because. Because I didn't know what the fuck you were gonna do."

He stares at me with a blend of fury and what feels like respect. Then he looks down at my hand,

"That's her?" he asks, pointing to the phone.

I look at the screen. It's a really nice app. Very clean and simple. So Christine is, predictably, a green dot labeled *Christine* moving along a cartoon map. "Yeah, that's her."

"Where?"

I blow out a breath, turn around in a circle, trying to get my bearings, and then point into the woods. "That way. Whatever that way is."

He stares at me. Still angry. Lots of questions. But there's relief too. Good old Danny can always be counted on to be good old Danny.

And then he changes again. He's a regular fucking chameleon tonight.

But it's fear I see now.

For the first time in my life I know what Alec van den Berg looks like when he's afraid of something.

"I don't know what's happening," he says.

337

"Yeah," I say. "Me neither. Let's go."

He takes a breath. Calms. Then says, "Yeah," and starts off in the direction I pointed.

We can't both be afraid at the same time. We have to take turns. And now that Alec is calmed down, his focus on what comes next… that's when the fear creeps under my skin. That's when I remember some words I told Christine a couple days ago. And they begin to repeat, over and over again, like a mantra.

They won't kill you, Christine. They'll rape you first. Torture you until you're begging for death.

When I said it, it was a scare tactic. Get her ass moving. Get her thinking clearly. Get her somewhere other than that tinfoil apartment. I believed it, but I never believed it would happen. Not with me there to keep her safe. Not on my watch.

Yet here we are.

Lars.

I don't know what Lars might do. I don't know what's going on with Alec and Lars. I've been gone too long. Too many things could've happened between then and now. All I know is that we were holding weapons on each other a few minutes ago. That Christine is with him, not me. That this feels like a setup from day one.

They set us up.

The blue inside me becomes a deep purple as I pick my way through the leftover weapons in Alec's cache. And by the time we're trucking off into the forest, both of us still shirtless and shoeless, like a couple of almost-Rambos or some shit, me staring at that little green dot on the app…

I'm red.

Nothing but red.

CHAPTER FORTY-NINE

Christine

I'm trying to pull free from this guy's grip on my arm, but he's stronger than he looks. He also seems even more scared and confused than I probably should be. Which is odd. Theoretically, he's the one in control. But then again, he is young. Maybe when I was his age I woulda looked that scared too.

Nah. I wouldn't. I'm pretty sure I've never looked scared.

"Are you OK?" A voice from behind me. Coming up fast. A voice I know. Alec?

Not quite. But close.

I turn to see the person I know is called Lars, but about whom I don't know much else. Bits and pieces pop into my brain. Fragments of conversations. Hints of a past that I maybe recognize. A Christmas tree and a young man with an angry expression. What do the images mean?

And his words make no sense to me. "Am I OK?"

"Are you hurt? I told them to make sure not to hit you. Although I will admit seeing you taking it from both Alec and Danny at once did inspire some feelings I wasn't quite ready for."

I don't even bother responding to that one. I want to say, *Who the fuck are you?* I want to say, *Why am I with you?* I want to say, *What are we doing?*

But that *we* part, oh, God. That *we* part makes me so sick.

Because I know who he is. I think. And I understand what just happened. Maybe. I might've been kicked out of seventeen or thirty boarding schools in my day, but it doesn't take a genius to figure this shit out.

I'm working with him. I did this. I planned this. I'm working with him.

No.

No, no, no.

That isn't true. It cannot be true.

"Lars," I say. But my voice comes out weak and squeaky.

"It's fine, nunu," he says, and I almost throw up. We're still moving, he's looking behind us as we jog. He gets beside me and kisses me on the cheek.

Oh, Jesus.

This is war, I decide. A civil war between brothers and I'm... I'm collateral damage.

But that's not true. I'm not *collateral.*

I don't want to know this stuff. I don't want to know what this is. I don't want to know what I did. I don't want to be here.

"This wasn't the plan," I finally manage, making it up as I go.

But Lars—who is so much like Alec it hurts to look at him—turns back to me and says, "It's fine," he says again. And he smiles at me. Alec smiles at me. *That's Lars. That's Lars. That's Lars. What the fuck is wrong with me?* "You're fine.

You did what you had to do. I understand. We'll sort it out."

I try to decide if he's fucking with me. Because I don't remember this plan. I don't even really remember him. I just know who he is.

"What are we doing?" I ask, unable to hold in the questions. "Why are we doing this? Lars!" I yell, because he's not looking at me now. He's looking behind us. And around in circles. Like we're lost.

"Mr. van den Berg?" the young guy who's still holding me asks.

And this is my chance. Suddenly, they're both focused on being terrible at their jobs. I can grab a gun, mow both of these motherfuckers down, and go find Alec and Danny. Because I don't know who Lars is supposed to be to me, but I'm absolutely certain who completes the triangle.

Except… More flashes of memory now. Me. Lars. Dancing. I'm laughing. Lars. Giving me flowers. Flowers? What the *fuck*?

Who am I?

What did I do?

Why did I do it?

And then… Christine. *Nothing. Nothing, nothing, nothing,* trying to convince myself. Because I love them. I love them. And there's no way I'd betray us. Our triangle is sacred. In no alternate reality is there an incarnation of traitor Christine.

"Gaan fok 'n bok!" Lars says. "This way."

And suddenly, for all the things I don't know, I know one thing. I know this direction we're headed. Because I was just there with Alec.

It's not the way out of the forest. If I let us get dragged in this direction, we'll be pinned against nothing for miles, and only one way back. The way that will eventually bring us crashing into Danny and Alec. And then someone else is going to die. No question. I can feel it.

That's when I realize it doesn't matter. It doesn't matter if I was somehow involved with Lars. It doesn't matter what I did. Or if I remember it or not. Or if I was just playing some secret double agent game.

Out here in the middle of nowhere…

Natural selection is about to sort everything out.

CHAPTER FIFTY

"This way," Danny says, looking at the green Christine dot on the phone.

I keep waiting for another black-clad fokker to jump out from behind a tree, or for a sniper's bullet to rip through my chest. If I were Lars and had gone through all the effort he's gone through to this point, I'd make sure that the job got done. But he's not me. And I'm sure that's part of the problem. So far, no sniper, no new ambush, nothing.

"What would you like to do when we catch them?" I ask Danny.

"What?"

"What would you like to do? What's the plan? What's the endgame? What are we fighting for, man?"

Our jog slows slightly, but we keep moving forward.

"Fuck are you talking about?"

"Why didn't he shoot her?"

"Dude," Danny says with exasperation, "I don't fucking know."

"And you're not curious?"

"No, it's Christine."

"You don't even know her anymore."

"I know her well enough."

343

God... I hate that I want to kill Danny right now. Because I love him so. That there is quintessentially Danny Fortnight. Black and white. Good and bad. Calls it as he sees it, loyal to a fault, and all that kak.

Yes, maybe he knew her. Once upon a time. He knew a little girl called Christine. But she stopped being a little girl so long ago. And he stopped understanding her when that change happened. So did I.

If either of us ever knew her at all. I'm not sure we even know ourselves anymore.

"He was never going to kill her," I observe.

"I know," he growls back. "Obviously. I mean, he's Lars. He's had a crush on her since he was fourteen."

"Yes. And that's sweet. But I don't know how much water their history carries. He's also my brother and he tried to kill me, bru. And you."

He says nothing. I don't take my eyes off him as I continue. "So what would you like to do? I'm giving you the reins, my china. This is your mission now. Following your lead and all that. What? Would you like? To do? When we find them? How do we handle this situation, Danny?"

He looks at me as if to say something, but then just glances down at the phone in his hand again and says, "This way."

344

CHAPTER FIFTY-ONE

Christine

We stumble into the clearing. The spot where Alec brought me earlier. It's so different at night. The panoramic view is now replaced by what feels like an endless blanket of black. The only way to know where the edge is is by observing the moonlight shining off the rushing waterfall.

"Fok!" Lars yells again. Then he turns his attention to the young guy. "Boy!"

The kid holding my arm stiffens at being called 'boy.' But then he says, "Yes, sir?"

"Let her go."

The kid does. He looks at me with eyes that just about scream, *I'm sorry*. Shit. Am I supposed to know who he is too?

Lars pulls out another pistol from an ankle holster and hands it to me. I stare at it, uncertain. I don't know why. Of all the things I still can't remember, how to use a gun is not one of them. In fact, holding a gun in my hands feels like the only thing that makes sense right now. But I hesitate.

"Take it," he says.

I reach my hand out slowly. Timidly. Lars shakes his head.

"Take the fokken gun, Christine," he says, grabbing my wrist and forcing the gun into my grip.

I look at it. I look at him.

"Not ideal," he says. "Not how I would've preferred this to go. But your fokken boyfriends are hard to kill, ain't they?"

Boyfriends?

"So I guess it's you and me now. Shame. All the fokken work we did. All the planning. All the effort we put in to make it look like it was a war between Brasil and my goddamn brother, and at the end of the day, we's just gonna have to shoot everyone in their bleeding faces ourselves, I reckon."

I've never experienced vertigo, but this must be what it feels like. Everything is swirling around in my head. I feel dizzy. I stumble back a step and the kid catches me.

"You OK, miss?" he asks.

"What's your name?" I say in return, looking up at him from where he holds me in his arms.

"Solomon, ma'am. Solomon Bophela."

"Thank you, Solomon."

"Brilliant," says Lars, snapping his head to look at us. "You're Solomon, then?"

"Sir?" Solomon says.

"Alec asked me about you. Why?"

"Sir?" Solomon says again. Lars is walking toward him now. Stalking him.

"My brother, boy. Alec van den Berg. He asked me if I hired you. I didn't. Where did you come from?"

"I... I..." Solomon stutters.

"Who fokken hired you, man? Where did you come from?"

"Sir, I was brought in by—"

346

But that's as much as he gets out of his mouth. Ever again. Because Lars lifts his pistol to Solomon's temple and splatters his brains out into the night sky.

I can feel my eyes go wide, and then I close them again. More images. Me and Alec, in bed. Making love. Me and Alec and Danny, earlier. Joined together as one. And then falling. Falling. The ground racing up to meet me. And something...

"Here," Lars says, bringing my attention back to now. When I open my eyes, he's handing me the rifle Solomon was holding. "This is better. Take this."

"Why did you do that?" I ask him.

"What?"

"Kill him. Why did you have to do that?"

"I didn't have to. But I chose to. I don't know him. I don't know why Alec was asking me about him. I don't know whose side he'd be on. I can't trust him."

Bullshit. I think this guy Lars just wanted to kill someone.

"And you think you can trust me?" I ask him.

He darts over to me and gets right in my face. I can feel his warm breath. "Why, Christine? Why not? Why shouldn't I? Is there a reason? You haven't let your feelings for those two enter back into things, have you? Because I thought that was done now."

My whole body is vibrating. I wonder if he can see it. "It is," I manage.

"Izit?" he asks.

I nod. "Yeah," I swallow. "It is."

"I hope so, luv." He strokes my cheek. "I hope so. I want to walk out of here together. I'll need you, at any rate, to deal with the Brasil Lynch of it all. We're not there yet, my sweet. Not yet."

What the fuck have I gotten myself into?

What kind of deal do I have going with Alec's brother? And why? God, why the fuck did I do this?

"Christine," Lars says. I turn my head to see him. Watch his lips move as he talks. But my mind is busy keeping track of what's happening around me, so I miss it.

"What?"

"Are you with me?" I nod. I don't know what else to do. "My girl," he says. Being called 'his' sends a chill down my spine.

Again, he brushes his knuckles down my cheek and smiles.

Everything in my body wants to revolt against that touch.

Everything except the one thing that controls me. Has always controlled me. Always been my best asset.

Instinct.

So I don't recoil. I smile back. Breathe out.

He grabs me by the back of the head and kisses me on the lips, hard. The kiss is surprising, but the pain from his fist brushing against my stitches is what grabs my attention.

"Ow," I blurt out, involuntarily.

"Sorry," he says on a laugh. "I forgot. You're lucky that Reggie and Lex was down there to break your fall. Ain't you?"

Reggie and Lex? Who—?

"Ain't you?" he yells this time.

"Yeah. Yes. I guess," I say.

From somewhere in the woods, we hear a sound. Two sets of feet. Running recklessly, without caution. The sound of two people fueled by emotion, not by reason.

348

Lars stands me up and presses the automatic rifle into my hands. He slaps a fresh clip into his pistol. He smiles.

"Here it comes. Go there. Behind that shrub." He points. I start to go where he tells me to. He grabs my wrist and stops me. I turn back.

"You don't remember a fokken thing, do you?" He squints.

I grimace. I don't want to, but I can't seem to stop it.

"That's all right," he says. "We'll get it sorted when this is done. Trust me, yeah?"

Trust him. Trust anyone. That's the stupidest request I've ever heard.

"Of course," I say with my most convincing smile.

"Because, luv, I'm trusting you." He nods at the rifle. And then he lets me go and takes his own place behind a tree on the other side of the clearing.

I duck down behind the shrub and close my eyes again, trying to remember anything. Anything that can help me understand any part of what's going on. Anything that can help me know what the right thing to do is. But all I see is me, Danny, and Alec again. But not from earlier today this time. From years earlier. From lifetimes ago. It's the only thing I can be certain of.

Or can I?

Fuck! I have no idea.

The sound of a gunshot causes me to open my eyes suddenly.

Oh, shit.

Oh, shit.

Oh, shit.

I fucking remember.

CHAPTER FIFTY-TWO

"Stop."

Alec does.

"What?" he asks.

Looking down at the GPS, it looks like we're almost at the end of the world right now. It seems like there's no more terrain. Just... nothing ahead of us. And Christine is floating there on the edge.

"What's that way? Do you know?" I ask him.

"Yeah, man. Looks like fokken Christine, don't it?"

"No. That," I say, pointing at what looks like nothingness.

"Hear that sound?" he asks.

I listen. "Yeah. What is that?"

"Waterfall."

"How far down is it? Can they keep going?"

"Their bodies can. Their souls, however, will be ferried off to heaven or where-the-fok-ever if they try to keep moving that way."

I stare at the map. That's what that nothingness is. It's nothingness.

"I'm going to ask again, man... What's our plan?"

"Jesus, dude. We're gonna get Christine—"

"Are we? Are we, now? Christine who it very likely seems has been playing us completely? Christine who's been playing the fokken damsel in distress, oh, woe is me, my poor memory is gone?"

"What are you—?"

"There ain't gonna be no happily ever after, man. Whatever happens next don't conclude with you, me, and Christine sitting on a fokken beach somewhere sipping piña coladas, slapping each other on the ass and laughing. So my question is, why the fok are we bothering?"

His eyes bore into me. I breathe heavily, trying not to punch him. Not because he's saying anything wrong. Because everything he's saying is right. He's telling the truth. Fucking Alec van den Berg is telling the truth. Jesus Christ.

Alec knows her better than I do, and Alec is worried. But maybe it's because Lars knows him better than anyone. Including me. Including Christine.

Brothers are like that. Even ones who spent most of the last ten years apart.

There is no way for this to end well. No matter what version of it runs through my head, they all end with at least one of us dead. I can't see a way around it.

I take a step away from Alec. Back in the direction from which we just came. We could just turn around now. Alec and I could march back, get in my Range Rover and drive the fuck out of here. We could leave Christine with Lars, assume that's what they wanted all along, and he and I could go back into the world together. Maybe we could start our own thing. Our own, new business, or...

Or maybe we could split apart. Go our separate ways. And then what? Spend the rest of our lives looking over our shoulders? I mean, shit, I figure we'll be doing that no matter what unless we kill everybody who threatens us. Or get killed ourselves.

He's right. There is no happy ending.

But still…

I turn back to face Alec. He bows his head and looks at me with an almost devilish gaze. I put my face in his face. I put my hands on his bare shoulders. I turn him around. He lets me.

And when his back is to me, I let my hands slide down between his shoulder blades and with my fingers, I trace the lines of the triangle. He tenses. I keep tracing. His head falls back and he looks up at the sky. Just like he did the first time I ever touched it. Actually, I don't know if his eyes are open or not, but his face is turned up and his shoulders drop.

I finish tracing the lines of the pattern on his back, let my hands drop from his skin, and stand there. Waiting. Waiting to see what happens next.

He doesn't turn around, and after a moment his head lowers back down again, he grabs his rifle up, racks it, and says, "Right then."

And before I know it, he's marching straight into the direction the GPS is telling us Christine is waiting.

And he's firing the rifle wildly as he goes.

CHAPTER FIFTY-THREE

We get the word "berserk" from the Norse berserkers. Warriors who were purported to have fought in a trance-like state in which they would eschew mail armor. Wild men. Crazy people. Men possessed. An army of Hulks marching unflinchingly in the direction of battle.

Naaiers must have been a sight to see.

No value in pretending we're not here. The whole point is to fokken make ourselves known. More than anything, what I want right now is answers. I want to know what the fok has been going on under my nose and how the hell I missed it. That's what I want. And I plan to get what I want.

"Lars!" I shout, marching into the clearing, firing my weapon as I do. "Lars! Come out now, bru! It's been fun, man, but playtime is over!"

I'm sweeping the rifle, making sure that if anyone tries to pop up and take a shot that there's a fair chance they'll get a belly-full of hot metal first.

And that's when I look over and see the laaitie Solomon. Dead. Brains well more outside his body than they were the last time I saw him. Damn, man. God damn it, Lars. Was that really necessary? The kid was so nervous

355

when we spoke on the flight over. So concerned he wasn't doing right.

That's all a lad like that ever wants. To do right. To please someone and feel like he's loved and appreciated. That's all most everyone ever wants. To feel a part of something.

I told him that he had a family now. Shit. But it wasn't a lie. I just failed to consider that some families have a great lot more dysfunction than others.

"Lars!" I scream as I continue firing around in a circle. I fire and fire and fire, until...

There's no fire left.

Throwing the empty rifle down on the ground, I plop down as well. Just sit square on my ass on the cold ground. And wait.

After a moment, Lars comes popping out from behind a tree that I've definitely marked up with my wanton shooting. He points a pistol at me.

"Hey, bru," he says.

"Bru," I say in return. "I get you?"

He glances quickly over his body and says, "Don't think so, man. Good one, though. Nice try."

I don't see Christine. I know she must be here, but I can't spot her. I have a fleeting panic that perhaps Lars threw her over the falls or something equally dramatic.

"Ask you something, bru?" I say.

Lars eyes me carefully and says, "Yeah. Go on."

"How long has this been on your mind?"

"What? Killing you?" he says, still holding the pistol on me. "A while, I suppose. I mean, after Mom and Dad died because of you—"

"Lars, man—"

356

"They fokken did!" He loses his cool quite a bit. "They did, man. Don't try to act like they didn't. You're the one who stole the diamond from Dad. *You* did that."

"Yeah. I did."

"Why? Was it just a joke for you? A fokken lark? Just to show you could?"

"Why we talking about this now, man?"

"When else, bru? You've never been there to talk before. You were always too busy jetting about the world with your dear, dear Danny and Christine."

"Jesus, man. Please don't tell me that's what this is about. Don't tell me you've been... what? Jealous? Fokenwil, man."

I'm reminded of a thought I had when I was fighting my way free of the cock-up with Wallace. Some people harbor their negative feelings far too close to their hearts. And that is simply terrible business.

"All right, man. I won't tell you that. Because that's not what this is about. I mean, I hated you for all that, but I wouldn't try to *kill* you over some kak *feelings*, bru."

I want to tell him that it makes me proud to hear him say that, but this ain't the time.

"No, bru. What I want is simple."

"What's that then?"

"Everything. All of it. All that you have, that's what I want. Because, big bru, as Dad once told me—before you got him and Mom killed—this world... all of it... is *mine*."

Fokken Zander van den Berg. Father of the fokken year.

"Christine? Come on out, luv."

I look over my shoulder and there comes Christine. From behind a bush. A goddamn shrubbery. She's lucky I didn't blow her silly head off with my berserker display a moment ago.

"Where's Danny?" she asks as she emerges.

I glance briefly in the direction from which I came. I know Danny is out there. I just don't know where.

"Went back," I say.

"What?" she asks.

"He said he didn't want any part of it. Said there was no point in pursuing. Figured there was no good way for us to resolve this and didn't want to do something he'd regret."

"Like what?" she asks. I think she just needs to hear it. That's fine. It's true.

"Like hurt you. He loves you. He didn't want to make an impossible choice. He loves you, Christine. He always has. He always will. So…"

There's a moment in which I watch Lars watch Christine. Then I turn back to look at Christine, who still stares at me.

"I remember," she says.

"You do?" I ask. "What do you remember?"

"Everything," she says.

"Oh, good. Well, your timing is just bang on, luv."

And at that, fokken Danny comes stepping out from the shelter of the trees, rifle at the ready. Danny, Danny, Danny. So very Danny of you.

"What do you remember?" he asks.

She looks around at the three of us. I'm not certain why Lars hasn't shot me yet. I suppose it's possible that he was waiting to make Christine do it. Either as some sort of test or simply because even after his little speech about resentment and power, he'd feel bad putting a bullet in his big brother.

"I remember you," she says, referring to Danny. "I remember you leaving."

Danny stares at her. She stares back.

"And you," she says to me. "I remember you betraying me."

She stares at me now. I know what she's talking about. I regretted it then just as much as I regret it now. But a fat lot of good regret does anyone.

"And you," she says to Lars. "I remember how you were there for me when Alec wasn't."

"I still am," he says. "I'm still here. Let's finish this now." He nods at me, gives Christine a tight smile.

I stand. Slowly. Saying, as I rise, "Tell you what. I've got a brilliant idea, yeah? How about this? Let's try to work this all out together. All of us. Yeah? We're all family. Family by blood, family by choice. It doesn't matter, does it? And this is a family business. So let's figure out how to bury everyone's hurt feelings and hang-ups about… whatever… and see how we can move forward as a unit. Kak, man. There's a whole bleeding lot of dead bodies back there and the four of us… we're the last ones standing. That has to count for something. We're survivors. All of us. I mean… imagine what we could achieve if we all just found some common ground."

I've never been much of a statistics enthusiast. Nor am I an "odds" oke. So I couldn't begin to lay a wager on what the chances are that my preposterous idea might gain some traction in this moment, but quite frankly, I'm all out of moves.

The only thing that can kill Alec van den Berg is Alec van Berg. Maybe. Maybe not. There are four of us standing in the clearing on this chilly autumn night. And at least one of us is not going to make it. Unless I can find the part of our shared desire that all of us can lock onto.

The sound of the rushing waterfall crashing into the earth below is the only thing I can hear. I breathe. Fill my lungs with cold air. I have goosebumps. Must be from the cold. I don't remember the last time that happened.

After what feels like quite a very long time indeed, Christine is the one to speak. She looks at Danny. Looks at Lars. Looks at me. I can't tell what she's thinking. And then finally, after several long moments...

"Sorry, Alec," she says. "Can't do it. A triangle only has three sides."

CHAPTER FIFTY-FOUR

Christine

"That's my girl," Lars says. His face so handsome. His body so perfect.

I feel sick. So, so sick.

But I wasn't lying. I do remember.

"Latch on to that anger, luv," Lars continues. "The memory of how it felt when your hero, Alec, burned you. How he smiled in your face as he turned his back."

"What the fuck are you talking about?" That's Danny. His rifle is hanging by his side. Like he's got no interest in killing anyone.

I back away, acutely aware that Lars and I are very close to the edge of the rushing river, the thundering sound of the waterfall down below like a soundtrack to a sick, sad ending. I trip over a rock and Danny, because he's the one I'm looking at, reaches out with his hand. Like he can pull me in across the distance and stop my tumble.

And it works. Because I don't fall.

"Where are you going?" Lars laughs.

"I remember you too," I say, not taking my eyes off Danny. "I remember the things you said. All the things you said to get me on your side."

"My side? Luv, this is our side. It's us against him, yeah? Remember that? That was you, Christine. That was all you."

I sigh, still backing away. I don't want to be here. I don't want to look at them. I don't want this rifle, I don't want this life, I don't want—"That wasn't me," I say. But it's a very weak denial.

"What the fuck," Danny spits, "is he talking about?"

"I'm talking about the—"

"Shut up!" I yell it. And even over the crashing waterfall, it is loud. "Shut the fuck up!"

"We talked about this, Christine," Alec says. I won't look at him. I refuse to look at him. I can't see that pretty face of his right now. Not now. "I told you I was sorry. And you forgave me, nunu. If you remember what I did, then you remember that part too, yeah?"

"Lies." Lars laughs. "All he's ever fed you was lies."

"Christine," Alec says, walking forward towards me.

Lars starts backing away now too. Trying to catch up to me. His pistol is pointed at Danny, not Alec. Which I take to mean… I'm covering Alec?

And I guess I am, because that's who I'm aiming at. Not real carefully, I admit. But this is an automatic rifle, so aiming isn't really necessary. I could rip his body in half with one squeeze of the trigger.

"Put the gun down, Christine," Alec says. "We're family, remember?"

Family. I almost laugh. But I'm still looking at Danny. Still focused on him for some reason.

"He betrayed you," Lars says. "You were so hurt. You cried for months, luv. You stopped eating, you stopped laughing, you stopped—"

"I said I was sorry," Alec says, voice calm. Too calm. "I made it up to you, Christine."

"With a diamond," I hiss. "You gave me a *bloody fucking diamond*!"

"It wasn't just any diamond—"

"Fuck you!" I scream. "Fuck you! I don't need another goddamned diamond!"

"That's right," Lars says. But I swing my rifle in that general direction and squeeze the trigger. A barrage of bullets rip through the trees. "Jesus fokken Christ!" Lars yells. "What the fok are you doing? We're on the same side!"

"Stay away from me," I say, my voice as shaky as my hands. "Stay the fuck away from me!"

"Look at me," Alec says. I've pointed the rifle back in his direction as I ease myself away from the river's edge and get my back to the woods. His body turns with mine. Lars turns too.

I'm still looking at Danny when I say, "Over there. Get over there by them."

"Christine," Danny says, our eyes locked. "What do you think you're gonna do here? Huh? Kill us all? For what?"

"Do it!" I yell.

He still has his rifle. It's still hanging by his side. I don't ask him to drop it and he doesn't make to lift it. He just exhales. I don't hear it as much as see it.

Danny deflates and walks forward. Stands to the right of Alec. I motion with the rifle. "Get closer together."

"Come on, Christine," Alec says. "Just… let's put the guns down and talk, OK? I didn't know you were still upset. I didn't know. We talked it through, yeah? You were fine. Lars is lying, and you just don't remember. He's feeding you—"

"The truth!" Lars says. "He fokked you, luv! He fokked you good and hard. And then he turned his back. And who was there to pick you up? Eh?" He laughs. "Wasn't Danny, was it?"

Danny shakes his head. "I don't know what the fuck is happening right now."

"Lies," Alec says. "Feeding you lies! You took a tumble, right? You hit your head, lost your memory—"

And that's when I stop listening.

That's when the whole world goes black.

And the questions start running through my head like ticker tape in an old movie.

Who are you?

What did you do?

Why are you here?

And then the final question comes to me like a slap in the face.

That's when the choppy lake goes still, and the hazy fog lifts, and the thunderheads surrounding me back away.

"Do you ever feel like... crushing pretty things?"

CHAPTER FIFTY-FIVE

When I look at Christine I see her sitting in the grass back at that foster home, poking the blue beetle with the stick.

I need to know what makes it so pretty.

She's been staring at me this whole time. Minutes, probably. That feel like years. Time has a way of doing that. Going fast and slow whenever it wants.

It's not supposed to be blue.

But now she's looking at Alec and Lars.

Two pretty, blue beetles.

It's a mutant. That's why it's blue.

I'm running towards her before I even realize I've moved. Time is funny like that. Because it's not a number, it's a series of events. It's motion, and I'm in motion. It's forward motion, and I'm moving forward.

But she's stuck in the past.

It shouldn't be possible. Not in this light. Just the moon hanging low overhead. There shouldn't be time. Me rushing towards her, frantic and afraid.

But none of that matters. Because I see what I see.

Her finger tightens and then the bullets scream out of her rifle in a spray of hellfire.

Christine

Danny barrels into me, but it's too late.

Who can you trust?

That's the final question I have in my head when the instincts take over.

When the world has conspired against you for so long you lose all sense of self and purpose, who can you trust?

The full weight of Danny's two-hundred-plus pound body made up of nothing but muscle slams into my chest. I hit the ground so hard, the stitches in the back of my head split open and...

Life leaves me.

I choke on its absence. Trying to inhale as Danny gropes and grabs for the rifle. I don't even have enough left to fight him for it.

I have lost all sense of self and purpose.

And then I'm still. My eyes closed. My head swimming in those flickering dots you see when you're about to lose consciousness.

It feels so good, too. So right. So much like home I want to embrace that darkness. Be that emptiness. Die right here and now and never think of anything ever again...

"Christine!" He slaps me across the face. "Breathe!"

I gasp, sucking in air. My throat burning, my chest screaming with fire. My eyes stinging with tears because I'm crying.

"Look at me!" He's sitting on my legs, leaning over my chest, hands flat against my cheeks on either side of my face as he presses his forehead to mine.

I open my eyes and look at him.

Who can you trust?

I answer that final question. Because there is only one truth left in my life.

Just one.

And his name is Danny Fortnight.

So I say, "You."

Danny

LONG TIME AGO

The Cook Islands are something to behold. I looked that word up when we first got here. Behold. Because it came out and I didn't really know what it meant. I just said it because I'd heard it somewhere. From someone. A book or maybe a movie.

Something to behold.

Something impressive and very much worth seeing.

Christine, even at age ten, was something to behold because she was impressive and very much worth knowing. A little girl with a stick and the desire to poke the pretty out of a beetle that wasn't supposed to be blue.

When we sailed into Aitutaki's main boat passage I held my breath and thought, *This is it. This is the real paradise. I thought, I might never leave. I might stay forever.*

Of course, we were coming off a job and even though we'd sailed into many a paradise over the last two years, we never stayed long. It was just meant to be a place to bask under the heat of the sun while the real heat died down back where we came from.

We stopped in Arutanga to pick up some supplies. Christine bought a yellow dress from an old woman selling them outside the fishing club.

She's wearing the dress right now. Been wearing it every day. The ruffled edge of the hem flutters along her tanned-brown thighs as I watch her trace letters in the wet sand down near the surf.

Alec, Christine, Danny.

She traces it over and over again. And every few minutes the waves come in and she jumps back, cursing nature for sweeping her letters out to sea.

But she persists.

Alec. Christine. Danny.

"So," Alec says.

"So," I say back.

We're lounging on chairs under an old palapa. The thatched roof has holes in it, so a stray beam of sunlight shines down on his arm.

"Wanna go to Europe?"

"Why not?" I laugh.

"I found another school for Christine."

"Oh," I say.

"I thought you wanted her in school?"

"I do, of course. But…"

"Yeah." He sighs. "I know."

Alec. Christine. Danny.

"What will we do?" I ask.

I kinda feel him shrug. He's not that far away from me. A few feet, maybe. "Whatever we want, I suppose."

I turn my head and look at him. So perfect. Well-muscled body. Sun-bleached strands of hair blowing in the breeze. He's not pretty. Not exactly. But he is at the same time. I don't think he knows what he's got. I don't think he even knows who he really is, for that matter.

I mean, yeah. He knows he's got more money than he could ever spend. He knows he's in charge of his own future. He knows he's unstoppable.

But he doesn't quite understand his privilege.

"Ya know," I say, "I never really asked you why."

He smiles. Eyes closed. "Why what, bru?"

"Why us?"

"You mean... why *you*?"

"Sure, I guess."

He opens his eyes and turns his head. Amber meets blue. He stares at me. For too long. So long I get an uncomfortable feeling, like he can see through me. "I'd been watching you."

"Yeah?" I say.

He nods. "About two weeks, I reckon. You were in that gym quite a bit. But you did other things too. Beat people up. Stole shit. Picked your little sister up from school every day and walked her back to that ratty motel. I thought she was your little sister. I thought you had parents. I thought... well, I thought a lot of things."

I wait for him to go on, but he doesn't. So I drop it for a while. But he never answered my question. So eventually I say, "Why then?"

"Because you had it all, bru. You had everything."

I laugh. "What are you talking about? I had nothing but Christine."

He juts his chin towards the surf. "She was all you needed."

"You wanted me for Christine?"

"No." He laughs. "I just wanted what you had. Her. You. Someone who was all I needed. I wanted to be part of that. Your family."

"Brothers then?"

"A different kind of family."

"What other kind is there?"

He shrugs. Turns away, then turns back. "The kind you choose, Danny. That kind."

"Oh," I say. "Yeah, then. OK. That's what we are. The kind you choose."

"I love you two."

I smile. Kinda huff out some air through my nose. "We love you back."

"I'll always love you two. It's a done deal, yeah?"

I huff again. "Sure. Done deal."

"No matter what happens, we're the only three who matter."

"What about Lars?"

"He can come along if he wants. One day, maybe. When he's old enough to understand what this is. But he's not part of us, is he? He's part of me, sure. But he's not part of us."

I nod, pretending to understand what it means to be us. Not quite getting it, but not wanting to break the moment and ask more questions, either.

Christine is suddenly under the palapa with us. She sinks to her knees, dropping into the sand. Picks up two handfuls, lets it flow through her fingers like an hourglass ticking off time. "I love it here."

I beam at her. And when I look over at Alec, he's beaming too.

It kinda hits me then. What he meant.

Alec. Christine. Danny.

"I wish we could stay like this forever," she whispers, picking up more sand so she can grab more time.

"Nothing lasts forever, nunu. Must enjoy things when they happen. That's all you can do."

I think about life before Alec and feel OK with it. It was hard, and we were scared, but... it was OK.

Then I think about life without Alec and find myself suddenly sad. Not for the loss of things he gave us, but for the loss of him. The loss of us.

I would probably be fine if we'd never met. Because you can't miss something you never had. But losing him... I mean, he gets on my nerves quite a bit. We argue plenty. And every now and then we even box until we're bloody. But I meant it. We love him.

I love him.

The thought of losing him feels like the end of something.

Something I'll never get back.

It feels like the loss of everything.

Something I'll never get over.

It feels like defeat.

Because there is no us without Alec.

RIGHT NOW

Did they die?

We ask ourselves that question every day. Or at least I do. I think Christine has moved on. It's been three months since she squeezed her trigger and blasted bullets at Alec and Lars.

Three months since we got up off the ground, walked over to the edge of the river, bent down to rub our fingers through the drops of blood on the rocks.

Three months since we looked at the water rushing over the waterfall.

Since I called his name, over and over and over.

"Alec!"

"Alec!"

"Alec?"

We made our way down to the pool at the bottom. It took hours to get there so we knew, even if we did find bodies, they'd be dead. We had to make ourselves leave the river first. And that was harder than it sounds. Leaving without him. Leaving him behind.

Then we found the house, got the Range Rover, found a road that took us close to the falls, then hiked back into the forest.

Christine didn't say a word the whole time. Not one word.

I talked to myself, mostly. "This way," and, "That way," and, "Over there."

But we didn't find bodies. We found nothing.

Alec once said, "Our love transcends everything."

Except betrayal, I guess. Because there's no love left now. Not in me, anyway.

I don't blame Christine. It's not her fault. It's my fault.

My fault for taking her out of the foster system.

My fault for pretending I could care for her.

My fault for introducing her to Alec.

My fault for letting her grow into a killer.

My fault for walking away and my fault for coming back.

Every bit of this is all my fault.

So why am I taking it out on her? When three months ago she was all I wanted?

I guess it's because... that's not all I want *now*.

There's three of us, not two.

There is no her without him. No me without them.

"I have to go somewhere."

I understand that this is the second time she's said that and there have been many minutes in between the two statements. But I'm sitting on a sand bar on the inside part of the Aitutaki atoll, looking over at One Foot Island where we left the boat, and all I can think about is that day back in paradise. "We should've just... stayed here," I say. "Stopped time and stayed here."

She says nothing.

So neither do I. More minutes go by. I can practically see her back then. Like she's right in front of me again. Picking up fistfuls of sand. Letting time slip through her fingers. I want to get up out of my chair, go to her. Make her keep that sand in her fists.

Make her stop.

But of course, she is right in front of me. Right now.

Except she's not her and I'm not him, and Alec is gone. Or dead. Does it matter?

"I have to——"

"I heard you," I say. Quietly.

She sighs. "I'm sorry."

"It's not your fault."

"Still, I feel... I know that, but... I'm... just sorry."

I asked her once what Alec did. What was it that sent her over to Lars.

She slapped me. "I wasn't with Lars! Everything he said was a lie!"

"I love you," she says now.

"I love you back," I say. Because I do. I don't feel it in this moment, but I love her. And if I lose her, well, I'll just die if I lose her.

"I think I should go. I have somewhere to be. And something to do and maybe..."

"Maybe what? Maybe you won't come back?"

"I'm coming back."

"Then why are you leaving?"

I get it. I mean know why. I'm not a whole lot of fun these days. And I don't really know what's bugging me. I just know it's something. Something I don't understand. Something that makes me want to sleep all day. Something that hates, something that wants to give up.

"I'm coming back."

Circles. I'm going in circles, not triangles.

"What did he do, Christine? Tell me." I whisper that last part.

And then I look at her. For the first time in days, I think. She presses her lips together and shakes her head. "I can't," she whispers back.

"Why?"

"Because it doesn't matter."

"It did that day."

That's what we call it now. *That day.*

"I'm leaving. I have to go but I'll be back. Please be here."

"Where would I go?" It's an honest question. Brasil is still looking for me. My fucking garage went up in flames that night we left. Oh, yeah, that was fun. Driving back to the city. To my home. Finding it gone. But then again, what did I expect? We left half a dozen dead bodies behind. Of course whoever sent that hit torched the place when they did the cleanup.

I don't know if that attack was Brasil or not. Probably was. Because we now know when Lars sends mercs in to kill you, he does it right.

Did, I guess. Past tense. Did it right.

I went to the other warehouse, packed up some things, grabbed the important contacts, a new burner phone for each of us. Money to get fake passports.

We picked up more money once we got to the Caribbean. And a boat. A big catamaran. One that can cross oceans. We didn't stop in South Africa. Went to Madagascar instead. Then off to the Seychelles, the Maldives, passed a bunch of fucking places in Indonesia, skipped Australia and kept going. New Caledonia, Fiji, and then... the Cook Islands. The only place we had left.

Two and half months we were on that yacht.

But time is so funny. Feels like yesterday we were standing in those woods looking at that river.

"I'll be back soon," Christine says, leaning in to kiss me on the cheek. "Please be here."

The next time I look up the sun is setting behind me, burning my back.

For a second I think, *Holy shit. Did she take the boat?*

But no. I see it. Across the lagoon where it's supposed to be.

So I swim back. Go inside. Turn on the lights, and make some ramen. Live, without really living.

Two days go by and I think she'll come back. Probably by morning.

Seven days and I'm a little less sure.

Ten days and I've got the GPS spooled up, food in hand as I scan the map. They have this little hut place on One Foot Island. Right next to the post office. Like a fucking snack bar if you were on a beach in the US. They mostly sell fish and crab, so that's what I'm eating. Fish taco. I ran out of ramen four days ago and I'm just not in the mood to take this boat out by myself and go to the market over in Aitutaki. I'll have to walk by the fishing club to get there and then I'll think of her yellow dress and the whole sad state of things will finally sink in.

She's not coming back.

Alec is dead.

There is no triangle, there is no us.

I am alone on the wrong side of the world.

So I look at the GPS map and eat my stupid fish. Try to decide where I can go that won't feel like death is calling me home.

I decide that place doesn't exist.

So I decide northwest.

I decide I'd like to kill Brasil. Take back what's mine. What's left, anyway.

And I come to terms with it. The loss, the sadness, the two holes inside my heart.

Because there's no way to fix this. There's no way to put that sand back in Christine's fist or those bullets back in her gun.

It's over.

I can either stay here and die. Or leave and fight to live another day.

If I quit… if I quit, Alec would never respect me again. I'd never get his voice out of my head.

So I stay up all night and plot the trip. And by the time dawn comes, I'm OK, I think.

I'm alone, but I'm OK.

It's taken a while, but I've come to terms with my new normal.

And that's when the boat tips slightly. And for a second I think, *Waves. Just waves.*

"Hey," she says.

But it's not waves.

I close my eyes and suck in a deep breath. Hold it. Then let it out and say, "Hey."

"I'm sorry."

I don't turn around and look at her. I can't do it. I just accepted things. Just started to feel whole again. And seeing her now. I don't know. I don't think I can do it.

She comes up behind me. She leans into my neck and she smells like wind. Like salt, and sea, and life. She kisses me and whispers, "I can fix this."

I just shake my head. She can't.

"He's alive, Danny."

"Lars?" I ask, unable to even consider—

"He's alive and I know where he is." She slips around and sits in my lap, her arms draped casually around my shoulders. A moment later she's kissing me on the mouth. "He's with Brasil. I can fix this, OK? Let me fix this."

Everything comes rushing back to me now.

Everything.

The hate. The love. The fear. The courage.

I picture this new life she's offering. One filled with many familiar things. Mostly guns, and death, and probably lots of fucking.

I sigh. Pull her into me. Wrap my arms tightly around her body.

She sinks into me.

I don't want her, I want us. I want the triangle. It's still true, what I told Alec when he asked me if I'd always need her to have him. That hasn't changed.

There is no her without him. No me without them.

379

This is the shape of our love.

For the first time since that day, I smile.

I feel… not whole. Not yet. As long as we're apart we're nothing but broken lines.

But I feel hope.

So I say, "Let's fix this."

Welcome to the End of Book Shit where we get to say anything we want about the book. Sometimes they're long and wordy, sometimes they're short and pithy. You never know. But they are never edited, so excuse our typos. And they are always last minute. Like… right before we upload. So don't mind us if we ramble.

It has been thirteen months since JA Huss asked me to write books with her. (It was the 3rd of August 2017, to be precise.) And this last (slightly more than a) year has been the most remarkable one of my career.

As I write this, I am in Las Cruces, New Mexico, shooting a movie, having just wrapped production on the first season of a Netflix series I'm thrilled to have been on.

381

I am also starting a new book with Julie while continuing to work on the TV adaptation of THE COMPANY, based on the world of Julie's books.

I am also talking with our audiobook publisher about multiple books I am working on with them both as an author and a narrator.

For those keeping score, that represents three full-time careers.

And I've never been happier.

(I'm not naturally given over to happiness, so it's not some impossibly high benchmark, but nonetheless — for me — I've never been happier.)

Here's why I bring it up: I don't know if there's some synergistic universal force at play that is creating a personal metaphor at this moment, or if I'm just forcing one, or a little of both, but here's what I do know: I've had the most abundant and gratifying year of my career because I seem to have triangulated my purpose in that regard. Before, there were pieces missing. And that disallowed the discovery of my fullest creative self. And now ... all the lines connect.

This happened in my personal world sometime back. I met my wife, who is very much the strong, unbending line that anchors my life, and concurrently, I met the friends I have (friends like Julie — true, steadfast, unwavering allies and champions) who keep me balanced and at peace as well. Me; Laura; Julie, et. al. That's my strength. I need all of those elements to truly occupy my best version of me. Because for a long time, I felt adrift. Like a single, unmatched line in search of something. And the universe was kind to me and painted onto my life my companion parts.

That feeling of completion and fulfillment is what this last year has been for my life in art. I am privileged to be constantly engaged and in the process of creating. And it is the greatest gift I could hope for. I don't know what next year will hold, but I'm not really thinking about it all that much at present because — right now — I feel whole.

Oh, I still find plenty to complain about. That's just who I am. That's part of the line that makes me me. But the previously missing parts coming together has ameliorated the carping voice in my mind to a greater degree than I've ever had happen before.

The trick to happiness, it seems to me, is to find the places where you and your loves, ideas, passions, and people all intersect and then *join* with them. Just touch them at the connection points and allow the power to flow back and forth between.

And, by the way, I don't know that I'm done adding elements. None of us are. There's nothing to suggest that the shape of *my* love isn't a myriagon. Or some other impossible-to-name polygon. I hope I'm able to just keep adding lines and re-shaping my life more and more and more and...

And I hope that for you as well. Both because you are you and you deserve happiness, and because ... I owe you. I am in your debt. You are the line that makes this all possible. That makes the work I do, and the work Julie and I do together, necessary.

There is no call for what we create if you aren't there to share in it. You are our third angle. Our completion.

Without you, there is no us.

So ... I hope that the discovery of new passions, new loves, new opportunities, and new discoveries leave their mark on you and allow the shape of the world you occupy to keep shifting and growing as you do.

Because, for all of us, every last one, no story is ever really over. The shape of the narrative just keeps changing as it moves along.

Alec, Christine, and Danny will be back.

And so will we.

We hope you will continue to join us.

-JM
19 September 2018

When Johnathan and I finished The Sexpert it was June. We had a serious deadline because we were taking ARC copies of the book to the Book Bonanza signing in July, which meant that we needed the book done very early so we could format and upload the paperback and get our physical copies to my house in time. I had just finished Play Dirty and there was so much going on with the signing, I just stopped writing. For like… weeks.

I have never done that before. Not since I first started writing non-fiction in 2008. I mean, I have literally been writing pretty much non-stop for the last ten years. It was kinda weird, to be honest. I kept asking myself... is this burn-out? Is this what that feels like?

But it's not that I didn't have ideas. I seriously had a new idea every single day. I'd write it down and say, "There. That's the next book." But then I'd get a new idea and that became the next book. I think I did this like eight times and pretty soon I started wondering if I'd ever be able to settle on another idea again. It was strange.

But The Shape of Love Series was in my head for a while. My problem was it started out as a run-of-the-mill ménage. My problem was... it was boring because I was thinking about following the "rules". My problem was I didn't want to write it. I loved the series title and the book title but the story I had plotted for it just... wasn't good enough.

I needed something more. I needed something like Junco. Or Rook & Ronin. Or The Company. A story that would inspire me. A story I could fall in love with. A story where I could give no fucks about how many copies I sold because this was about ME again.

And that's not what my story started out to be.

AND – this was the first time in like two and a half years that I didn't have a pre-order up with a deadline.

I seriously wrote EIGHT BOOKS from January to June. Eight. Angels Fall, Flesh Into Fire, Passion Rising, Total Exposure, Pleasure of Panic, The Boyfriend Experience, Play Dirty, and The Sexpert.

I published over half a million words in seven months. And not ghostwritten words, bitches. All my words (and Johnathan's too).

I needed time to THINK ABOUT SHIT, ya know?

So I stopped writing and that's why I was coming up with new ideas every day. Did I want to write this book instead? Or that one? Or hey, how about these six ideas over here? We just wrote a pretty funny rom com, should I write another one of those?

But I didn't want to do that either. The Sexpert series (Which, from this point on, will be called The Tall, Dark, and Handsome series) is a world. A world I love, I'm excited about, and I'm looking forward to more books in that world. (In fact we started Pierced, the next TDH book, two days ago and we're already on chapter three. Fuckin Pierce and Myrtle are gonna kill you.)

And all my other worlds have been wrapped up with pretty bows. There were no messy dangling threads for me to grasp onto and insert one of these ideas into.

I also knew I did NOT want to write another standalone. I've been writing standalone series for a couple years and you know what? I need more right now. I mean… when you get three books to tell the story about the same characters it's so much more amazing. But readers love the standalone, I guess. I dunno.

I kept thinking back to the Rook & Ronin series and The Company. And Junco. And how I loved, loved, loved writing the "long story".

And I had just come off The Misters, and The Turning Series, and Jordan's Game. And sometimes when I get to the end of a book I know it's "over". Like… it is. It's over. But I wish I could skip the marriage and the baby and just say, you know what? This ride isn't over yet, bitches. Give me a fuckin' minute, OK? I'm not done with these people. And besides, no bitch gets off that easy anyway. Time for a reality check.

And so once I decided this was not going to be a standalone series I felt a whole lot better about things. I wrote the prologue and chapter one. But I wasn't getting excited yet because I had written like five chapter ones in the past three weeks and all of them got put on hold for another idea.

But fuck it. I started it and I had Christine's name, but no names for Danny and Alec. And Johnathan and I were on the phone one morning and he said something like, "Tell me about your book. What are you writing?"

So I took a deep breath and said… listen to this… Which was a big deal because once I told someone about an idea it became real, ya know? And I was still a little worried that I wouldn't be able to get to chapter two.

But I told him about Christine. And I said, "I don't know where it goes from there, I don't have names for these two guys, I just know it's something like 321 meets the Company. And there's a kid, but she's grown up now. And there's a James/Ark, but he's kind of a bad guy. But there's a James/JD too, because all the bitches loved JD." And then I said, "You wanna read it?"

Which… one year ago, would never have happened. EVER.

No one read my words until the book was done and then only RJ, my editor, got to have opinions about it that I would give fucks about. Like, I literally remember this phone convo Johnathan and I had last summer and it was an hour-long conversation of me having a meltdown because he was gonna get to read my words before I was done.

Poor Johnathan, lol. He was a champ on that phone call. He really was. It was a bunch of "It's OK. It'll be fine. We'll get through this."

It wasn't that easy but you know, by this time Johnathan and I had written five books already. And a script for The Company TV show. We were getting better at this collaboration thing and I respect his opinion.

So I asked him if he wanted to read it.

And he said, "Fuck yeah. It sounds amazing. Like this sounds like something I'd love to write." (Or something to that effect, because I have a terrible memory when it comes to conversations.)

So then I said, "You want in on this?" lol

And he said, "Yeah. Let's do it." (He really said – man, I got a shit ton of work right now and it's cray. And this is insane to even consider but, yeah. Let's do it.) ☺

So I send him the blurb, the prologue, and chapter one.

Like an hour later I go outside to feed my donkeys. I'd told him that I think the one guy is into something illegal. Like all of them are obviously outlaws, but this one guy, he's doing something. Not Italian mob. Not mob at all. Something... classier. If there's such a thing in the criminal world. So I'm outside scooping beet pulp into a bucket for my donkeys and it hits me.

Diamonds.

And I swear to God, my phone dings and I get a text from Johnathan. Like in that same instant. It's a business text about something business-y. But I reply back, *I got it. Diamonds.* And he says, *Blood Diamonds? Can I be South African?*

lol

So I said fuck yeah.

And that was it. I was writing again.

WE. We were writing again.

And over the course of the next six weeks The Triangle came to life. And holy fuck, man. I love it.

I know what romance IS.

I get it.

I know what you have to have in the story to make people feel "satisfied". I know what the dude can and cannot do. I know the rules. I do.

But no one write romance the way I write romance because I have a very particular view of what's romantic in a book and it's not always the standard "two people fall in love and live happily ever after" kind of romance.

I mean, I can write that. The Sexpert is definitely that. But the whole point of The Sexpert is to make you laugh and I wasn't in the mood to make you laugh. I wanted to make you feel some shit. I wanted to confuse the fuck out of you, and twist your brain, and make you throw your damn Kindle at the wall.

And if I have to write nothing but rom coms for the rest of my career, well, I'm gonna go do something else, OK? I am. I love the TDH series and I'm having a bunch of fun writing about Pierce and Myrtle. But I can't do it every single book. I'll die.

I am just Julie's dark, twisted mind. That's all I can say.

If people don't like that, it's all good. But I am not a formula writer. And when I write a story like Junco, or The Triangle it comes from somewhere else. Somewhere deep inside. There is no formula for The Company. Or Rook & Ronin. Or 321.

And there is no formula for The Triangle either. We're building a new world here and we're gonna do it right. So if that means we have dangling threads at the end, so be it.

This is the shape of our writing.

You'll also notice we do not have book two up for pre-order. We only get 90 days on an Amazon pre-order and the second book won't release until January. We're not releasing in December because I have another book I'm working on for December called The Dirty Ones (about the twisted world of erotica writers, ironically enough). And Pierced, book two of the TDH series, is slotted to release October 30th. So it's four months between books one and two.

I hate making you guys wait but again... this is Junco. This is Rook & Ronin. This is The Company. And these things take time. Writing the "long story" requires a lot of daydreaming. It requires time to get inside your characters and figure them out. And four months isn't that long anyway.

So January, unicorn bitches. January. Follow us on the websites below or on our socials to get the first look at the rest of the story. And if you'd like to try another one of our books, give Sin With Me a go or if you're looking for another MFM book like The Triangle while you wait, try Taking Turns (Which is FREE right now) or 321.

J.H. 9-20-18

www.JAHuss.com
www.HussMcClain.com

SPECIAL THANKS

Johnathan and I would like to express our heart-felt thanks to the following people who have helped us with our books.

Laura McClain for many obvious reasons, but also for being our proofer for books one-five.

Charlotte Istel for proofing this book.

RJ Locksley for editing *all* the books. ☺

Everyone at Podium Publishing for making our audiobooks special. Victoria, Tamara, Emily, Jessica, and Greg.

Nicole Alexander, my assistant, and her husband Tim for just... all the things.

Michell Hall Casper and Melissa Fisher for their super-proofing powers.

And all you superfans who take time out of your day to hang out with us.

We are so grateful.

J&J

about the authors

Johnathan McClain's career as a writer and actor spans 25 years and covers the worlds of theatre, film, and television. At the age of 21, Johnathan moved to Chicago where he wrote and began performing his critically acclaimed one-man show, Like It Is. The Chicago Reader proclaimed, "If we're ever to return to a day when theatre matters, we'll need a few hundred more artists with McClain's vision and courage." On the heels of its critical and commercial success, the show subsequently moved to New York where Johnathan was compared favorably to solo performance visionaries such as Eric Bogosian, John Leguizamo, and Anna Deavere Smith.

Johnathan lived for many years in New York, and his work there includes appearing Off-Broadway in the original cast of Jonathan Tolins' The Last Sunday In June at The Century Center, as well as at Lincoln Center Theatre and with the Lincoln Center Director's Lab. Around the country, he has been seen on stage at South Coast Repertory, The American Conservatory Theatre, Florida Stage, Paper Mill Playhouse, and the National Jewish Theatre. Los Angeles stage credits are numerous and include the LA Weekly Award nominated world premiere of Cold/Tender at The Theatre @ Boston Court and the LA Times' Critic's Choice production of The Glass Menagerie at The Colony Theatre for which Johnathan received a Garland Award for his portrayal of Jim O'Connor.

On television, he appeared in a notable turn as Megan Draper's LA agent, Alan Silver, on the final season of AMC's critically acclaimed drama Mad Men, and as the lead of the TV Land comedy series, Retired at 35, starring alongside Hollywood icons George Segal and Jessica Walter. He has also had Series Regular roles on The Bad Girl's Guide starring Jenny McCarthy and Jessica Simpson's sitcom pilot for ABC. His additional television work includes recurring roles on the CBS drama SEAL TEAM and Fox's long-running 24, as well as appearances on Grey's Anatomy, NCIS: Los Angeles, Trial and Error, The Exorcist, Major Crimes, The Glades, Scoundrels, Medium, CSI, Law & Order: SVU, Without a Trace, CSI: Miami, and Happy Family with John Larroquette and Christine Baranski, amongst others. On film, he appeared in the Academy Award nominated Far from Heaven and several independent features.

As an audiobook narrator, he has recorded almost 100 titles. Favorites include the Audie Award winning Illuminae by Amie Kaufman and Jay Kristoff and The Last Days of Night, by Academy Winning Screenwriter Graham Moore (who is also Johnathan's close friend and occasional collaborator). As well as multiple titles by his dear friend and writing partner, JA Huss, with whom he is hard at work making the world a little more romantic.

He lives in Los Angeles with his wife Laura.

JA Huss never wanted to be a writer and she still dreams of that elusive career as an astronaut. She originally went to school to become an equine veterinarian but soon figured out they keep horrible hours and decided to go to grad school instead. That Ph.D wasn't all it was cracked up to be (and she really sucked at the whole scientist thing), so she dropped out and got a M.S. in forensic toxicology just to get the whole thing over with as soon as possible.

After graduation she got a job with the state of Colorado as their one and only hog farm inspector and spent her days wandering the Eastern Plains shooting the shit with farmers.

After a few years of that, she got bored. And since she was a homeschool mom and actually does love science, she decided to write science textbooks and make online classes for other homeschool moms.

She wrote more than two hundred of those workbooks and was the number one publisher at the online homeschool store many times, but eventually she covered every science topic she could think of and ran out of shit to say.

So in 2012 she decided to write fiction instead. That year she released her first three books and started a career that would make her a New York Times bestseller and land her on the USA Today Bestseller's List eighteen times in the next three years.

Her books have sold millions of copies all over the world, the audio version of her semi-autobiographical book, Eighteen, was nominated for a Voice Arts Award and an Audie Award in 2016 and 2017 respectively, her audiobook, Mr. Perfect, was nominated for a Voice Arts

Award in 2017, and her audiobook, Taking Turns, was nominated for an Audie Award in 2018.

Johnathan McClain is her first (and only) writing partner and even though they are worlds apart in just about every way imaginable, it works.

She lives on a ranch in Central Colorado with her family.

Printed in the USA
CPSIA information can be obtained
at www.ICGtesting.com
LVHW040859010524
778989LV00024B/98